# The General's Tribune

## A Legion Archer
## Book #8

## J. Clifton Slater

Blending history with fictional stories that joins the two into a single cohesive narrative requires a love of the process. I have, however, been known to go off on tangents in my first draft. Acting as my lighthouse, Hollis Jones shines her light and aims her red pen at the intersection where I veer off track. Through her knowledge and ability to focus my interest, she guides the books from the edge of disaster, and helps me create a compelling story. For her, I am eternally grateful.

As always, my warmest 'thanks' goes to you. My readers are the reason I can spend my days doing research and writing stories. Rendering a hand salute to you for being there for me. Ready, two!

If you have comments, contact me:
GalacticCouncilRealm@gmail.com

# The General's Tribune

## Act 1

*The twin winds of greed and lust for power blew out of the west, racing eastward across the Mediterranean.*

*Although secure in his foreign position and made rich from his conquests, Cornelius Scipio retreated to Rome. The architect of the victory in Iberia, being too young to be a Senator of Rome or a Consul, began a new campaign. Too proud to serve under another General, Cornelius switched tactics. From directing infantrymen on a battlefield, he used political influence and charity to grow in popularity with the elites of society and with the citizens of Rome. To what end, few knew, and even less would understand his impossible plan.*

*With Carthaginian forces removed from Iberia, the reinforcements, and supplies for Hannibal Barca dwindled to a trickle. Even so, Hannibal held onto the southwest quadrant of the Italian peninsula and remained a danger to the Republic.*

*The twin winds blew ever eastward.*

*Philip V of Macedonia cast his greedy eyes on the Island of Rhodes. And while the fabled phalanxes of Macedonia were formidable on land, to conquer an island nation, he hired pirates to interfere with shipping. Some of the privateers raided for coins, others for pride, and one pirate, Diceärch of Aetolia, joined the*

1

King's war as a way to quench his hatred of priests and temples, and to satisfy his yearning for cruelty.

Ever eastward, the winds blew.

After smoldering in the desert sands along the Nile River, a rebellion flared up. And while Cretan Archer Jace Kasia worked a contract in Alexanderia, his days of sleeping under a roof were numbered. War was coming, but first the rebels needed to emerge from the shadows and declare their intentions. When the rebellion materialized, God/King Ptolemy IV would raise an army of the Pharaoh and march south to meet his fate.

And somewhere in transit, a letter traveled to Crete. The message, if it ever reached the Archer, will direct Jace Kasia westward against the winds to the Roman Legions. Once there, he will take his place as the General's Tribune.

Welcome to 205 B.C.

## Chapter 1 – Protector of Society

Deep in the night, a two-banker rowed from the western arc of Serifos Island. Bypassing the industrial town of Megalo Livadi, the ship traveled onward until the torchlights of the iron mines in the hills faded.

Farther around the island, a white tower glowed in the moonlight. Shortly after the ship rowed into view, a ridge running from the Aegean Sea to the hill with the white tower blocked the line of sight.

Any guard able to separate the dark shape of the liburna from the black water needed to shift his view to follow the ship's progress. Yet, no matter how much he scrutinized the settlement of Paralia on the other side of the ridge, he would never locate the two-banker or its crew.

"The dark blemish on the rocks is Cyclops' Cave," the rear oarsmen whispered. "This is the blind spot I was telling you about, Captain."

"I don't think anyone is close enough to hear us, except the water fleas," Diceärch said, his voice carrying down the length of the two-banker. "And if there is anyone, we'll take his life and leave his soul and body to rot."

"Starboard, bring in your oars and mind the rocks," the navigator ordered.

The liburna drifted forward until the right side bumped against a steep rock bank.

"Turn us around," Diceärch instructed. "When we leave, I don't want to be troubled with backing away from shore."

"Planning our escape route, Captain?" Corporal Ambrus inquired.

The oarsmen on the pirate ship backstroked in a half circle. When the port side scraped against the weathered rock face, the Captain replied.

"Rule number six, Corporal," Diceärch confirmed. "Always know your exit. Give me lookouts on the ridge."

Ambrus tapped four rowers on the shoulders. They grabbed weapons, whistles, and climbed to the rock shelf. A moment later, the five vanished into the darkness.

"Are we ready, sir?" Sergeant Sarpedon asked.

"We'll wait for a little light," Diceärch advised. "It's a mile to Paralia, and I don't want anyone to get lost in the dark."

Sarpedon turned away from the black outline of his Captain and mumbled, "or miss the look on the priest's face."

There was no secret to why Diceärch chose Paralia. Although this raid was second to his personal reasons, the raid offered a good balance between risk and reward. The majority of the hamlet's garrison lived in the white tower as part of a regional defense force. Their absence left the mining settlement almost unguarded. If the garrison knew a raid was in progress, the soldiers could run downhill and engage. But, with the ship in a neighboring cove, the garrison would remain in the tower, on the hill, and unaware of the robbery.

As with any worthy challenge, Diceärch weighed his cunning and the gathering of mining riches against the chance of death. Success would feed and reward his crew and please his patron, Philip V of Macedonian. Yet satisfying both parties, and the mission, were secondary to the Captain's peculiar crusade.

*** 

When sunlight brushed the sky, Diceärch studied the ridge. Once sure he couldn't see the top of the white tower, and confident the guards in the tower couldn't see his ship in the cove, he instructed.

"Sarpedon, take your squads to town. And remember to get in quickly, get out faster, and what you can't carry, destroy. As our Macedonian Admiral said, our job is to deny supplies to Rhodes, Egypt, and Athens wherever we find them."

"Yes sir. I take it you'll be at the Shrine of Venus?" the NCO guessed.

"The Goddess of Copper, it's fitting don't you think?" Dicëärch hissed out the rhetorical question.

Sergeant Sarpedon walked away. He recognized the signs when madness took his Captain. Other than his propensity for inhuman acts, Dicëärch was a good leader. And most days, he put the welfare of the crew first.

Even if they were hated by King Philip's enemies, and shunned by his allies, the Captain was making everyone rich. Besides, it was war where fortunes and foes were made. That thin thread of wisdom was enough to settle the Sergeant's conscience.

"First squad, hold your positions and defend the ship," Sarpedon ordered. "Squads two through five, let's go raiding."

As the forty-one pirates scrambled up to the rock ledge, Dicëärch waved the ship's sailors into motion. Of the four, one carried a pair of broken oar blades with a single word etched on each piece of wood. The five men stepped on the rail and mounted the rock shelf, coming level with Cyclop's Cave.

From there, they jogged onto dirt, reached a gravel road, turned right, and followed the same route as the raiding squads. Had they gone straight, the Captain and sailors would be heading for the white tower. The same road the garrison would use if they detected the raid. But danger and reward and the mission were secondary to Dicëärch's true passion. Primarily, he chose Paralia because the village had a shrine and a cleric in residence.

Clouds softened the sky to a light blue. In the distance, the Aegean Sea sparkled a deep blue green, and a gentle breeze sent ripples across the cove. The empty bay should have raised an alarm. But the morning guards were only slightly more senior than the inexperienced overnight watchers.

"Are you up there?" a garrison NCO called from the courtyard. "Are you awake?"

Eighteen feet overhead at the top of the white tower, a sentry answered from the walkway, "Both of us are up and alert, Sergeant."

"Maybe we should stand up," the other guard whispered.

"Don't worry," the first said while his legs dangled over the edge of the walkway, "he won't come up until he's had breakfast."

As a result of their negligence, the absence of fishing boats from Paralia, rowing out for a day of casting and pulling nets, went unobserved.

***

After a night at a narrow beach on a small rocky island, two Roman quinqueremes launched early. They traveled westward, the sails of the warships rippled in the morning breeze before filling with a new wind. The beat of the musician ended along with the stroke count of the Second Principale. In the quiet, Proconsul Valerius Laevinus moved to the ship's commander.

"Centurion. Explain to me again, why we have to stop at Serifos," he grumbled. "I'd hate to lose this stiff breeze."

The five-banker's Centurion held a hand over his eyes as he gazed at the island they were approaching. He didn't respond to Laevinus' inquiry. The Proconsul inhaled, preparing to deliver a verbal lashing to the inattentive commander of the warship.

"General Laevinus, you were Admiral of our fleet in the Adriatic Sea," his adjutant, Tribune Rasinia, reminded Valerius. "Refilling the ships', and the crews' waterskins is important before a long crossing."

Laevinus exhaled and nodded.

"I know, Rasinia. I know," he admitted. "It's just I expect a fleet from Pergamon to come over the horizon at any moment and take her back. The sooner we reach Republic waters and pick up more warships, the sooner I can relax."

"Sir, I believe your handling of the negotiations with King Attalus was a lesson in diplomacy," Rasinia offered. "So, while I understand the weight of your responsibility, I don't see the Pergamon King going against the agreement."

"And yet, we took her from her people," Laevinus warned. "If a foreign power came to Rome and snatched away the Sacred Flame of Vesta and took six Vestal Virgins, there would be rioting in the streets. And the men who allowed it, by necessity, would have to retreat to Capitoline Hill and hide behind temple guards."

"General, I know nothing about the Sibylline Books, prophecies, or the ten chosen to read the text and interpret the writings," Rasinia stated.

He indicated a circle of six men dressed in bright saffron robes. Two had metal cymbals in their laps, another pair rested copper horns across their arms, and one clutched a skin-tight tambourine.

A second tambourine lay on the deck beside the last priest. While the others held instruments, he embraced a shiny, black, misshaped sky rock. Pulled tightly against his chest, his hands squeezed the ungiving stone as if he feared it would float away. The pose resembled a parent hugging a child or a lover wrapped in the arms of a companion. While the six priests sat motionless, the robes of the Galli of Cybele (*cy-be-lee*) danced in the wind.

"But what I do know, sir," Rasinia concluded while looking at Laevinus, "the Goddess Cybele is guarded by six of her priests, two of the Republic's best warships, and you, a master tactician. My concern is with your health. We're ten days from Ostia. And sir, if you don't let go of the tension, you'll invite a visit from Morbi, and fall to one of the God's illnesses."

"You're correct, of course," Laevinus agreed. The General turned to the Ship's Centurion and inquired. "Which way around Serifos?"

"We could go with the wind to the north of the island, sir," the ship's commander answered. "But if any Pergamon warships are following, they'll figure we took the easy route."

"But we'll row to the south, and throw them off our scent," Laevinus said, summing up the tactic.

"Yes, sir," the Centurion confirmed. He addressed the ship's first officer. "First Principale. We're about to lose most of our air. Standby the oars."

8

"Second Principale, stand by the oars," the First bellowed.

Leaning in close to the General, Rasinia commented, "You weren't the only one worrying about King Attalus going back on his word."

"It's a relief knowing the Ship's Centurion also thought of it," Laevinus confessed. "And we are ten days…"

Before the Proconsul/General could finish, the Galli of Cybele erupted in a mantra, accompanied by a disjointed, rhythmless musical score. Even their voices were pitched to accent the disharmony of their song.

*"The erratic flight of the bee*
*The erratic flight of the bee*
*From flower to bloom*
*From flower to bloom*
*Flying about crazily*
*Flying about crazily"*

Cymbals clashed, horns blared, and tambourines thumped double time, all completely out of sync with the voices and with the other instruments.

*"Strikes by an enemy*
*Strikes by an enemy*
*From hikes to spikes*
*From hikes to spikes*
*Spear tips all bloody*
*Spear tips all bloody"*

Again, the cymbals clashed, horns blared, and tambourines thumbed out of rhythm. And the voices of the Galli purposely conflicted with each other.

*"Floods the river mighty*

*Floods the river mighty*
*From trickle to tragedy*
*From trickle to tragedy*
*Washed away in misery*
*Washed away in misery"*

After the last verse, the priests fell silent. The Gallus holding the sky stone passed it to another priest. The pause held until the symbol of the Goddess Cybele was settled in the arms of next man. Then, in harmony, and as good as any trained choir and rehearsed orchestra, the Galli crooned and played.

*"Goddess Cybele giver of life*
*Guardian and mediator*
*From disorder, from wilderness*
*From uncertainty*
*Guide us from the natural order*
*To harmony, to calm, to shelter*
*To safety*
*Goddess Cybele*
*Protector of society"*

Despite increasing the volume, the Galli maintained the professional sounding music and song.

*"The erratic flight of the bee*
*From flowers to bloom*
*Flying about crazily*
*But in your hands, Cybele*
*They return to the hive*
*Make sticky honey*
*And create wax*
*From wild activity*

*View the useful bee*
*Blessed by Cybele*
*Goddess Cybele*
*Giver of life*
*Guardian and mediator*
*From disorder, from wildness*
*From uncertainty*
*Guide us from the natural order*
*To harmony, to calm, to shelter*
*To safety*
*Goddess Cybele*
*Protector of society"*

To overcome the chanting and playing, the First Principale crossed the deck and dropped down to the rower's walk.

"Second Principale," the first officer shouted in the ear of the rowing officer, "have the oarsmen use the rhythm set by the priests."

"Are we going into battle?" the Second Principale teased.

"What?" the First asked.

The rowing officer laughed and began clapping to the rhythm. In moments, the rowers fell into the new stroke rate.

*"Strikes by an enemy*
*From hikes to spikes*
*Spear tips all bloody*
*But in your hands, Cybele"*

Powered by the oarsmen, even with the wind slacking off, the five-banker maintained her heading. The volume increased again, and the Galli swayed with the chant.

11

On the island, a white tower, high on a ridge, appeared.

A signal from the Centurion directed the navigators to steer into a bay. Not until the warship rounded the point did Valerius Laevinus notice the village of Paralia and the flames dancing within the walls of a shrine.

*"The shield walls hold*
*Stopping steel*
*And saving lives*
*From wild to cozy*
*The gift of safety*
*Blessed by Cybele"*

"Please be silent," Valerius Laevinus shouted. But his battle tested voice could not top the song of the Galli. Yet, he tried again. "I said, be silent."

If anything, the volume of the priest increased.

*"Goddess Cybele*
*Giver of life*
*Guardian and mediator*
*From disorder, from wilderness*
*From uncertainty*
*Guide us from the natural order*
*To harmony, to calm, to shelter*
*To safety"*

"Enough. I said, be silent," Laevinus bellowed.

The General took a step towards the circle of priests. Rasinia placed a hand on his arm and halted the forward motion.

"Sir, don't," the Tribune yelled in Laevinus' ear. "Each Gallus has a thin knife with a sharp blade."

"What do I care about knives?" an enraged Laevinus barked. "I am a Roman General."

"Sir, each Gallus carries the knife he used to castrate himself with," Rasinia informed Laevinus. "In short sir, I don't think they care if you die or they die, as long as the Goddess is honored."

*"Goddess Cybele*
*Protector of society*
*Flood the river mighty*
*From tickle to tragedy*
*Washed away in misery"*

Giving in to the reality that he was dealing with fanatics, Laevinus instructed, "Signal the escort warship and have them land infantry and investigate the fire at the shrine."

*"But in your hands, Cybele*
*As land drains empty*
*Rich dirt remains*
*From high to dirty*
*Wheat to barley*
*Crops grow hardy*
*Blessed by Cybele*
*Goddess Cybele*
*Giver of life"*

The second Roman warship raced to the shallows. But rather than backing to the shoreline, the quinquereme spun parallel to the beach and dropped twenty Marines over the side. A Centurion accompanied the infantrymen. They splashed to the beach and jogged to the burning shrine.

*"Guardian and mediator*

*From disorder, from wildness*
*From uncertainty*
*Guide us from the natural order*
*To harmony, to calm, to shelter*
*To safety*
*Goddess Cybele*
*Protector of society"*

General Laevinus didn't notice when the song ended. Events on shore held him rigid and focused.

"Centurion of the ship, put us on the beach," Valerius Laevinus ordered. "I need to know what caused that."

***

At the burning shrine, the combat officer bent forward and vomited. Rushing to the aid of their ill Centurion, the two squad leaders and a battled scarred Optio reached the stricken officer and extended hands to support him.

Shaking off the arms, the Centurion indicated the doorway to the shrine. After peering into the inferno, the NCO puked. Both squad leaders reeled back, dropped to their knees, and they vomited.

On the General's five-banker, Tribune Rasinia questioned, "What would cause that?"

"*Asebeia,*" one of the saffron robed Galli answered. "To burn a temple is blasphemy."

After his announcement, and while the warship backstroked to the beach, the Galli chanted softly.

*"Goddess Cybele giver of life*
*Guardian and mediator*
*From disorder, from wildness*
*From uncertainty*

14

*Guide us from the natural order*
*Goddess Cybele*
*Protector of society"*

## Chapter 2 – Ten Days to Ostia

For all the dipping and rising, the two-banker may as well have been a piece of driftwood. But rather than the tide, the raiders vessel was held against the rock face by the hands of the port side rowers. Bobbing below Cyclop's Cave, the liburna made no move forward to leave the cove. And while the outboard hands of the port side stabilized the ship, on both sides, the rowers held their oars low and ready with their inboard hand.

"Captain Diceärch, I think those were Roman warships," Sarpedon stated. "We need to get out of this place."

The crew understood the situation and a section of oarsmen nodded in agreement with the Sergeant.

"We do and we will, once Ambrus reports," Diceärch replied. "Right now, Sergeant, your attention would best be used to properly stow the bags of raw copper and the pumice stones."

Heavy bags of copper concentrate and lighter sacks of pumice stone lay scattered on the walkway between the rowers' benches. Dropped haphazardly when the oarsmen returned from the raid, the lighter packages of pumice took up more room. Yet, the less bulky bags of copper had more effect on the balance of the ship.

While Sarpedon directed a work party, shifting the heavier bags to the center of the two-banker, four oarsmen appeared at Cyclop's Cave. Three hopped down from the rock ledge but one remained on the shelf. Squatting, he turned his back on the ship, and watched the road that led to the white tower.

"Corporal Ambrus said to hold," one of the returning lookouts reported. "The first Roman war ship dropped Legionaries at the beach. They went to investigate the fire in the shrine."

"Where's the second five-banker?" Sarpedon demanded.

The NCO locked eyes with Diceärch to be sure his Captain was paying attention to the reply.

"The other warship is floating just offshore."

The navigator cleared his throat and offered, "If both warships were dry, we could be long gone before they launch. But smoke from the shrine will bring the garrison down long before that. In short, Captain, we should leave now."

Diceärch pointed in the direction of Paralia.

"Not while the five-bankers are afloat," he remarked. Then, he asked. "Navigator, what do you figure our profit will be from the raid?"

The shift from talking about the immediate danger to the economics of their mission baffled the navigator.

"Once the concentrate is smelted into copper ingots," he guessed, "we'll make a tidy profit, Captain."

"Did you hear that?" Diceärch announced to the crew. "Our navigator said we'll make a tidy profit. I disagree.

Because of our work and the raids by other ships employed by Philip V, the price of copper and pumice has risen. Buyers in marketplaces claim the higher prices are naked piracy."

Laughter rippled through the pirate crew, settling nerves, and buying Diceärch extra moments before they mutinied. He might be a good leader, but self-preservation and panic always overrode loyalty in a crew of brigands.

Diceärch preferred desperate men who threw off the façade of civilization to pursue coins and pleasures. Beyond the control of his authority as a Captain who delivered wealth and took care of his men, he had Ambrus and Sarpedon to enforce discipline. And because of his choices, none of the crew were in a position to cast moral judgement about the proclivities of their Captain.

On the rock ledge, the oarsmen waved while keeping his arm low. Diceärch noticed and pointed at the navigator.

"Stand by oars," the man shouted.

Relief washed over the rowers and sailors. They waited, anticipating the order to extend their oars.

\*\*\*

The fourth oarsmen dropped from the rock ledge and rushed to his rowing station. A moment later, Corporal Ambrus raced into view, jumped off the ledge, and landed facing Diceärch.

"The soldiers are jogging down from the tower," Ambrus described. "The second five-banker is being pushed onto the beach. We should leave, Captain."

In a gesture meant to relay thoughtfulness, Diceärch brought a blood encrusted hand to his equally soiled chin and bared his teeth. Pieces of flesh caught between his teeth dangled over his lower lip. Seemingly obvious to the horror he portrayed, the pirate Captain licked the pink meat.

"Sailors, raise your mast," he ordered.

"But Captain, the soldiers will see it," the navigator cautioned.

"And run to Cyclops' Cave where they will stop to taunt us," he explained. "Better that than the soldiers racing to the Romans and begging them to launch the five-bankers and chase us."

When the clang of armor and shields announced the arrival of the garrison from the white tower, Diceärch instructed, "Push us off gentlemen, and toss out your oars. We don't want to overstay our visit."

Rowers used their oars to shove the two-banker away from the rocks and the sailors unrolled the sail.

Once clear of obstructions, the navigator shouted, "Blades down, stroke, stroke. All together stroke, stroke."

A moment later, soldiers appeared on the rock shelf. By then, the liburna had moved out of javelin range. Shouts and insults were the only things to reach the pirate ship.

On the steering platform, Diceärch noted the receding shoreline and watched dispassionately as a group of agitated soldiers shook spears and danced around. Next, using his tongue, he scooped the pink meat back into his mouth and chewed contentedly. The sail filled with air and his ship glided away from Paralia, the white tower, and the garrison.

*** 

On the beach at Paralia, Valerius Laevinus stomped down the ramp and strutted across the beach. Behind him, Tribune Rasinia jogged to catch up. At a full sprint, ten heavy infantrymen spread out to form a protective screen around their General.

"What's going on at the shrine?" Laevinus questioned.

"Not sure, sir," Rasinia admitted before adding, "but it can't be good. I know the Optio. He's a veteran. There are few sights or vile deeds he hasn't seen."

Ahead of them, the combat officer, Legion NCO, and the squad leaders milled around, embarrassed by their displays of weakness. Even so, the four averted their eyes from the now smoldering shine, looking anywhere else except into the scorched interior.

"Centurion, report," Laevinus demanded.

"Sir, I can explain about the vomiting," the combat officer started to say.

Laevinus cut him off, "We'll discuss your delicate constitution later. Right now, tell me about the shrine."

"General. We splashed ashore, and seeing no threats from the village, I directed my squads to the burning shrine," the Centurion described. "As I approached the structure, the aroma of beef in a hot iron skillet combined with the fragrance of roasting pork made my chest pound and my mouth water. The smells brought back memories of my wedding feast and my family."

"I'll ignore the facts that you are a poet and a romantic with a weak stomach," Laevinus mocked. "What took you from the sweet memories to blowing breakfast like a vino-soaked barbarian?"

"Sir, if I might have a say," the NCO requested.

"Go ahead Optio," Laevinus invited. "Maybe you can tell me without the forlorn language."

"General, I will try, sir. When we reached the burning shrine, the smells in the air were frying beef and roasting pork," the Optio related. "But there was an odd tinge to the aromas. I've fought battles in burning towns. And although I'm familiar with the stink, I didn't associate it with the shrine, until I looked through the flames. There were two bodies cooking on the altar. Like the Centurion, I had the taste of meat on my tongue when I understood the only thing grilling was a single priest. The conflict between sight and smell revolted my stomach and I puked."

"But you said there were two bodies," Laevinus reminded the NCO.

"Sir, it was only one victim," the Centurion confirmed. "The second figure was the skin of the priest draped across the altar next to his skinned body."

"Blood from the execution covered his robe," the Optio added. "It's on the floor under the altar, sir."

Laevinus gazed into the interior and gasped at the two images burned into the altar. Almost as if an artist had drawn two men and the charcoal got smudged. Yet, it wasn't a drawing, or charcoal, but melted flesh and the charred remains that marred the pale granite.

"General, the garrison is coming," Rasinia alerted him.

From the west, files of soldiers ran through the village. While the inhabitants tried to stop them and talk about the raid, the garrison ignored them. At their front, a young officer ran faster than his men. Before the Greek officer arrived, the General's Legionaries closed in and formed a shield wall.

\*\*\*

About the same height as Rasinia, the Greek Captain appeared younger by years. In a glance, he observed the altar, spit on the ground, and sneered at Laevinus.

"This has to be the work of Diceärch," the Greek announced.

"You know who did this evil thing?" the General questioned. He spoke while looking over the Legion infantry shields.

"Diceärch is one of King Philip's raiders," the Greek officer replied, using a superior tone. "About a year ago, we began receiving reports about a pirate who hates the Gods, their temples, and their priests. But today, we're in luck."

"It wasn't lucky for the priest, or the shrine," Rasinia interjected. "Why would you be the recipients of blessings from Occasio?"

Using the name of the God who personified opportunity, luck, and favorable moments, let the Greek know the Tribune was puzzled by the statement.

"Not this tragedy, but the aftermath," the Captain tried to clarify. "Diceärch just launched from a cove a mile from here. His crew is rowing a liburna westward. With your five-bankers, you can easily catch him."

Rasinia flinched, every fiber of his being screamed to put the pirate up on a cross. But he didn't say anything. Rather, the Tribune looked to his General for guidance.

The aide wasn't the only one with visions of bringing the vicious pirate to justice. Valerius Laevinus flexed his jaw and crinkled his brow while holding an internal debate. After a moment, the contortions fell away, and his features went slack.

"We can't do it," he stated.

"But you Romans are the reason for the raids," the Greek growled. "The least you can do is help us."

"How is Rome to blame for pirates and raids in the Aegean Sea?" Tribune Rasinia asked.

In a move intended to deflect any scorn or insults from his General, Rasinia strolled around the infantry shields and faced the Greek.

"After Philip V signed a treaty with Hannibal and Carthage, he moved his army against city-states in western Greece. But you rallied the Aetolian League and shipped Legions across the Adriatic Sea to oppose him," the Greek lectured. "After Philip signed a treaty with Rome, he wasn't satisfied with Macedonia. He turned his attention eastward and set his eyes on Rhodes. The King has hired pirates to break Rhodes by destroying trade to the island nation."

"I still don't see the connection or the extension of blame," Rasinia pushed back against the narrative.

"As you witnessed here, they don't restrict their piracy to merchant ships. This is Rome's fault, and yours to remedy. Now launch those warships, and end Diceärch."

"We can't do that," Rasinia said, repeating General Laevinus' words. Going further, the Tribune pointed at the two warships. "We are charged with transporting a Goddess to Rome and dare not stray from our holy mission."

As they talked, a Gallus raced by the officers. With the bright saffron robe flying behind him, his passage was noticed by everyone. On the north side of the shrine, the Priest of Cybele came to an abrupt stop. Lifting his face to the heavens, he screamed.

On the five-banker with the Goddess Stone, the other five Galli began praying and playing their instruments. The priest at the shrine, while singing with the other priests, kicked over a pillar of stones. As it toppled, a broken oar blade fell to the ground. He shifted to another pair of pillars and knocked one of those over. A second oar blade crashed to the ground.

Rasinia sprinted to the makeshift altars and picked up one of the boards.

"*Paranomia*," he read a word carved in the oar blade. "Why would anyone create an altar to self-delusion and lawlessness?"

The Greek captain arrived and picked up the second piece of wood.

"This is the first one I've seen but I've heard of them," he announced. "You have *Paranomia*. And this is *Asebeia*. Reports tell us that Diceärch leaves two altars when he raids. One to self-delusion. And if you miss the target of his claim, the second altar is to *Asebeia*, honoring sacrilege and blasphemy. Surely after witnessing the depravity of the man, you can't refuse to go after him. You must stop Diceärch and end this scourge."

"We can't do that," Rasinia repeated the General's decision.

"Unfortunately, we cannot," Laevinus confirmed. "Rome's protection is more important than stopping a single pirate."

***

Late in the afternoon, the two warships pushed off the beach. Standing near the village, the Greek officer seethed at the Romans failure to stop the threat prowling the Aegean Sea.

On the flagship, Laevinus turned his back on the island of Serifos.

"If not for the Goddess," he remarked, "I'd have gladly gone after the pirate."

"Your decision is understandable, sir, our mission is more important," Rasinia assured him. "But I do wonder where the pirate learned his tactics. He arrived without being detected and escaped after we were on the beach. That reflects the patience of a talented commander."

"Don't go soft on me, Tribune. From what we saw, crucifixion is too good for Diceärch," Laevinus said. He inhaled sea air and faced west before the warship reached the mouth of the bay. "We should make Ostia in ten days. Once we hand off the Goddess and her priests to whatever delegation the Senate sends, I'm heading for my villa. It'll be good to sleep in my own bed."

"General, I believe every Roman commander since the founding of the Republic has felt the same way."

***

Two thousand miles to the west, Optio Decimia watched the fleet of merchant ships row out of Cartagena Bay. Flanking the transports, Roman warships assumed escort positions around the ten heavily loaded merchants. Turning, Sidia started to address Cornelius.

"General Scipio, this is…"

Cornelius raised a hand to stop his bodyguard. Then he lifted an arm and pointed a finger at the shoreline of Iberia.

"Over there, I am a General. Out here, and especially when we reach the border with Gaul and then the Republic, it's Dominus Scipio. Both my military title and authority vanish with each stroke of the oars. Behind me rests all the victories I commanded and respect I built in Iberia. Ahead. Well, ahead is a curtain, shrouding the future."

"Ahead is Villa Scipio," Sidia offered hoping to pull his General out of the melancholy. "In ten days, General. I mean Dominus. We'll reach Ostia. A day later, you'll be home."

Cornelius lifted his chin and gazed at the overcast sky. Between the movement of the clouds and the travel of the five-banker, the world seemed to shift. As if puzzle pieces, banks of clouds rotated, separated, and recombined as the ship sailed under them. The effect made Sidia dizzy.

"Can you feel that?" Cornelius inquired.

"I feel unsteady, sir," the bodyguard answered. "Should I be experiencing something more?"

"Remember when we first arrived in Iberia," Cornelius stated, ignoring Sidia's question. "No one expected me to survive, let alone thrive."

"But you did, Dominus," the bodyguard recalled. "You fought the Carthaginians and pushed them out of Iberia. Is that your plan for Rome? Are you going to conquer the Senate and the people of the Republic?"

"Yes, but not with a gladius and a shield," Cornelius advised.

"Then how, sir?" Sidia asked.

"I have no idea," Cornelius admitted. "I had hoped for guidance from the Gods."

"And did you receive any?"

"None. Absolutely no hint of a solution or a plan," Cornelius said. "The Gods are silent this morning."

Overhead, banks of clouds ripped apart, then joined with others to create new, more impressive formations. On the sea below, the wealthy fleet of Cornelius Scipio sailed with the wind, heading for Ostia in the Roman Republic.

***

A thousand miles to the east, the sky over Rome was as cloudless as the oracles were silent. But the ten men, who departed from individual carriages, weren't aware of the void, yet. They peered around Capitoline Hill in the manner of conspirators. Once finished with the visual inspection, they lined up. Then in a solemn procession, the ten men marched up the steps and entered the Temple of Jupiter.

At the end of the file, one of the men asked, "Did we do the right thing? What if our actions angered the Gods."

The other nine men continued to walk. Although silent about the statement, their steps weren't as confident as when they climbed the stairs to the temple. No one could answer the questioner because none of them knew the answer.

At the back of the temple, they approached an armored guard stationed in front of a doorway. The sentry stepped to the side, extended his spear arm, and opened the door. As was fitting, the ten men brushed by the Legionary's shield before crossing the threshold and descending a set of steps. The shield symbolized the limited access allowed to the underground room. While the door remained open, the guard moved to secure the entrance. His shield and spear served as a barrier, preventing unauthorized admittance.

***

Candles flared to life, casting illumination on the curved ceiling of a brick chamber. The ten men circled a table containing two bound stacks of ancient parchment.

*"To spare the city, seek a mother from the east,"* one of the ten guardians recited while placing his hands on the two books of Sibylline prophecies. "It is written by the oracles, and we all agreed, a new protector was needed. Required in fact to save Rome from Hannibal and to deflect the awful omens."

"By introducing a new Goddess into our society," the one who questioned their actions reiterated, "will we suffer retribution from Vesta, the protector of Rome? Perhaps the Sacred Flame will be extinguished. Or could the war Goddess Bellona, in protest to a new Goddess, abandoned us during the next battle?"

"Need I remind you that two snakes glided through the doors of the Temple of Jupiter in Naples," another guardian pointed out. "Or that recently, a pig with two heads was born. At Alba, two suns were seen, and in Campania it became light during the night. Here in Rome an ox spoke, and the temples of Ceres, Salus, and Quirinus were all struck by lightning. And to refresh your memory, the Sacred Flame of Vesta did go out and our Legions have lost every battle to Hannibal Barca."

"It's why we consult the books," an older advisor remarked. "As the Sibylline Books directed, to spare Rome further disasters, we sent Valerius Laevinus to Anatolia to

27

seek a Protective Mother Goddess. No God or Goddess should take offense at our steps to protect Rome."

"A new, dignified Goddess will be welcomed by the populace, I'm sure," another guardian proposed. "But now we need to find the proscribed method of welcoming the new Goddess."

The ten men whose duty required them to protect the books, and to decipher the prophecies, bent to the task of reading the pages. Even when the candles burned low, and the flames flickered, they continued. Finally, one spoke up.

"We have failed to find the proper ritual for a new Goddess," one announced. "Therefore, I vote that we turn the problem over to the Senate and allow them to decide on the formalities."

The ten agreed and extinguished the stubs of the candles. Then in a dignified manner, they took the steps to the rear of the temple. When the last guardian left, the guard sealed the chamber and positioned himself in front of the door.

They didn't know it, but they had ten days before the appearance of Cybele, and her fanatical priests, the Galli. And ten days before Cornelius Scipio, the conqueror of Iberia, landed his vast fortune at Ostia. Or that the arrival of both would trigger monumental changes in Rome.

### Chapter 3 – Lynx with Kittens

"Bad omens, undefeated enemies, and malevolent spirits abound. I know. What is needed. To change. The fortunes. Of Rome," the speaker stated.

Although spoken softly, the emphasis displayed certainty, even if the volume didn't. From atop the pedestal, his voice carried to a small crowd gathered around him.

"Tribune, what would you suggest?" Fulvius Flaccus inquired.

"Senator, thank you for asking," Marcus Cato acknowledged. The question from a Senator gave legitimacy to Cato's arguments. Using a louder voice, he answered. "We must return to the old way. Our founders revered the Gods and weren't afraid of extreme sacrifices. To show our adoration, we must bury living humans to honor the Gods. Perhaps then we will be heard as we entreat them for assistance. Yet, once we have the attention of our Roman Gods, what will they see? Our men in Greek robes conversing in Aetolian. I spit on the notion. Will our Gods recognize us if we parade around in Egyptian linen, speaking as the desert dwellers do? No, I say, never. We must reclaim our Latin ways. Else, our own Gods and Goddesses may perceive us as strangers and not answer our prayers."

Marcus Cato paused to allow his audience to focus on the last part. He started to speak again when an aide to the attending Consul of Rome appeared on the porch.

"Consul Philo has called an early start for the afternoon session," the assistant shouted. "Let the citizens of Rome and visitors to our city know an important matter has arisen, and it demands the attention of the Senate."

Having lost his audience, Cato jumped down from the pedestal. He was two steps from the stand when Senator Flaccus hooked his arm.

"Come to the session as my guest," Flaccus encouraged. "I'm sure my faction will want to hear your take on Philo's latest crisis."

"It would be my great honor, sir," Tribune Cato declared.

Joining the crowd, Flaccus and Cato navigated the steps up to the porch.

"We can't wait until you take the purple stripe," Flaccus remarked.

"I'm just twenty-eight, sir," Cato pointed out. "Four years short of qualifying for a Senate seat. But the Senate did lower the age for one of the Consuls. Maybe by next year, you'll also lower the age requirement for a Senator."

"Don't gamble your coins on that," Flaccus informed him. "We need our young men out fighting Hannibal and the Gauls. The only battles in Rome are old men fighting each other."

They climbed the steps together. But when they reached the porch, a pair of aides raced to Flaccus and began filling him in on Senate gossip. Who was the latest to verbally stab who in the back, and which coalition had disagreements and defections in their ranks. Fulvius Flaccus and the aides entered the Senate chamber with Marcus Cato following as a special guest.

\*\*\*

Consul Veturius Philo stood at the dais. Looking down, he studied a piece of parchment he had already memorized. The pose kept him from making eye contact with the Senators as they returned from the lunch break.

A couple of rows back from the front, a pair of older Senators shuffled to their seats.

"This better be a hot out of the charcoal, flaming problem," the eldest Legislature remarked, "to interrupt my midday nap."

"You know those cavalrymen," the one next to him remarked, "everything is full gallop and flying capes."

"How we ended up with two horsemen as Consuls," the first grumbled, "I cannot figure out."

"Infantrymen are steadier and not given to panic. That's for sure."

The same conversation, or close to it, floated under the sounds of sandals rasping on travertine floors and the whispers of aides passing information to their patrons. And the question was the reason Consul Philo occupied himself with the small piece of parchment. Because he too marveled at how a pair of cavalry commanders becoming Co-consuls of the Roman Republic.

*\*\**

Almost two years before, Veturius Philo, and his Co-consul Caecilius Metellus, had commanded Legions light in infantry but heavy with cavalry. An unbalanced and unnatural state, General Claudius Nero complained. But the entire eastern region of the Republic required mounted riders to effectively cover the territory. And both Legions were kept busy trying to maintain law, order, and control.

Yet, after months of keeping Hannibal Barca's army pinned up in southern Bruttium, nights spent chasing Gaelic raiders, and wild pursuits of rebellious Samnites back to their villages in the Apennines mountains, all enemy activity stopped.

"What do you mean nothing to report?" Nero exploded on his commander of scouts.

The airy room in the villa suddenly felt small and suffocating.

"General, it's a fact," the senior scout assured the Governor of Bruttium. "I've doubled my scouting parties, but they can't find any marauders or signs of recent raiding."

"I feel like a naked bather at the seashore and the tide has gone out leaving me exposed and sitting on the sea floor," Nero scoffed. "And it's left sand in the crack of my butt. I'm irritated and want to know what happened?"

Battle Commander Caecilius Metellus marched in, holding his head, and scowling.

"And where have you been, Colonel?" Nero demanded.

"Sir, Colonel Philo's Legion is patrolling south and mine to the north. We haven't had a chance to socialize. Last night, when he got in, we got caught up."

"Caught up in an amphora of vino, no doubt," Nero guessed. "I hope it was good Roman red."

"Actually General, it was Greek and not so good," Caecilius Metellus admitted.

"Why do I put up with you and Philo?" Nero complained. "I don't even like cavalrymen."

Something banged into the door, it swung wide, and knocked against the wall. Battle Commander Veturius Philo strutted in, trying to hide his intoxicated state. Bouncing off the door allowed him to right himself and to strut more or less straight to the Pro-consul's desk.

"Good morning, General Nero," Philo said, his words not in sync with his mouth. "It's a beautiful day. Isn't it, sir?"

Nero twisted around to judge how hard it was raining and the lateness of the morning.

While he was turned, the senior scout remarked to Philo, "My patrols are coming up blank on raider activity."

"We still see scavenging patrols from Hannibal's mercenaries down south," Philo responded. "Who is missing? Is it only the Samnites?"

"No, the Gauls have vanished as well as the tribesmen," the scout stated.

"Hold up," Metellus announced.

For long moments, he remained silent. Nero faced his senior scout and his two Battle Commanders. One had nothing to report, and the two Colonels were unsteady and barely on their feet.

"Caecilius, what are you thinking?" Philo questioned.

Caecilius Metellus licked his lips and squinted his eyes as if facing a bright light.

"My father and I hunted a lot while I was growing up," he described. General Nero snorted. But Philo held up a hand, asking for patience for the other Battle Commander. "One day, we couldn't find any game. Not a small mole, a marmot, hare, shrew, or a deer, all the wildlife had vanished from the area."

"Why?" the scout commander asked.

"A female lynx with three kittens," Metellus told him. "She was teaching the young ones to hunt."

"What has that got to do with our missing raiders?" Nero inquired.

Veturius Philo squared his shoulders before saying, "there is something big and dangerous heading this way, General."

"All the small bands of raiders and bandits are hiding," Metellus added.

"And if something is coming towards us, what do you propose we do about it?" Nero questioned.

"Allow us to take our Legions north," Philo said. "I'll take the seaside route and Metellus the inland track. Whoever it is, we'll flank their vanguard, get a measure of them, and come back with a description."

"How drunk are you two?" Nero demanded.

*** 

Four days later, Veturius Philo rode ahead of three hundred Legion and auxiliary cavalrymen.

"What do you expect to find, Colonel?" the Legion's senior combat officer asked.

"Senior Centurion, I don't know," Philo admitted. "Because we have no reports of a slow-moving land army, it might be an invasion from the sea."

"If those Macedonians want a taste of our steel, let them come," the combat officer maintained. "Their King Philip tried in Antolia when he made a pact with Hannibal. We showed him our shields and he ran. I never did get my blade wet."

34

"I have a feeling that will change soon," Philo commented.

His assurance was bluster as neither he nor Caecilius Metellus had confirmation of an enemy army coming from the north. After a tirade by General Nero about bad and reckless plans, he ordered the two Battle Commanders to investigate. Allocated only three hundred cavalry each, and no infantry, the Colonels in effect were reduced temporarily to Tribunes.

"Leave my infantry in place," Nero ordered. "Maybe a week of roughing it in the field will remind you about the hardships of a campaign. Take three hundred cavalry and go find me the Lynx with kittens."

\*\*\*

Philo and Metellus had enlisted a unit of light cavalrymen for courier duty. As the mounted Legions moved parallel to each other, the riders carried messages between the Battle Commanders.

"Riders coming, sir," the Senior Centurion notified Philo.

Shortly after the sighting, two of the light cavalrymen reined in.

"Colonel Metellus sends his regards, sir," one courier stated. "He wanted to notify you that he is setting up a marching camp at the Esino River. And that you shouldn't be jealous, sir."

Philo glanced at the sun, and decided it was too early to end the march.

"Tell Battle Commander Metellus that while he is bathing, we will continue hunting for the enemy," Philo directed.

"Yes, sir," the cavalrymen acknowledged.

The messengers headed off in a westward direction.

"If we turned east for ten miles, we could swim in the sea," the Senior Centurion mentioned. "If we continue straight, we'll reach the Esino River in ten miles or so."

"Now that is a good idea," Philo stated.

"The sea, the river, or both sir?"

"I want to put our camp near the river," Philo replied. "We can swim and water the horses. And while we're there, put our best fishermen to work. I favor fresh fish for dinner."

"Yes, sir."

The sun dipped low in the sky, forcing Philo to increase the pace. For a marching Legion, the distance would have required jogging. But with a mounted patrol, they caught sight of the river with plenty of daylight remaining.

"We'll put the camp at…," Philo stopped talking and looked over the Senior Centurion's shoulder. "Aren't those the same messengers we talked with earlier?"

The combat officer twisted around for a moment to study the approaching riders.

"I believe they are, sir. But who do they have tied to the extra horses?"

\*\*\*

Four mounts trotted to Colonel Philo and reined in. One of the couriers smiled and stated, "We didn't deliver your message, sir."

Veturius Philo eyed the two extra horses and the men tied to the mounts.

"I depend on you to keep me in contact with Colonel Metellus," he reminded the light cavalrymen. "But you seemed to have added to your duties. Can you explain them?"

"Battle Commander, I'd like you to meet Lieutenant Bōdasht," the courier replied. He indicated a Carthaginian. Next, he used a toe to nudge a Gaul. "And his guide, and not a good one, Ealadha."

"Bōdasht and Ealadha," Philo repeated their name before asking. "Why were you heading for Cisalpine Gaul?"

"Colonel, they weren't traveling north, sir," the other light cavalryman informed Philo. He lifted a pouch from a saddle horn and handed it to the Senior Centurion. "They were heading south for Hannibal Barca's camp."

The senior combat officer pulled a scroll from the pouch, blinked when he saw the addressee, and re-rolled the parchment. While handing the scroll to Philo, the Centurion offered, "Congratulations, Colonel."

Confused by the compliment, Philo read the message and understood.

*To the most honorable General Hannibal Barca,*

*Greetings from Iberia. I propose a meeting in the town of Perugia in Umbria. The topic will be combining my troops, siege engines, grain, and war elephants with your veteran forces. With our armies combined, we will fulfill destiny.*

*All glory to the great God Baal Hammon. Together with his blessings and our superior army, we will end the Republic and achieve our father's dream.*

37

*Until we meet, I am your loyal brother, General Hasdrubal Barca.*

Philo rolled the scroll and tucked it into his pouch.

"Senior Centurion, set up our camp at Iesi, double the guards, and run patrols over the Metauro River. Watch for the Carthaginian vanguard, I'll want a report," he directed. Then to his couriers, he questioned. "I know it's late. But can you guide me to Battle Commander Metellus this evening?"

"Yes, sir."

\*\*\*

By sunrise, Caecilius Metellus rode west to alert Consul Marcus Livius and his four Legions to the threat of Hasdrubal Barca. Shortly after he left, Veturius Philo led a patrol south with extra mounts and Hasdrubal's messengers. In two days, Philo would verify for General Claudius Nero the existence of a lynx with kittens in eastern Campania.

Out of necessity, both Colonels rode hard. For as the scroll stated, if the Carthaginian brothers met, the Republic would end.

Act 2

## Chapter 4 – The Brothers Barca

Veturius Philo, his patrol, extra mounts, and Hasdrubal's courier arrived at   Grumentum exhausted. Expecting to find ordered Legion camps and Legionaries doing normal duties, Philo halted on a rise above the town.

Almost extending to the town's wall, new stockade fencing outlined a separate camp. Although deserted, the less than perfect shape told the Colonel the encampment had to be the work of Carthaginian mercenaries. They were gone, but deserted and scattered gear displayed signs of a rapid retreat. Also missing from Grumentum were the Legions of Claudius Nero. Their tracks followed the discarded items heading south, meaning the Legions pursued the mercenaries.

"We'll rest for the night with the teamsters, get fresh mounts in the morning, and follow the Legions," he informed the members of his patrol.

To the weary cavalrymen's delight, in the morning, when Philo went to file a report with the Legion clerks, General Nero and his command staff came to them.

\*\*\*

Philo rode to the villa in Grumentum where Nero had set up his headquarters. At the entrance, he and the

Carthaginian took the steps to the porch. Before entering, Claudius Nero and his personal guards rode up.

"Colonel Philo, I could have used you," Nero complained as he dismounted. "Hannibal tried to recapture Grumentum. After we pushed his forces away, they tried me again at Venusia. But they were disorganized."

Nero reached the top of the steps and stopped to examine the Carthaginian.

"Sir, where is Hannibal?" Philo inquired.

"The scouts tell me he's running for Metapontum," Nero answered. "I've left a Legion and a Battle Commander to watch him. I'm back here to organize the wounded and rest the Legions. That's why I'm back. Why are you here?"

Philo pushed the Carthaginian messenger forward, "General I'd like to introduce you to Lieutenant Bōdasht."

"Did he get by my Legion lines?"

"No sir, not exactly," Philo informed Nero as he handed the General the scroll. "He never made it to your lines."

*** 

Messengers with letters and a copy of the scroll left for Rome at midday. By evening, Legionaries were collecting supplies for a long march. Morning found Battle Commander Philo, his infantry, and his cavalry racing ahead of the remainder of Nero's Legions. For speed, they left their supply wagons with the main column.

"Two hundred ninety miles, sir?" his Senior Tribune asked.

"That's what the map to Senigallia shows," Philo confirmed, "And we need to get there fast if we're going to stop Hannibal's brother at the river."

Whether an infantryman, skirmisher, or a cavalryman, covering almost three hundred miles rapidly takes a toll. But the Legion of Veturius Philo pushed through the pain. As did the Legions of Claudius Nero who were not far behind.

\*\*\*

While Nero had three times the distance to cover, the Legions of Marcus Livius were relatively close at one hundred miles from Senigallia. They should have arrived in time to stop Hasdrubal Barca before he crossed the Metauro River. But Consul Livius had learned, just a few years before, a harsh lesson about too much initiative.

\*\*\*

Battle Commander Caecilius Metellus entered the town of Narni, asked directions to General Livius' headquarters, and rode directly there.

"What's this about, Colonel?" the General's senior staff officer inquired.

"We intercepted a message from Hasdrubal Barca to his brother Hannibal Barca. Hasdrubal wants to meet in Perugia. We have a chance to stop him before he joins with Hannibal," Metellus rushed while answering. Then he insisted. "I must see Consul Livius."

"The Consul is busy with meetings and correspondence all afternoon," the Senior Tribune informed Metellus. "Why don't you go have a bath, find some decent clothes, and come back around midday tomorrow. I'll see if I can move the Consul's schedule around and fit you in."

"Did you not hear what I said," Metellus questioned his voice rising with each word. "The brother's Barca are a threat to Rome and the entire Republic. I must talk with the Consul."

"I'll let your outburst pass as you aren't under the Consul's command," the staff officer pushed back. "But if you persist in such disorderly conduct, I'll send a letter of reprimand to Consul Nero. And let him deal with you."

"My apologies, Senior Tribune," Metellus stated. "It's been a long ride and I got over excited. With your permission, I will see you tomorrow at midday."

"Certainly," the staff officer allowed.

Caecilius Metellus walked from the villa, his temper barely under control, and his hand a short distance from the hilt of his cavalry sword.

*** 

Washing and scraping took the road dirt from his body and the warm soak helped his attitude. Refreshed and dressed in a clean tunic, Colonel Metellus located the Tribune's mess and went for dinner.

"You're stationed down south with Consul Nero's Legions," an older man told him.

"I am, sir," Metellus confirmed between bites of lamb. "Caecilius Metellus. And your name?"

"Tiberius Longus, absentee Senator of Rome, former Consul of Rome, and once a General of Legions," the man replied.

"All the titles are in your past, sir," Metellus noted.

"Twelve years ago, I left the Legion as a Senior Tribune and went to my farm. While there, the Senate elected me to a

Consulship. I only visited Rome once during my year," Longus told him. "After my Consul year, I retired to my country estate. Three years later, they drafted me as a Proconsul and sent me to Lucania. I defeated the Carthaginian General Hanno and liberated the Lucania Region. Any idea what I did after that?"

"You retired to your country estate?" Metellus guessed. Longus plucked a small piece of lamb off the platter, popped it into his mouth, and began chewing. Metellus probed. "Unless your country villa is on the outskirts of Narni, I have to ask why you're here with Consul Livius' Legions."

"Very astute, Colonel. My villa and farm are directly north of Rome. I'm here as a character witness."

Metellus sat very still while considering the meaning. After a long pause, he asked, "Just what does that mean, Senator Longus?"

"Eleven years ago, Consul Marcus Livius commanded a successful campaign against the Illyrians," Longus answered. "When he left Illyria, he went to Carthage on a diplomatic mission. He and several Senators, unfortunately for Livius, very few thought they could make a deal with Carthage to recall Hannibal. His mission failed and when he returned to Rome the Senate tried him for malfeasance concerning war supplies."

"I don't understand, Senator," Metellus admitted.

"At the trial, the prosecuting side said Livius witnessed Roman merchants and transports from our allies in the harbor doing business at Carthage. But he didn't report the merchants or do anything to punish our allies," Longus explained. "They came very close to accusing him of taking bribes. But they didn't need to go that far. The Senate stripped Marcus Livius of his Consulship and he retired to his country villa."

"But, sir, he is a Consul now," Metellus pointed out.

"A reluctant and timid Consul," Longus clarified. "He doesn't lack courage and has an astute knowledge of tactics. He is a superb military commander. But Livius doesn't trust the Senate. I'm here to sit in on meetings to be a character witness in the event the Senate accuses him of something."

"Can you get me in to see him, Senator?" Metellus inquired.

"Once we finish eating," Tiberius Longus assured him.

The old Senator took another piece of lamb and chewed it while Colonel Metellus barely touched his food.

\*\*\*

Early the next morning, Battle Commander Metellus and his personal escort trotted out of Narni on the eastern road. Shortly afterwards, four Legion couriers galloped westward towards Rome and the Senate.

"Colonel Metellus, I thought you couldn't get a meeting with Consul Livius until today," his Centurion of Cavalry mentioned. "Aren't you going to see him?"

"Last night I learned an interesting lesson about politics," Metellus informed the cavalry officer.

"What's that, sir?"

"If you can avoid them, do," Metellus stated. "If you can't avoid politics, stay out of the Senate."

"But that's where they engage in the most politics, sir," the Centurion remarked.

"It's like a laundry service," Metellus commented. Confused, the cavalry officer cocked his head to the side. Understanding the look, Metellus explained. "If you act too independently, you'll suffer retribution. When you get revenge, your target will get avenged. Now repeat the steps endlessly, as of dealing with soiled linen sheets. That is Roman politics."

"Isn't that a rather cynical viewpoint, Colonel?"

"It is," Metellus agreed.

They rode in silence as the hills wrapped the city of Narni in green branches, while the path descended to the Esino River Valley.

***

One hundred miles to the east, a patrol galloped into the forward operating base of Philo Legion in the town of Iesi.

"Senior Centurion, we spotted their scouts twenty miles north of the Metauro River," the NCO reported. "We have maybe four days before their infantry reaches a crossing at the Metauro."

The combat officer faced south, then mentally called Colonel Philo asking when he was going to return. Two hundred cavalrymen could deal with scouts. But not an entire Carthaginian army.

"Good work," he complimented the patrol. "Go eat, clean up, and get some rest."

"Are we going north again tomorrow?" one of the cavalrymen asked.

"No, I'm sending you west along the Esino," the Senior Centurion told him. "You'll be looking for signs of their scouts crossing. I need to know if Hasdrubal changes course."

"So, you can tell the Battle Commander?"

"Go eat," the senior combat officer snapped, "and stop asking questions."

He wasn't angry. The Senior Centurion just knew the next question, and he didn't have any idea when Veturius Philo would return.

*** 

Three days of patrolling and hearing about the Carthaginian army getting closer, put the Senior Centurion on edge. The next patrol to come in, he met at the entrance.

"Pack your gear and head south to our fallback position," he ordered. "Don't clean up or eat. Pack and go."

"Bad news?" the NCO asked.

"Not yet, but I want us out before it gets bad."

"No argument from me, Senior Centurion."

He had half the patrols gone when a new group of riders appeared on the riverbank of the Esino. For a moment, he panicked but then the face of Battle Commander Caecilius Metellus came into focus.

Maintaining the vigil at the gate, Philo' senior combat officer saluted when Metellus trotted up to the entrance.

"Welcome to Iesi, Colonel," the Senior Centurion greeted him.

After scanning the camp, the Colonel inquired, "Where are your cavalrymen?"

"I've sent most of them south."

"How far out are the Carthaginians?"

"They'll be splashing across the Metauro by mid-morning. And I've seen no sign of our infantry."

"The Legions of Marcus Livius should be along any day."

"My patrols report Iberian and Ligurain heavy infantry in the march. Even with our combined cavalry, we don't have the weight to stop infantry. So, pardon me, sir, but any day sounds weak.

"Any day is all I have, Senior Centurion," Metellus admitted. "How far are we from the Metauro River?"

"At this location, there's seven miles between the Esino and the Metauro."

"We'll concede the seven miles to Hasdrubal," Caecilius Metellus declared. "But this is as far as his scout will go. The Carthaginian can't prepare for the unknown, and our cavalry will keep him blind."

"Rah, sir."

\*\*\*

Dirty might have been part of the discomfort, or soreness, or hunger for a full meal. Hard camp biscuits, and dried meat, gnawed on while on the move were not satisfying. But none of those came close to the bone deep weariness from long days and short nights of traveling.

"In the name of Consul Marcus Livius, identify yourself," an Optio demanded from the top of the stockade wall. The mounted scout reined in, blinked, then laughed. From inside the marching camp, the NCO asked. "Is something funny?"

"I was told to locate Iesi on the other side of the Esino River," the scout informed the Sergeant of the Guard. "But here in the dark, a Legion camp appears."

"Identify yourself," the Optio repeated.

"I'm the forward scout for Philo Legion, under authority of Consul Claudius Nero," the scout answered.

"The last report we had was Nero's Legions were at Grumentum," the NCO challenged, "some three hundred miles from here."

"General Nero is on the trail," the scout assured the NCO.

The sounds of approaching horses came from the dark before a Battle Commander and his staff reached the Legion camp.

"Open the gates and break out the cooking pots," Veturius Philo shouted. "My men need to eat, and I need an update on the Carthaginian advance."

No one spoke for a moment until a familiar voice scolded, "Took you long enough. Where's my Legion?"

"Colonel Metellus, I regret to inform you," Philo responded, "but your Legion is guarding General Nero's supply wagon caravan. A fitting position for a leaderless herd."

"There's no one else in the Republic who would dare to insult me like that," Metellus stated. "Open the gates for Colonel Philo."

\*\*\*

Predawn Marcus Livius moved his Legions across the Iesi River. Before they reached the Carthaginian camp, Livius ordered a right turn towards the coastal city of

Senigallia. In a curved maneuver, the Legions touched the coast on the outskirts of the city before angling inland on a northwest heading.

The movement put them downriver from where the Carthaginians had crossed the Metauro. With the Legion cavalry alongside the river, the Carthaginian mercenaries were cut off from their fording location. In a perfect sweep, Livius had prevented a retreat. Next, his heavy infantry swung wide sealing an area between the river and a set of steep hills.

Near the steep hills, Colonels Veturius Philo and Caecilius Metellus sat on their mounts. Behind them, rows of Legion cavalry waited on nervous mounts.

"This battle will make our reputations," Philo announced. "After our victory, we'll be famous. Never again will we buy our own drinks in Rome."

"Maybe they'll make you a Consul," Metellus remarked. "If we win. If not, you'll be cold and dead by the Metauro river."

Philo grinned to show he had no fear when trumpets blared from behind them. Metellus glanced back then faced Philo.

"We'll live," he assured the other Battle Commander. "General Nero has arrived. His Legions might be exhausted, but the Carthaginian doesn't know it."

Whistles shrieked, trumpets blared, and flags waved.

"Colonel Metellus, be careful today," Philo offered.

"Every day," Metellus assured his friend. "Out of curiosity, why today, specifically?"

"Because I'll need a trustworthy Co-Consul."

"Not me," Metellus stated. "I have no desire for politics."

"Too late to back out now, Consul Caecilius Metellus," Philo teased. Then he waved his arm and shouted to the Legion cavalry. "Squadrons, forward."

\*\*\*

Consul Veturius Philo pulled his mind from the past and peered around the Senate chamber. The Senators blamed the Consul for the ills of the Republic. Even though it wasn't really personal, they would have held anyone in the position to the flames, the thought still made him angry. Studying the legislatures, he took relief in the fact they only had mental lances to jab at him.

"Senators, take your seats," Philo encouraged. When only a handful paid attention, he shouted. "After the battle at Metaurus, I cut Hasdrubal Barca's head from his dead body and presented it to General Nero. If you don't want me to start harvesting heads, get to your seats. We have at hand the business of Rome."

The aggressive Senators sneered, and the passive ones nodded. But all went to their seats because foremost to each was the welfare of Rome.

## Chapter 5 - Most Virtuous

If Consul Philo wanted to be a Proconsul in the future and become a General of Legions, he'd need the support of the Senate. As it stood with only a couple of months left in his Consulship, he would never get the votes.

After his outburst of temper, Veturius Philo paused to study the makeup of the Senate. There were gaps and chasms he needed to bridge if he was going to save the remainder of his term. And that required finding balance between two disgruntled factions.

Battles with Hannibal had taken men in their prime, leaving an age gap in the Senate. Many of the older members of the legislative body wore bitterness like pieces of armor. That group slung words as if they were in combat and protected by their obligatory presence. Others, while they preferred to be retired, accepted the continuing duty as their fate.

On the opposite side of the age gap, younger ones resented being in the city and not on their farms or with Legions fighting the Carthaginians, the Illyrians, or the Gauls. To them, serving in the Senate fulfilled a family's tradition and not their ambition.

Between the old and the young, Veturius Philo and his contemporaries were mostly absent. Being prime military age, a seat in the Senate took second place to being officers in the Legions.

While the age gap presented issues, the real problem was the ravine between philosophies. Whether young or old, they embraced the principles of one side or the other. In popular discord, speakers referred to the philosophies as the Latin Ways versus Hellenization.

***

Pushing his thoughts aside, Philo announced, "We have been handed a delicate matter. The ten guardians of the Sibylline books have reached an impasse."

"Maybe they should have reached an impasse before sending Proconsul Laevinus to Athens for a new Goddess," an older Senator complained.

Across the chamber, a young Senator shot back, "He didn't go to Greece. The ten who decipher the oracles sent him to the east to find a Mother Goddess to protect Rome."

"Call it what you will, pup, but he went to Anatolia," the old legislator pointed out. "And those people are mostly Greek."

"Senators, if you please, let's keep it civil," Philo called for order. When the two shifted from glaring at each other to frowning at the Consul, he continued. "What's done is done and now we have a quandary. How do we greet the new Goddess?"

"Send the Priestesses of Vesta," a Senator declared. "Let the Goddess of the Hearths of Rome bring the Mother Protector into the city."

"That seems reasonable," another said, seconding the idea.

"If I might?" an older Senator requested.

Philo almost missed the soft-spoken man. Recognizing him as one of the chamber's elder statesmen, the Consul conceded, "The floor is yours, sir."

Pushing to his feet, the Senator related, "I have three daughters. They are a blessing to me and my wife. And they have filled my villa with laughter, for the most part."

"Is there a purpose to this rendition of a happy home?" a Senator, soured on his duty, demanded.

"If you wish a say, I'll call on you next," Philo proposed. "For now, please remain quiet and respectful. Continue Senator."

The old man cleared his throat and swallowed before saying, "My daughters have blessed me with three strong and successful sons-in-law. Daughters are a joy until required to make a unified decision."

"Is there any point to this?" Senator Flaccus inquired. "I'm seventy-seven years old, and I fear I'll be seventy-eight before the tale of his three daughters comes to a conclusion."

"Have you no sense of a good parable?" Senator Alerio Sisera asked.

"What parable?" Flaccus questioned.

As if misunderstanding Flaccus, Senator Sisera explained, "A parable is a tale with a lesson. Although some call them fables, such as Aesop's Fables, where a story has a moral to teach."

"I know what a parable is," Flaccus shouted.

"Then why did you ask?" Sisera inquired.

Frustrated by the exchange, Fulvius Flaccus sat back and folded his arms across his chest. Alerio Sisera saluted and passed the floor back to the Senator with the daughters.

"As I said, daughters are a joy until you ask them to make a decision. Then they squabble, argue, and create havoc."

"I believe, I understand," Crassus Dives announced.

"Please Pontifex Maximus, if you'll clarify for the Senate," Philo invited Crassus to speak.

As a Senator, and the head of all the temples in Rome, Crassus Dives had the admiration, or the begrudging respect, of most citizens. Religious politicians had different effects on different people.

"He is saying to have the Goddess Vesta meet the Mother Goddess would create friction between the Goddesses," Pontifex Maximus Dives summed up. "Just as daughters will disagree, so would two Goddesses with overlapping responsibilities."

"Where does that leave us?" Philo questioned.

"If I might?" Alerio Sisera requested.

"The chamber recognizes, Senator Sisera," Philo granted.

"I have a son and a daughter. Twins in fact," Alerio told the Senate. "Other than the occasional squabble, they support each other. I believe we need to advance a supporting God to welcome the Mother Protector."

All eyes turned to the Pontifex Maximus. Crassus put his face in his hands as if prostrating himself while seeking wisdom. The Senate fell silent, expecting him when done, to forward a God that complimented the new deity.

"The answer lays in Senator Sisera's example," Crassus Dives proposed as he dropped his hands and raised his face to the ceiling. "Gods are jealous of their domains. Sending another could be a mistake."

Bewildered, a younger Senator asked, "If not a Priestess of Vesta, or a priest from another temple, then who do we send?"

"We send our best," Dives proposed. "Our finest example of Roman manhood, and our most virtuous maiden. If the new Goddess is to protect us, she should be greeted by the ones under her care."

Veturius Philo developed an immediate headache. The solution was as simple as it was complicated. If he opened debate on the finest example of Roman manhood, the factions would tear the Senate apart. Should the man be steeped in The Latin Way, or could he embrace The Greek Style? The arguments, already thrashing from side to side in the Consul's mind, increased the mounting pressure.

"Consul, if I might make a suggestion," Alerio requested.

"Senator Sisera, please."

"I propose the Senate lean on the Pontifex Maximus to choose the finest man and the most virtuous maiden," Sisera recommended. "He can, after all, consult with the temples of Rome about his decision."

"The motion to have the Pontifex Maximus choose the welcoming committee is put before the Senate of Rome," Philo exclaimed. "Do I hear a second?"

"I second the motion," stated the old Senator with the three daughters.

\*\*\*

Passing through the cattle market to reach the shrine, Nasica Scipio dodged livestock on his hiked to the Temple of Hercules. Nasica always liked the temple because travertine columns surrounded the structure. Without a grand entrance like Jupiter's temple, it seemed unpretentious and welcoming from any direction.

"What can Hercules do for you?" a priest inquired.

"Give me strength to deal with my mother," Nasica said while laughing. As he handed a coin to the temple cleric, he clarified. "I received a message to come here.

However, it wasn't signed, nor did it explain the purpose of my visit."

"Please go inside," the priest directed. "It was a pleasure to meet you, Dominus Scipio."

Being called Master by the priest felt odd as did the used of his family name by a stranger. Nasica stared at the cleric for a long moment. Then, fearing he was being rude, he bowed to the priest, strolled between a pair of columns, and entered the temple.

"Nasica Scipio come sit with me," Crassus Dives invited.

The Pontifex Maximus reclined on one sofa and indicated another across from his. The seating wouldn't have been out of place in a feasting hall or a public room. But the couches were under the statue of Hercules, making it a unique setting.

"In a temple?" Nasica inquired. Then he remembered his companion managed all the temples in the city. He attempted to rephrase. "I mean casually lounging in a temple can't be proper, sir."

"Under different circumstances, I'd agree," Dives replied. "But this isn't a social visit. Sit."

Rather than sprawling on the sofa, Nasica perched on the edge of the cushion.

"You don't drink much or go out with friends for rowdy nights on the town," Dives stated. "Why?"

"Well, sir, since my father was killed in Iberia, I stay home to take care of my mother and the affairs of the estate," Nasica told him. "Is that a problem?"

"Not that I know of," Dives assured the young man. "You don't abuse the household staff from what I can tell. And you pay your family's bills on time. Although you use an uncle to sign contracts."

"I'll be twenty-five in a few years, Pontifex Maximus. Then I can take care of my own finances."

"Of that I have no doubt. But let me ask," Dives questioned, "can you resist free vino, temptations of the flesh, and sacks of coins for personal appearances and endorsements?"

"Are you going to put me in the gladiator games?" Nasica inquired. "Those are the only people who get paid to attend parties and social functions."

Crassus Dives elevated his eyes and gazed at the statue of Hercules.

"Lend him the strength to perform the labors of a hero," Dives prayed. Lowering his face, he peered into Nasica's eyes. "I need your word that for the next five months, you will not become a public speaker or a paid public figure."

"It's not much to ask," Nasica informed the Pontifex Maximus, "because no one wants me for either of those."

"Oh, but they will, Nasica Scipio. They will indeed."

\*\*\*

Clouds moved over the sun, dulling the afternoon. The gloom matched the mood of Quinta Claudia. As a little girl, Quinta dreamed of being a Vestal Virgin. She aspired to tend the sacred fire and to protect the Temple of Vesta, just as the Goddess protected the households of Rome. Plus, the Priestesses of Vesta dressed beautifully. And when they stately paraded by in a procession, spectators inhaled the rare and lovely fragrances that marked the passing of a Vestal Virgin. Alas, she wasn't chosen for the honor. And the dreams of a child faded while waiting for her father to find a suitable husband.

Round like the Temple of Hercules, but elevated above street level, the Temple of Vesta was open to all citizens during the day. At night, only women were allowed inside. Guards made sure of it.

Quinta approached one of the armored sentries and extended the letter her family had received.

The sentry examined the letter, stood erect, saluted her, then gestured towards the steps. Feeling as proud as a Vestal Virgin, Quinta Claudia marched up the first few steps while resisting the urge to turn around and wave at the pedestrians on the street. Giggling, she ran to the top of the stairs and entered the temple.

***

Even after the muted light outside, the interior of the temple became murkier, making it hard to see. Two figures came out of the darkness to stand on either side of the girl. For a moment Quinta panicked, but a sniff informed her the figures were Priestesses of Vesta.

"What can Vesta do for you child?" one cooed.

"I'll be fourteen in the spring and will soon be married," she protested. In an embarrassing flash, Quinta realized where she was and who she was lecturing on the legal age of womanhood. "My apologies, Priestesses of Vesta. My father received a letter, instructing him to send me to the temple. I'm overly excited and forgot my manners."

"Then come with us," they encouraged.

A curtain parted and the trio entered a room filled with burning candles.

"She's delightful," a priestess announced.

On a sofa, a man sat upright in a dignified pose. He bowed his head acknowledging the pair of priestesses. Then he examined Quinta from her freshly washed hair to the new sandals on her feet.

"Quinta Claudia, do you have a lover?" the man asked.

His bold question caused Quinta to stagger back towards the curtains. One of the priestesses extended an arm and stopped the retreat.

"It's not what it seems," she eased out the words.

The feel of her arm and her smooth voice calmed the girl.

"I do not, sir," Quinta told the man. "I am waiting for a husband who will benefit my family."

"Spoken like a true daughter of Rome," Crassus Dives declared. Then he asked. "Have you spoken blasphemy about any Gods or Goddesses, desecrated a shrine, or spoken harshly to your elders?"

"Sir, I can assure you that I have never and will never act in such a disgraceful manner," Quinta swore.

"Priestesses, can I get your opinion?" Dives inquired.

"She's cute, has the right credentials, and the proper attitude," a Vestal Virgin replied.

The other hugged Quinta and announced, "I believe Pontifex Maximus, that this is the most virtuous maiden in Rome."

"Keep her safe until the caravan is ready and the chaperone comes to take her off your hands," Dives directed. He stood and added. "She is the most virtuous, keep her that way."

## Chapter 6 – Family Reunion

Veturius Philo sat on his horse watching the wagons roll away.

"We did the best we could," Crassus Dives remarked.

Philo looked down into the carriage of the Pontifex Maximus.

"You did it," the Consul admitted," and saved me from the debate from Hades."

"Or a civil war," Dives advised. "There's nothing to do now but prepare for the arrival of the Mother Goddess."

"Where are you going to house her?"

"Until we get the new temple built on Palatine hill," Divis replied, "I'll have the Temple of Victoria share space. I figure a Protective Mother can't be too insulted being close to the Goddess of Victory."

"They are two sides of the same coin," Consul Philo proposed. "Have a healthy and prosperous day, Crassus."

"May the blessings of the Gods go with you, Veturius."

Consul Philo nudged his mount and the horse trotted forward, circled the guardhouse that marked the extreme edge of the city and circled back towards Rome's defensive walls. As he came around, he issued a salute to the Pontifex Maximus.

Crassus Dives returned the salute as his driver hauled back on the reins, forcing the horses to step back. The carriage traveled in reverse until it reached a broad section of the roadway. There the teamster snapped the whip, and the team walked a half circle before trotting forward to the gates in the Servian Wall.

As the Consul of Rome and the Pontifex Maximus approached the city, the best man and most virtuous maiden of Rome traveled southwest towards the city of Ostia.

***

Seventeen miles from Rome, the seaside city of Ostia had five major features. Three were gifts from the Gods and two emerged from Roman ingenuity.

Osita sat near the mouth of the mighty Tiber River. At non-flooding times of the year, merchants could bypass Ostia and row directly to the docks at Rome. But when The Blond flowed high on its banks, shipments were dropped at Ostia and transported to the city by wagon. Additionally, the area was a natural harbor with miles of flat shoreline. The beach space allowed the Roman Navy to train oarsmen, sailors, and ships' officers on the coast. And in the low area between Ostia and the Blond Tiber, salt flats allowed for the harvest of the precious mineral year-round. Those three features were gifted to the citizens of Rome by the Gods.

From the muscle and ingenuity of the Republic, manmade structures included the Legion fort. Built to stop a land invasion and to guard the mouth of the Tiber, the walled fortress and barracks occupied a large swath of land. And on the shoreline, but of economic importance, were the original wooden wharfs. Centuries of wooden poles and boards, many rotten and split by seawater were in a constant state of repair. And for the future, inventive posts adjacent to the old dock were under construction, using a new material, poured concrete.

***

The first warship in Cornelius' fleet rowed by the docks, heading for the beach. His second five-banker cut a half circle and rowed farther from the land.

"You could watch the unloading from on shore, sir," the Ship's Centurion suggested. "It would be more comfortable."

Cornelius Scipio didn't speak until the warship completed the full circle and faced the docks. Rowers held their oars in the water to steady the warship.

"Centurion, I don't think my presence in the middle of that would be welcomed," Cornelius offered.

On shore, wagons of lime and ash backed up to what resembled a dry pond. Men scooped the elements into the pond and mixed them with short paddles. Once the gray ash was streaked through with ribbons of white lime, porters carried buckets of seawater from the Tyrrhenian to the pond.

"What are they doing?" Sidia Decimia inquired.

"The engineers are building a new pier," Cornelius answered.

"That can't be right," the bodyguard protested. "I've watched the Legions build bridges. First, they cut down trees and trim them into poles. Then they hoist them under a tall tripod and drop a rock on top, driving them into the mud. But maybe they've finished setting the pilings."

"No log pilings," Cornelius explained. "The concrete will be poured into forms and left to harden."

From the beach, a large flat boat, almost raft-like, was paddled into a position between the land and a structure poking out of the water. Unfortunately, the presence of the construction boat blocked part of the wooden pier, hampering the docking of Cornelius' transports. His first merchant ship struggled to reach the wooden dock.

"I don't see any forms, Dominus," Sidia offered.

"It's the pieces of wood beside the flat boat just poking out of the water," Cornelius pointed out the forms. "What I can't figure is how they're going to get the concrete from the pond to the form."

Boards were laid from the land to the flat boat and tied down. With the raft stabilized, buckets of concrete were scooped out of the pond and dumped onto a flat piece of leather. Four men folded the corners over the concrete and tied them in pairs. Porters inserted a pole, lifted the load of concrete, and carried it onto the flat boat. With the space cleared, the four other men spread a new piece of leather for another load.

"There's your answer, sir," Sidia noted.

On the raft, a foreman guided the leather sling of concrete over the form. He shoved two corners off the end of the pole and held the other two. The sling flopped open, and the concrete fell into the form. The leather was taken away for another load. Laborers began shoveling an equal amount of gravel into the form.

"Centurion, how long will it take to unload my transports?" Cornelius inquired.

Stretched out to the north, nine merchant ships drifted along the coast. Each hauled valuables secured in Iberia. After maneuvering with its oars, ropes were tossed from the first merchantman to a team of dockworkers.

"Sir, with the limited docking space, it could be the rest of the day," the ship's officer replied. "Unless we double stack the transports."

"Why didn't you bring that up before?"

"It depends on the current from the Tiber, sir," the Ship's Centurion explained. "We won't know until the first transport docks. And even then, we have no way of knowing when heavy rains in the mountains will wash down. A sudden current could strip away the outboard ship."

For several moments, Cornelius studied the workers as they filled the piling. Finally, he inhaled and resigned himself to not supervising the unloading of his treasures from a warship.

"Take us to the beach," he ordered. "At least I can arrange for wagons while I wait."

A squad of Cornelius' infantrymen dressed in nondescript armor and holding Iberian shields, jogged to the dock from the first warship to beach. They stood guard as bars of silver were offloaded from Scipio's first transport.

***

The Priest of Victoria shifted, trying to find a more comfortable position. Each bump in the road sent a jolt through the wagon to his backside.

"One would expect a good Roman road to connect Ostia to Rome," Priest Ceionia complained.

64

"Capable cleric," Nasica Scipio proposed, "I don't mean to criticize, but the road is made of the finest materials and laid with the expertise of the Central Legion. There is possibly no better roadway in the entire Republic."

"I will endeavor to persevere," Ceionia vowed. "How much longer do I have to withstand the assault of the wagon bed?"

Their teamster answered without turning his head.

"We just passed the four-mile marker, priest."

"We could get out and walk," Nasica offered. "It's a lovely day and a walk will stretch our legs and fill our lungs."

"Is nothing ever a problem for you?" Ceionia questioned.

"I do get irritated when the farm manager is late sending his reports," Nasica admitted. "But I find a sternly worded message cures him of that ill for a few months."

The priest stared at the young man for a while before stating, "You just might be the best man in Rome."

"But I'm not in Rome. We're almost in Ostia with no idea when the Goddess will arrive. Therefore, it stands to reason, I cannot be the best man in Rome."

"Ouch," Priest Ceionia uttered when the wagon hit another bump.

*** 

In the transport behind Nasica Scipio, Bestia, the chaperone sneered at Quinta Claudia.

"I've heard you are not chaste, or an honest person," Bestia accused Quinta.

"But, ma'am, I am a dutiful daughter," Quinta pleaded her innocence.

"And it's rumored you spent time alone with numerous men."

"By the Gods, that's a lie," Quinta protested. The young girl fought back tears while begging. "Why would you say such mean things?"

"A soiled maiden for a soiled Goddess," Bestia answered. "After the word gets out about you, Rome will never accept the Greek deity."

Quinta crowded into the back of the wagon as if she was a small animal trapped by a hungry wolf. The reason she was on the way to Ostia to greet a new Goddess rested on her reputation. If tarnished, her life would be ruined and her future bleak.

From the front of the wagon, the teamster announced, "Four miles to Ostia, ma'am."

***

Cornelius Scipio led the horse out of the stable and glanced at the sun. Half the day had slipped by and most of his merchant ships were still waiting to unload.

"Stableman, where can I find an agent?" He called into the barn. "I need to rent a villa, a walled villa."

If he was a Pro-consul / General, or traveling under Legion orders, the fort would provide security for his shipments, wagon teams, and overnight housing. As a private citizen, he needed to rent a villa, acquire transports, and buy food for the men in his security detail.

"The town Magistrate handles rentals, sir."

Cornelius handed the stockman a pair of bronze coins, mounted the horse, and rode for the center of Ostia.

***

By midafternoon, the villa manager finished showing Cornelius the lower levels of the estate.

"Come and let me show you the highest room in the house, Dominus," the manager invited. "From there, you get a lovely view of the ocean and the horizon."

"This is not a vacation," Cornelius said, turning down the offer. "I only expect to be here one night before my transports head for Rome."

"Still, sir. Such a view is not to be ignored."

"In this case, I will ignore it. I need to get to the dock."

Cornelius wanted to be polite and gracious. But he had wagons being filled with bars of silver, iron, and gold, and slabs of copper and lead coming off the ships. Once across the docks, the problem started. Wealth drew criminals, and vast wealth would draw a horde of thieves. To protect the metals, Cornelius either had to keep it moving and heading to Rome or house it behind walls for the night.

He rode away from the villa remembering as a General in Iberia, he had Tribunes and Centurions to handle these issues. As a citizen of the Republic, it fell to him.

***

Trotting from the residential avenue to the main road, Cornelius started to guide the horse to the left. But he spotted an odd caravan coming down the road and reined in at the intersection. Four wagons composed the bulk of the convoy. Escorting the wagons were six temple guards, their clubs hanging from saddle horns. If it was only a supply caravan from a temple heading for Ostia, there'd be no mystery.

But it was more, much more. Four Lictors of the Republic accompanied the wagons and temple guards. And for anyone not sure of the convoy's importance, the Lictors rode with the symbols of their office resting on their left arm. An ax with the handle surrounded by rods of elm, and tied with bands of red leather, the fasces represented a dire warning. Any of the Lictors could execute an offender for any offense, meaning the wagons were under the protection of the Senate of Rome.

Cornelius looked with curiosity at the approaching convoy. Then realizing if he remained motionless, the wagons would pass him, and he'd be stuck behind the slow-moving vehicles. He put heals to the horse's flanks. At three paces forward, a voice called out.

"Cousin Cornelius. Cousin Cornelius. Over here."

Vainly glancing at the villas on either side of the avenue, and then at the open fields along the roadway, Cornelius was unable to locate the source of the voice.

"Cousin Cornelius, I'm in the wagon," Nasica Scipio directed.

Gnaeus Scipio died with his brother, Cornelius' father, in Iberia. A chance meeting with Gnaeus' son, Nasica, on the road to Ostia in a Lictor protected caravan caught Cornelius by surprise. Confused, he jerked on the reins and the horse stopped in the middle of the roadway.

"Nasica?" he questioned.

"In the name of the Senate of Rome move out of the way," a Lictor threatened, "or suffer the consequences of your actions."

Delaying the family reunion, Cornelius kicked the horse to get the beast moving before the Lictor reached him. Trotting towards the dock, he glanced over his shoulder and inquired, "We need to catch up. Where are you staying?"

Nasica ducked into the wagon, apparently seeking an answer. When he reappeared, he shouted, "Near the Shrine of Bellona in the Legion fort."

"I'll see you once my cargo is secured," Cornelius promised.

blank page

## Act 3

## Chapter 7 - The Goddess of War

Harnessing the authority of the Lictors, the convoy rolled into the Legion fort unquestioned. At the Shrine of Bellona, the best man in Rome and the most virtuous maiden were assigned quarters adjacent to the shrine.

"This is your home while we wait for the arrival of the Mother Protector," Ceionia informed Nasica. The Priest of Victoria strolled into the suite, sniffed then held his nose.

Nasica Scipio walked into the public room of the two-bedroom apartment. Rustic and unadorned, the accommodations were previously occupied by fanatical Bellonarii, priests of the Goddess of War. And the rooms smelled of sweat, minted rubbing oil, and vinegar as if the place was a gymnasium.

"The accommodations are better than I expected," Nasica proposed. He walked to a spear, shield, and gladius hanging on the wall and considered the war gear. "At least we have some privacy. They could have put us in a barracks with eighty infantrymen."

"You sound disappointed," Ceionia noted.

"I am," Nasica admitted. "Mostly I only get to hear about the outside world from visitors to the villa."

\*\*\*

In the next apartment, Quinta Claudia huddled in the corner of a bedroom. Bestia stood over her.

"Raise your voice, tell anybody about my plan, and I'll stab you," the chaperone warned. "Better, yet, I'll slash that face of yours. No quality husband will want a soiled, disfigured woman."

"But I'm the most virtuous maiden in Rome," Quinta protested. "The Pontifex Maximus chose me."

"And now he's casts you aside. Remember, I have a knife and a duty to kill you if I choose to protect the accursed Greek Goddess," Matron Bestia shot back. "And I don't need you alive to accomplish my mission."

"Then why keep me alive?"

"A living example of bad behavior is better than the memory of a dead girl," the matron answered. "Remain silent and you'll live. Speak out and be martyred along with the Goddess."

Sobs racked Quinta and she remained huddled in the corner as if hiding from reality. The matron closed the door to shut out the sounds of misery.

"She worships at the altar of Coalemus," Bestia mumbled to herself. "Blessed with the gift of stupid by the God, and too sheltered by her family, she has no backbone. Thank you, Quinta Claudia, for making my job easy."

***

In the town of Ostia, neighbors in the villas around the rented compound watched as armed men escorted six wagons down the avenue. They assumed, based on the cargo, the people renting the place would stay for a while.

"One night, Tribune," Cornelius assured the staff officer. "Keep the metals safe overnight and we'll be in Rome tomorrow afternoon. And you'll be with your family by the evening."

"You can count on me, General," Gordian replied. "The Centurion and I have assigned a watch rotation."

Cornelius wanted to remind the young nobleman that he was no longer a General. But correcting him seemed petty compared to the duty of guarding a fortune.

"I'll be at the Shrine of Bellona if anything comes up," Cornelius advised.

After returning a salute, Cornelius took the reins from Sidia. The former General and his bodyguard walked their horses through the entryway. Behind them, the gates closed, and the locking bar dropped into the brackets. They mounted and rode from the rented villa.

\*\*\*

Where an open roofed shrine in Rome might accommodate thirty people at the most, the Shrine of Bellona in Ostia could welcome one hundred Legionaries, Marines, rowers, or sailors. To serve the Goddess of War and to disburse her blessings, the shrine supported ten Bellonarii. Two of the priests marched to the quarters where the guests were housed.

A knock brought Ceionia to the door of the apartment.

"May I help you?" the Priest of Victoria asked a young man with scabbed lines crisscrossing both arms.

"The venerable priests of Bellona invite the best man in Rome and his escort to our evening service," the Bellonarus replied. "There will be a reception afterwards."

73

"Considering the generosity of the shrine," Ceionia responded, "I don't see how we could turn down your offer."

"I will inform the head priest," the young cleric said.

Ceionia closed the door and shuddered.

"Priest Ceionia, who was at the door?" Nasica Scipio inquired.

"We're going out this evening. To the shrine, to witness a ceremony honoring the Goddess of War."

"Euge," Nasica exclaimed, voicing a cheer. "The worship of Bellona is so often shrouded in secrecy. It'll be interesting to see a ceremony firsthand. Should I leave my knife in the room or wear the blade?"

"From what I just saw, the priests of Bellona won't care."

\*\*\*

The second Bellonarus rapped on the door to the other suite.

"What do you want?" Bestia demanded.

"The most virtuous maiden in Rome and her escort are invited to a ceremony honoring the Goddess Bellona," a man with multiple scars on both arms replied. "There will be refreshments and a reception after the service."

"We will not be attending," Bestia snapped. "Leave us alone."

She slammed the door, but something prevented it from closing all the way. In a snit of anger, Bestia pulled the door back and slammed it harder. The door hit and bounced away from the frame.

"This door," Bestia started to complain when she noticed the bleeding knuckles of the priest.

Despite the painful injury, the Bellonarus kept his hand on the frame. In a calm, but resolute tone, he informed the chaperone, "The head priest of Bellona is not accustomed to having his invitations turned down."

"We have traveled far today," Bestia explained. "We are too exhausted for socializing."

The priest glanced at his bleeding knuckles. Next, he stared into Bestia's eyes and stated, "The most virtuous maiden in Rome and her escort are invited to a ceremony honoring the Goddess Bellona. There will be refreshments and a reception after the service."

Agents of disharmony and subterfuge aren't swayed from their mission by much. An intense, unfeeling, and committed priest constituted one of them.

"We'll be there," Bestia uttered before gently closing the door. Turning around, she advised. "Quinta Claudia, pull yourself together and get dressed in your long robe. We're going out. But remember, what I said."

***

Cornelius and Sidia galloped to the gate of the Legion fort.

"Open in the name of the Governor of Iberia," Sidia announced. "He has a meeting at the Shrine of Bellona."

The last thing an afternoon sentry wanted was anything involving the Officer of the Guard. And by delaying a high-ranking official, he would draw the attention of his Centurion. The Legionary hoisted the cross bar and saluted the Governor as Cornelius and Sidia rode into the Legion fort.

"Not a Governor anymore," Cornelius remarked.

"I'm still an Optio of Legions," Sidia countered. "And it's still my job to open doors for you, sir."

***

A good engineer could fit a full-sized temple into the footprint of the shrine at Ostia. But the main Temple of Bellona rested to the west of Rome, outside the Servian Wall, on the Field of Mars near the Tiber River. Barely eighteen miles away, the Pontifex would not allow another temple to the Goddess in the region.

"It's a big shrine," Sidia mentioned.

"If you were the Goddess of War and you built a shrine in the Republic's largest naval fort, would you make it average?"

"No, sir," Sidia described. "I'd push the boundaries until the head of the temple threatened to ride down here and demolish it."

"It appears someone did just that," Cornelius confirmed.

He slid down from his horse, and a priest, with slash marks on his arms, rushed over to take the reins.

"Welcome to the Shrine of Bellona, Dominus," the priest greeted him. "I'm afraid the shrine is closed for a private ceremony."

"If it includes Nasica Scipio, then I'm invited," Cornelius told the cleric. "And where I go, my bodyguard goes."

"The best man in Rome is expected," the priest told him. "In the name of Pontifex Terrigenus, you are welcome to the Ceremony of Blood."

Sidia handed the priest a coin. Then he and Cornelius strolled alongside the shrine, moving towards the entrance.

"That answers that," Cornelius remarked.

"What does, sir?" Sidia inquired.

"The size of the shrine. They have a Pontifex in charge, as if this was a full temple."

"Seems the only thing the shrine's missing is a roof and columns," Sidia offered.

A man stepped around the far corner and blocked their progress.

"A roof and columns would make this a temple," he speculated, "and that would conflict with the temple at Rome. And the Temple of Bellona there holds an important place in the history of the Republic."

"And today, as well," Cornelius added. "The war column is there, plus the territory near the Tiber is considered non-Roman territory. Consuls and Senators can meet with enemy ambassadors on the Field of Mars. And the fields are the marshalling area for triumphant parades."

"For one so young, you are well versed in the use of the Field of Mars," the man acknowledged. "Your name?"

The stranger raised his arms as if to say inquiring about a name was an afterthought, an innocent question. Cornelius noted deep cuts, some old and others almost healed, on the man's limbs. And he recognized the challenge inherent in the inquiry.

"Cornelius Scipio, Governor and General of Legions for Iberia," Cornelius informed him. "And I am the cousin of Nasica Scipio."

The arms dropped, the hand clasped, and the man's eyes widened.

"General Scipio, welcome to the Shrine of Bellona."

"Your name, sir?" Cornelius asked.

"Pontifex Terrigenus, head priest for the Shrine of Bellona at Ostia. The other guests have yet to arrive. Please go right in."

*** 

Unlike most shrines with a couple of free-standing columns at the entrance, the front of Bellona's shrine displayed spears, shields, and gladii.

Before they entered, Sidia asked, "General, what is the war column?"

"Before Rome declares war, a Fetiales priest must throw a javelin into the enemy's territory. To save weeks of travel, the priest goes to the Field of Mars and throws the javelin over the war column."

"That's convenient," Sidia concluded.

They walked through the doors and found a typical shrine. Seating for worshipers and a granite altar for sacrifices. Cornelius guided them along the side to a spot near the altar.

***

Nasica Scipio and a priest entered. The cleric was soft and unscarred like the Bellonarii. Nasica saw Cornelius, lifted an arm in greeting, and headed in his cousin's direction. But two priests intercepted the young man and led him to the other side of the shrine.

"We'll catch up later," Nasica remarked.

Although spoken low and respectfully, his voice bounced off the walls and echoed down the length of the shrine. At that instant, Quinta Claudia, and her chaperone Bestia, walked through the entrance.

"We'll catch up later…" faded and Bestia pulled Quinta close.

"Is that one of your male friends?" the chaperone accused her. "Oh, but this is delicious. Not only aren't you clean, but you've taken the best man in Rome down with you."

Quinta attempted to pull away, but Bestia jerked her back.

"And remember what I said," she warned. "I'll cut that pretty face and leave you beside the road like an empty husk after the harvest. Now dry your eyes and keep your mouth shut."

In an attempt to dry her tears, while walking, Quinta dipped her head and lifted the sleeve of her robe. Not watching where she was going, the most virtuous maiden in Rome tripped over a bench and fell. Sprawled between two rows, she cried out.

"Stupid girl," Bestia growled, "get up, you're embarrassing me."

As Quinta struggle to untangle her legs from beneath the benches, a form shoved between the chaperone and the girl. A deeply scarred arm reached down and extended a helping hand to Quinta.

"Now see here," Bestia protested, "I am the girl's chaperone and I protest."

Two of the scarred priests shouldered in front of her, moving Bestia farther from her charge.

"Allow me to help you up," Pontifex Terrigenus insisted. "You are a guest of honor in Bellona's shrine. We can't very well have you sitting on the floor. Now can we?"

When Quinta Claudia touched the hand, she felt a power run through her body. All the way to her feet, she grew in strength. But when Terrigenus released her, the old fears flooded back, and Bestia appeared at her side.

"Come child, we'll take our seats," the chaperone insisted. To the priests, and the Pontifex, she scolded. "I told you the maiden was exhausted from the trip."

***

Terrigenus stood silently in the shrine. Five priests in a semicircle formed a backdrop for their Pontifex. None moved or even breathed hard.

"Goddess of War, we bring you two representatives from the Pontifex Maximus. One a man and one a woman. They are here to greet a new Goddess," Terrigenus stated. Because of the walls, his voice reverberated as he spoke, giving the words power and depth. "While she will be a Mother Protector of Rome, you will always be Bellona."

At the name of their Goddess, the five priests and the Pontifex drew knives. They held the blades up as if showing them to the Goddess.

"To honor your bloodlust and madness in battle, we offer blood for blood," Terrigenus and the five priests pulled up their robes and extended a leg. Then slowly, they drew the sharp steel across their thighs. Blood ran from the deep cuts, down their knees, shins, ankles and over their feet. Pools collected under each man.

Quinta Claudia began yelping, making sounds as if she was a wounded puppy. Bestia hissed at her, but Quinta ignored the admonishment.

"When going to war you bring companions to spread terror among your enemies. Bellona, accept this blood for blood," Terrigenus bellowed. The seven men extended their other leg and sliced deeply on that thigh. Blood ran to the floor and as if the fluid was guided by an unseen intelligence, the pools grew and linked together. In moments, the priests and their Pontifex stood in a lake of blood. "You take Discordia to war. Hail the Goddess of Discord & Strife. But she is not and never will be the Goddess of War. Bellona, accept this blood for blood."

The six slashed their forearms and as the blood flowed for the new wounds, they switched their knives to their other hand.

"We call on the female spirits of justice and vengeance to join with you in battle," Terrigenus said, dropping his voice to a deep rumble. "Protectors of mothers, fathers, and elder siblings, the Furies fly to punish wrong doers. But they will never be the Goddess of War. Bellona, accept this blood for blood."

They sliced their other forearm. The circle of blood grew, and the Pontifex and his priests lowered their heads, signifying the end of the ceremony. Unwounded priests rushed forward with vinegar-soaked bandages.

A hush fell over the shrine.

Then a yelp, sounding much like a puppy, came from Quinta Claudia. Next, she stood and howled as if possessed by a fully grown she wolf. With her arms extended, Quinta turned and faced Bestia.

"Bellona, accept this blood for blood," Quinta screamed at the chaperone. "If you are going to cut me, do it now. Do it here, so I can draw strength from Bellona, the Goddess of War."

No one moved because almost none of them had experienced the horror of war or dealt with frightened and wounded Legionaries during battle. Two men in the shrine understood Quinta's trauma. They rushed forward to separate Quinta Claudia from her chaperone.

## Chapter 8 – Our Daughter

Cornelius draped an arm over the distressed girl's shoulders. In a gentle manner, he guided her away from the bench. Bestia tried to follow but Sidia blocked her path.

"Sit down," the Optio ordered. "We are guests in a shrine. Be respectful."

He dropped onto the bench beside the chaperone, the meaning of his actions clear. Stay in place, unless you can get by a big bodyguard.

While bandaging his wounds, Terrigenus offered, "The sight of a blood sacrifice has different effects on those who witness the ceremony. Some shy away from the gore, fearing the pain. Others understand the significance of sacred blood and recognize its value. Between them are men accustomed to battle and feel at ease with the sight. Most are just grateful it's not their blood being spilled. And finally, there is a rare observer who is transformed by Bellona's intervention."

The Pontifex of the shrine pointed at Quinta Claudia and beckoned her to him. As if in a trance, the most virtuous maiden in Rome tread lightly across the stone floor until the hem of her robe floated on the surface of the red lake.

"From today, you are a daughter of Bellona," Terrigenus announced. He drew his knife, bent, and moistened the tip in the lake. Next, he cut a shallow, but bloody line, on Quinta's forearm. After the cut, the Pontifex pressed the hilt of the knife into her hand and declared. "Let no God or Goddess, no man, nor woman doubt your fierceness, Daughter of Bellona."

Bestia grunted to show her displeasure, and instructed, "Come here child. This show is over."

Quinta cocked her head to the side, turned to face the chaperone, then stared at Bestia as if seeing her for the first time. Without looking away from the matron, Quinta said, "Pontifex Terrigenus, I require a new chaperone while I await the arrival of the Protective Mother."

The Pontifex signaled two of the Bellonarii and the priests stepped to the edge of the lake.

"Our daughter is here on a mission important to Rome, its citizens, and the Republic," Terrigenus instructed. "You will guard her from harm and lend any assistance required for the completion of her mission."

"Yes, Pontifex," they agreed.

"This concludes the ceremony. Please adjourn to the reception room," Terrigenus informed the guests. "I will join you once I've cleaned up."

Cornelius met Nasica in the center aisle and the Scipio cousins walked out together. Priest Ceionia followed along with Quinta and her two scarred priests. Behind them, Sidia stood from the bench.

"What about me?" Bestia inquired.

"It seems," Sidia informed her, "your services are no longer required."

While Optio Decimia hurried to catch up with Cornelius, Bestia bared her teeth.

"My services are already paid for, Optio," she hissed. "Without wasting days with the brat, I'll be free to spread rumors about the most dishonorable maiden in Rome."

The Bellonarii mopping up the blood heard Bestia laugh as she strolled down the length of the shrine. Even when she was outside, the evil tone drifted to them as they went about erasing any sign of the blood sacrifice.

*** 

For a stoic sect, the food on the table was surprisingly varied and hearty. And the wine plentiful and a deep, satisfying red.

"My compliments on the refreshments," Cornelius offered to the Pontifex.

"One thing you learn after years of sacrifice is the need to nourish the body," Terrigenus replied. He indicated Quinta and the two Bellonarii. The girl was in a deep conversation with the Priest of Victoria. "The Bellonarus who delivered the invitation told me there might be a problem between the girl and her chaperone. I didn't expect it was bad enough for a threat. Did you talk with Quinta?"

"In the wagon from Rome, Bestia accused her of ugly crimes and said the shame would be passed to the Protective Mother," Cornelius told him. "Quintas didn't know who to trust until you opened her eyes to the courage of Bellona."

"The Goddess of War does have that effect on people," Terrigenus professed. "But Quinta's situation presents a problem for the temples of Rome."

"How does one chaperone present a problem?"

"If it was only one person spreading evil gossip it wouldn't be," the Pontifex explained. "I've got to think someone replaced the chaperone with an anti-Hellenistic operator. That would require coordination, meaning they had more sympathizers in the convoy."

"And more in the Capital," Cornelius projected. "I thought to arrest Bestia and send her to the Senate. But I'm thinking that would be a waste of manpower. What can we do to salvage the arrival of the Protective Mother?"

"Do what Quinta did," Terrigenus advised, "trust in Bellona."

***

Cornelius Scipio prayed several times a day and regularly asked the Gods for guidance. While he trusted in providence, the conqueror of Iberia also acted to bring about positive results. In the rented villa the next day, he spoke with the Centurion of the five-banker that brought him from Iberia.

"The navy says Valerius Laevinus and the Goddess from the east should arrive any day," Cornelius informed the commander of the warship. "I want a controlled arrival. To do that, I need to know General Laevinus' location."

"You want me to sail down the coast and locate him," the Ship's Centurion assumed. "I can do that."

"When you find him, tell the commander of his warship to use the dock and not the beach," Cornelius instructed. "Then get back here and warn me."

"I can do that General Scipio."

"You realize, this is a request and not an order," Cornelius stated. "I'm no longer in command."

"I know that General Scipio," the warship commander replied.

Then he saluted and marched from the room.

Sidia stepped away from the wall with a grin on his face.

"What's so funny?" Cornelius asked.

"You claim not to be a General, but you've taken control of the arrival of a Goddess," Sidia answered. "And you're working on a solution for dealing with the Bestia situation. But in all this, you're missing an opportunity, sir."

"If there's an opportunity here, please tell me. Because I don't see it."

"How did the Pontifex Maximus plan to introduce a new Goddess to the citizens?"

"I hadn't thought beyond getting her across the dock," Cornelius admitted, "let alone into the consciousness of the citizens."

"How about a parade through Rome, sir?" Sidia suggested.

"That would help introduce her," Cornelius admitted. "But I've been forbidden to hold a parade. And threatened with punishment if I do."

"General Scipio, sir, what if a champion of the Goddess led the parade?" Sidia proposed. "You know, bought bread to pass out to the crowds? Maybe hired criers to announce the wagons?"

Cornelius turned to the window and stared at the horizon.

"We only have me on horseback, and a wagon with Nasica, Quinta, and the Goddess. Not much of a parade."

"Gold, silver, copper, lead, and iron would make nice displays," Sidia corrected, "especially if each wagon of metal was guarded by an armored Legionary."

"A champion of a Goddess, Legionaries to guard the Goddess and infantrymen to protect valuables," Cornelius rolled the phrases around in his mouth as if savoring a honey cake. "Lictors and temple guards, and priests of Bellona and Victoria as escorts."

"I don't know much about politics, General," Sidia admitted. "But I can't see how the Senate of Rome could condemn a holy procession."

"Run and find me Tribune Gordian," Cornelius directed. "I need to know if he wants to go to his parents' villa straightaway. Or unpack his parade armor and be the personal escort for a Goddess."

\*\*\*

Cornelius' Legionaries put away their Iberian gear and opened their luggage. Over the next two days, they buffed armor, polished helmets, and brushed fresh coats of paint on their shields. Procured wagons were painted bright colors, and those with problems were repaired to assure each transport would roll properly during the parade. Draft horses enjoyed extra hay and were groomed until their coats gleamed. Only after much of the preparations had been made did Cornelius face one of his biggest obstacles. He called the Lictors of Rome to a meeting.

"From what I gather, you have no orders beyond escorting the Goddess to the Temple of Victoria on Palatine Hill," Cornelius told them.

The four enforcers sat in the great room of the rented villa. All four had been Legion Optios or Centurions. Medals displayed on their chests exhibited lifetimes of war and discipline. Although stern public servants, they gladly took glasses of wine. And they ate with relish from trays stacked high with cheese and sausage.

"I assume you didn't call us here to verify our instructions from Pontifex Maximus Dives," one stated.

"I have more to say," Cornelius offered. He had hoped the sight of brightly colored wagons, healthy animals, and Roman war gear would sway the Lictors. But the response reminded Cornelius of the Lictors strict adherence to duty. "I have a proposal that doesn't interfere with your mission. It only requires you to accept a longer route."

"We know about your procession," another enforcer uttered. "And we're all aware of your victories in Iberia. Your history of taking care of your Legionaries and your veterans proceeds you."

"Then you agree to an extended route to Palatine Hill?"

"No, General Scipio, we do not," the third Lictor disclosed.

As silently as hobnailed boots can heel-and-toe across a travertine floor, Sidia clicked his way to the door and left the room. The mild interruption caused the five men to pause. Cornelius was first to break the silence.

"It's an extension," he reiterated. "Not a delay or a pause, only a different route."

"The length of the path is not the problem, General Scipio," the fourth enforcer explained. "What you're suggesting is a public display of confidence in you from the Lictors of Rome. It becomes political. We must decline and insist that you release the Goddess to us for immediate transportation to Rome."

Of all the maneuvering he'd devised, and battle plans he'd created over the years, Cornelius didn't have any idea how to change the minds of the Lictors.

"General Scipio, permission to speak, sir," Sidia Decimia announced from the doorway.

Cornelius glanced quickly, then focused on his bodyguard. Sidia had returned with his medals displayed on his chest.

"Lictors of Rome, may I present Optio Sidia Decimia."

"You have something to add Optio Decimia?" A Lictor invited.

"Two items, sir," Sidia listed as he crossed the floor. "Two of you have referred to Dominus Scipio as General, knowing he is no longer a General. Can I assume it's out of respect and not a jest?"

"Consider it a sign of respect for his actions in Iberia," an enforcer told Sidia.

"If you respect General Scipio, why is there a problem allowing him to organize a procession for the Goddess?"

"We fear the woman, Quinta Claudia, is tainted."

Another Lictor advised, "there are rumors of her vile deeds. We can't be involved if there is a hint of scandal."

"And having the Goddess reject the representative of Roman womanhood is more than a hint, it's a disgrace," the fourth Lictor vowed.

With the challenge defined, Cornelius had an objective, if not a solution. He tried persuasion.

"The rumors are false," Cornelius promised. "I know the young lady and she is innocent of the charges. It's the people spreading the rumors. They're attempting to use Quinta to separate the Mother Protector from the citizens of Rome."

"If you could prove the Mother Protector accepts Quinta Claudia, we would have no objections to the procession."

"How can we do that?" Sidia inquired.

The question landed heavy in the room. It seemed to be an impossible barrier to the procession. But Cornelius, being a man of faith, answered, "We will trust in the Goddess Bellona."

At the mention of the Goddess of War, the Lictors all nodded in agreement.

**Chapter 9 - Champion of the Goddess**

In the middle of the night, the duty Optio flipped the sand-dial and sent out Legionaries to relieve his sentry posts. The fort and the docks at Ostia lay in soft moonlight from a full moon. People slept peacefully under blankets in the cool spring air.

Yet, sixty-five miles up the Tiber, the citizens in the hamlet of Ponzano Romano huddled together in fear. Lightning lit the night, thunder shook the ground, and the constant downpour threatened to collapse the thatched roofs.

High in the mountains, rain collected and flashed down dry creek beds. The river valley downhill from the village filled. As if poured from a million pitchers, the rainwater came at such a rate, the volume quickly exceeded the capacity of the riverbanks. When the river valley could hold no more, a mighty flood rolled down the Tiber River.

***

Just past daybreak, Tribune Gordian rousted his Legionaries. Once fed and dressed in their best war gear, the staff officer marched the men to the fort. By the time the Legionaries arrived, Cornelius Scipio had the best man in Rome and the most virtuous maiden waiting with their escorts. They joined the Legionaries in the trek to the docks. Shadowing the greeters, the four Lictors rode through the gates, walking their mounts behind the crowd.

"I'm afraid," Quinta Claudia whispered.

"A daughter of Bellona need not fear," one of her Bellonarii assured her. "Everyone is afraid before a fight. But the Goddess will be with you in battle."

"But I don't know where the enemy is," Quinta whined. "The liars seem to be everywhere."

"As is the virtue of the Goddess," the other priest told her.

The mass of people reached the dock at the same moment the construction workers rowed the flat boat into position. They would be pouring the new pier next to the old wooden dock. It made for a tight fit, but wouldn't prevent the unloading of cargo, or the debarkation of a Goddess.

***

The sun perched in the east, halfway between the horizon and the peak of the morning. Shadows of those facing west crossed the dock and vanished over the edge of the boards. Porters hauled leather sheets of concrete to the low barge and the foreman dropped the loads into forms.

Two five-bankers glided into view from the south. Once close to the docks at Ostia, the quinqueremes rolled their big sails and extended their oars.

"Foremen of Concrete," Cornelius shouted. "Out of respect, we need you to back your crews away."

"Yes, Dominus Scipio," the man acknowledged.

Shooing his workers off the flat boat and up the embankment, the foreman moved the construction workers away from the docks.

"I've sat with you when battles were going wrong, sir," Sidia commented to Cornelius. "And I've watched you save the day with masterful orders or daring acts. I've never seen you fail."

They both looked back at the four Lictors.

"There's always today," Cornelius warned.

Visible on the first warship, men in saffron robes danced on the upper deck. Out of sync notes and disjointed voices carried across the water.

"Who are they and why are they making that racket?" Tribune Gordian asked.

"Our Ship's Centurion told me about the Galli," Cornelius answered. "They are the priests of the Goddess Cybele."

"The priests have no restraint," Gordian remarked. "Or any sense of propriety."

"You're not the only one who thinks so," Cornelius pointed at the approaching warship. "The First Principale is having trouble communicating with the rowing officer and the navigators."

In an undignified sprint, the first officer of the five-banker raced to the steps leading down to the rowers' walk. After dropping onto his belly, and most likely speaking to the Second Principale, he pushed upright. Then, the officer sprinted back to the rear oarsmen.

Because the orders were delayed or misheard, the quinquereme slipped sideways. The rowers were stroking contrary to the direction being steered by the rear oarsmen. Again, the first officer ran to the opening in the deck. On this circuit, he vanished down the ladder to the rower's deck.

One hundred and fifty feet long and twenty-four feet wide, the warship almost floated on top of the water. There were nine feet of hull underwater, but the twelve feet above sea level gave purchase to any winds.

Seeing the end of their journey approaching, the Galli clashed cymbals, blared horns, and thumbed tambourines, and they sang louder.

*"Goddess Cybele giver of life*
*Guardian and mediator*
*From disorder, from wilderness*
*From uncertainty*
*Guide us from the natural order*
*To harmony, to calm, to shelter*
*To safety"*

The First Principale appeared, ran to a sailor, shouted in his ear, then dashed to another. The sailors picked up ropes. At the steering platform, the first officer leaned into the ear of the Ship's Centurion.

The commander of the vessel waved his arms in frustration. Believing it was the signal to throw, the sailors on the bow section hauled back and flung their ropes into the air. For an instant, the ropes floated in the direction of waiting dockworkers.

*** 

Created from the heavy rainfall in the middle of the night, the flood waters washed down the Tiber River and gushed into the Tyrrhenian Sea. The volume wasn't enough to raise the sea level, but the flood water did push below the waves, sending swift currents away from the mouth of the Tiber. One finger of the strongest current ran under the flat boat and smashed into the hull of the warship.

*"Goddess Cybele*
*Protector of society*
*The erratic flight of the bee*

*From flowers to bloom*
*Flying about crazily*
*But in your hands, Cybele*
*They return to the hive*
*Make sticky honey"*

Along with the current from the flood water, the wind, its moisture now gone, caught the flying ropes and the side of the warship. As the warship twisted in the current and the breeze, the hull boards jerked then glided towards the new concrete piers.

The ropes, the only way to haul in the wayward ship, were pushed far to the side. Missing the dock, the ropes plunged down, draping across the flat construction boat. In heartbeats, the great ship carrying the Mother Goddess to Rome would be a wreck, spiked on concrete piers.

\*\*\*

No one reacted, enough moments hadn't past for anyone to understand the disaster. Yet one person saw the developing catastrophe and acted.

"Daughter of Bellona," a Bellonarus whispered in Quinta's ear. "Grab the rope, save the ship."

Prompted into action, the much-maligned maiden raced down the embankment, sprinted across the flat boat, and at the edge of the water, snatched up the ropes. Alone in the blowing wind, her face contorted with effort, hair whipping around her head, the maiden hauled on the ropes with all her strength.

And to the amazement of Cornelius Scipio, his Legionaries, Nasica Scipio, the Priest Ceionia, the temple guards, and all the constructions crews, the warship steadied and drifted away from the hard tips of the concrete piers.

Sidia peered behind Quinta Claudia to see the two priests of Bellona hunched at the foot of the embankment, pulling on the ropes with all their might. As dockworkers rushed to Quinta and joined her in pulling the five-banker to safety, Sidia swung around in his saddle.

The four Lictors of Rome sat on their horses, their eyes wide, and mouths opened. They couldn't see the base of the embankment or the Bellonarii adding their strength to the maiden's. All they could see was the most virtuous maiden in Rome harnessing the blessings of a Goddess.

*"Goddess Cybele*
*Giver of life*
*Guardian and mediator*
*From disorder, from wildness*
*From uncertainty*
*Guide us from the natural order*
*To harmony, to calm, to shelter*
*To safety"*

Sidia had no doubt the rumors would vanish, and the parade would go on, now that the Lictors believed Quinta Claudia was a champion of the Goddess Cybele.

## Act 4

### Chapter 10 – A Fine Procession

As if an army had marched on Rome and bivouacked, the Field of Mars became covered with tents to accommodate the participants in Cybele's procession. At the headquarters tent, the tent flap opened, and the four Aediles of Rome entered. They braced and saluted.

In his hand, Cornelius Scipio held an unread scroll from Senator Alerio Sisera. After weighing the importance of the message against the influence of his visitors, he placed the message on his desk, still unread.

"You do realize, I am not a General of Legions anymore," Cornelius mentioned.

"Here on the Field of Mars, considering the host you've gathered for the Goddess Cybele," one of the public servants explained, "you are a Legion commander to us."

"Thank you," Cornelius said. He handed each a large sack of coins. "We'll need bread for the crowd, announcers to tell the crowds about each wagon, and awareness spread through the city about the welcome parade for the Goddess Cybele."

"You'll have attendees along the parade route," one assured him. Then the Aedile notified Cornelius. "The Pontifex Maximus is waiting for you, by the gates."

"Is there a problem with the procession?" Cornelius inquired. "I'd like to be ready for his objection."

"I don't believe so," another of the Aediles replied. "I think he wants to be in the parade."

"In that case, I better not keep him waiting," Cornelius said as he moved to the exit. "If you have questions, Tribune Gordian has answers. And if he doesn't, I'll back up everything he makes up."

Once out of the command tent, Cornelius mounted his horse and rode for the western gate in the Servian Wall.

***

A moment after he left, Sidia galloped up beside him.

"Is there a problem, sir?" the bodyguard asked.

"Not unless me being replaced at the head of the procession, and being overlooked by the crowd, is a problem," Cornelius told him. They trotted through the gates to find Crassus Dives waiting in his carriage. Aside, Cornelius remarked to his bodyguard. "The parade lead has just been claimed by the Pontifex Maximus."

"You can't know that for sure, sir," Sidia offered.

Cornelius reined in and saluted.

"Pontifex Maximus, a good and healthy day to you, sir," Cornelius greeted the head of all the temples in Rome.

"Dismount and walk with me, General Scipio," Dives instructed.

If anyone should know his status as a citizen and not a military leader, it was the Pontifex Maximus of Rome. Cornelius glanced at the thirty feet high defensive wall, the Legionaries on duty at the gateway, and the sprawling city. Everyone within the walls knew of his demotion. Confused by the continuing use of the title, he slid off his horse and met the Pontifex Maximus as Dives stepped out of his carriage.

"Am I missing something important, sir," Cornelius asked.

"That will depend on if you consider having your property in Rome seized by the Senate, and you being exiled from the Republic as important."

***

From some temples, the Pontifices rode to the Field of Mars, while other temples sent large groups of priests. They wanted to be part of the procession introducing the Goddess Cybele to Rome. When approaching the gateway, the temple heads, and the clerics, stopped to exchange greetings with the Pontifex Maximus.

To speak without interruption, Dives and Scipio left the main road and strolled down a side street. Behind them, Sidia Decimia and a bodyguard for Crassus Dives kept up while maintaining a respectful distance.

"Considering the number of enemies I have in the Senate," Cornelius suggested, "being seen with me in public might not be the best idea."

"The job of Pontifex Maximus is a lifetime position," Crassus reported. "I may not be the most popular man in Rome, but I am the most difficult to unseat."

"I suppose when you reach the pinnacle of an occupation, you can relax," Cornelius concluded. "Unlike an Iberian General in Rome."

"There are drawbacks to any position," Crassus remarked. Then he emphasized. "For instance, there are civil projects I'd like done. But a Pontifex Maximus only has so much political sway."

"Right now, I can identify with the feeling," Cornelius sympathized.

"And that's why I wanted to speak with you," Crassus said, dropping his voice so it didn't reach any of the nearby pedestrians. "The Senate had laid traps for you, my young friend. Both legal and civil, but you avoided them. And in the most unusual manner. You created a trap of your own making."

"You mean the procession?" Cornelius guessed. "I've invested a fortune in the parade."

"I can appreciate the mountain of coins you've disbursed," Crassus empathized. "But if you ride in the procession, the Senate will have you on trial the next morning."

"Even if I'm a champion of Cybele?"

"Even if you're accompanied by Jupiter himself."

They walked a few more steps as Cornelius digested the information. With a huff, he mumbled, "Then I should pull my support for the procession. It doesn't make sense to back a venture with no profit or benefit."

"I didn't say there were no advantages," Crassus Dives countered. "I've got to get to a meeting. You do what your heart tells you. But think back over this conversation. When you figure it out, come see me."

At a hand signal, the bodyguard for the Pontifex Maximus blew a whistle. Two mounted guards appeared at the end of the block. They cleared the street for Crassus Dives' carriage.

"Another benefit of being head of all the temples," Crassus said as he stepped into his carriage, "I have the power of the Gods to clear a path for me wherever I want to go."

The Pontifex Maximus of Rome left Cornelius standing on the side of the street confused yet intrigued by their exchange.

"Does the Pontifex want to be in the parade, sir?" Sidia questioned.

"I don't know, we never got to that," Cornelius answered. "What I know is he does not want me in the procession."

"Then he wants you to step aside and let someone else sponsor the Goddess' parade?"

"Optio Decimia, I have no idea what the Pontifex Maximus wants of me," Cornelius admitted.

*** 

Two days later, Senator Alerio Sisera sat in a wagon bed along with three other Senators. Being elevated, they had a decent view of the forum even if the wagon was behind the crowd. And owing to the wooden benches placed in the bed, they were seated comfortably.

"I hear the first announcers. It sounds like they're approaching Capitoline Hill," one commented. "The procession can't be far now."

The four old Legislators glanced right, looking up the forum searching for the leader of the parade. As the sponsor, he would command the second loudest cheers while collecting adoration of the masses. The loudest cheers would greet the Goddess Cybele as was proper. Both were

101

powerful political statements for the honorees. Unless it was Cornelius Scipio.

"Did Scipio receive your warning?" a Senator asked Alerio.

"I don't know, he didn't respond," Alerio confessed.

Rounding the base of Capitoline Hill, wagons piled high with bread rolled into view.

"Feeding the animals at the zoo," one Senator scoffed.

"Be kind," another scolded. "The citizens have been trained to expect bread at public spectacles."

"Feeding the citizens wins hearts and minds," Alerio suggested. "Too bad it doesn't work on the Senate of Rome."

"Here's the sponsor," one announced.

The four gawked to see who led the procession.

"All hail the sponsor of the parade for Cybele. The man who brought you bread and the following spectacle," a man ahead of the mounted leader bellowed. "All hail, Crassus Dives."

***

Senator Sisera relaxed, knowing that Scipio had not tempted his detractors in the Senate by riding in the parade. With the General of Iberia safe from trial for defying the Senate, the tension eased from Alerio Sisera's neck. Now in a festive mood, he anticipated the parade of established temples and looked forward to seeing the priests of the new Goddess.

"Senator Sisera, how does the parade look?" Cornelius Scipio inquired from beside the wagon.

"Come up and see for yourself," Alerio encouraged. "Stand behind me so we can talk."

Cornelius climbed over the sideboards and took a position behind the senior Senator.

"The Pontifex Maximus looks good at the front," Cornelius remarked. "But to be truthful, I didn't know he wanted to lead."

"That's usually a step towards a run for Consul," the Senator beside Alerio mentioned.

The breath caught between Scipio's nostrils and his lungs. In his mind he remembered Dives saying, *"For instance, there are civil projects I'd like done. But a Pontifex Maximus only has so much political sway."*

"What else did you say?" Cornelius whispered out loud.

"Did you say something, Scipio?" a Senator inquired.

"Just expressing awe over the number of loaves of bread," Cornelius lied.

In front of them, the guards on the bread wagons pushed back greedy people while bakers flung bread out into the crowd. Cheers swelled up as people caught the loaves.

"All hail, Crassus Dives."

"Dives sure appears to be a man positioning himself for a Consulship," another Senator proposed.

"Can Dives run for Consul?" Cornelius inquired.

"The Pontifex Maximus is a Senator as well as the head of the temples," Alerio Sisera answered. "There's no reason he can't be a Co-consul of Rome."

Cornelius chuckled as he recalled Dives's comment, *"I have the power of the Gods to clear a path for me wherever I want to go."*

"Between my coins and the Goddess Cybele's authority," Cornelius hissed at Crassus Dives. "I'd say you have a wide path to the Consulship. Enjoy the bread."

"Scipio are you hungry?" asked one of the Senators, hearing only the last word. Without waiting for a reply, he ordered his bodyguards. "Go and get a loaf for Cornelius Scipio."

Dives rode by while the former Legionary shoved his way into the crowd. The bodyguard located a man with a loaf, took the bread, and pushed his way back to the wagon.

"Euge," the Senator cheered as he took the loaf. Handing it to Cornelius, he encouraged. "Enjoy."

Cornelius ripped off a piece and popped it in his mouth.

"How does it taste?" the Senator inquired.

"Like four thousand coins," Cornelius replied.

And it should, because Cornelius Scipio had purchased eight thousand loaves to be passed out during his parade.

\*\*\*

Next, a pair of announcers shouted from either side of the procession, "All hail the Bellonarii, the scarred clerics from the Temple of Bellona."

Dampened slightly by the reputation of the priests, the crowd lowered their cheering, as if to avoid drawing attention to themselves. In return, the twenty Bellonarii paid the attendees no mind as they walked down the Forum.

"Hail silver and iron taken from Iberia," the next pair of announcers called out.

After the addition of so many temples, Cornelius had reduced the number of wagons hauling metal. Silver and iron seemed to go well together, as did a later wagon with gold and copper. He sent the lead to market figuring his contribution to someone else's parade already exceeded any charitable obligation.

"All hail the priests of victory from the Temple of Victoria."

Priest Ceionia and his brethren blessed the onlookers as they strolled by.

As if a flowing river, the temple priests and Pontifeces blended together as they moved along the avenue. Then, among all the sameness, just in the middle of the procession, the crowd became deadly quiet.

A new group of priests chanted in a melodic tone.

*"Nenia Dea*
*You hover just out of sight*
*But death is called*
*To claim life"*

It's been an impressive parade, don't you think, Sisera?" a Senator questioned.

But Alerio Sisera didn't respond. In his younger days, Senator Sisera earned the nickname Death Caller. As if in a trance, he chanted along with the priests of the Goddess of Death.

*"With gentle hands so light*
*Take him with care*
*As is a worthy man's right*
*Goddess of Death, Nenia Dea*
*Hear our plight*
*As you hover just out of sight"*

A shiver ran through the masses until the followers of Nenia Dea moved farther down the route. When a new temple came forward, the crowd returned to their normal exuberance. Except for Alerio Sisera, who remained motionless. Only his lips moved as he held a private conversation.

"If it's my time," he spoke to the Goddess of Death, "Nenia Dea take me quick."

So many times, over his life, Alerio Sisera had deadly encounters. At each, he'd plead with Nenia for a quick release if injured. To date, she had not taken his soul from his body.

"Another day perhaps?" he questioned.

She didn't answer. The Goddess of Death, his personal deity, never did.

*** 

For a Roman crowd, stuffed with bread and shared vino, they were loud but not riotous. The presence of the dignified temple priests and Pontifeces reminded the populace of the reason for the holy procession. Their city and the Republic quivered under the threat of Hannibal Barca. To protect Rome, a new Goddess from the east had arrived and they were there to welcome her.

To emphasize the importance of Cybele, the Mother Protector, the next to last, and the biggest contingents of priests came from the Temple of Jupiter. In a display designed to demonstrate support, the Pontifex and a hundred clerics of the Sky Father marched in the parade.

"All hail the Temple of Jupiter," the announcers called out. "All hail the Temple of Jupiter. All hail the Temple of Jupiter."

They repeated the proclamation for clarity. They had to as the following pair of announcers shouted directly behind the last row of priests from the Temple of Jupiter.

"All hail the Goddess Cybele," the next set of announcers shouted. "All hail the Goddess Cybele."

"Why are Cybele's announcers so close to Jupiter's priest?" a Senator in the wagon complained. "I've never seen such disrespect."

"Never mind how close. The new Goddess should be good," another Senator asserted. "Good for the city, and good for the people of Rome."

***

"All hail the Goddess Cybele."

Then loud music reached the Senators in the wagon and the spectators along the Forum.

"What is that commotion?" Alerio asked.

While Capitoline Hill hid them from view, the manic music of cymbals clashing, horns blaring, and tambourines thumping proclaimed the arrival of the procession's honoree.

"Senator Sisera," Cornelius answered, "those are the priests of Cybele, the Galli."

Jerking as if having fits, leaping as if walking on hot ashes, and tossing their heads around like mad bulls, the priests of Cybele rushed into view. With saffron robes flowing, their exuberance burst on the citizens of Rome.

Accustomed to inflexible rituals and orderly worship ceremonies, the Romans recoiled from the onslaught of near madness.

*"Strikes by an enemy*
*From hikes to spikes*
*Spear tips all bloody"*

The Galli shouted the words as if to challenge a competitor. And while no temple opposed Cybele, the spirited celebration of the Mother Protector did defy the normal process of honoring the Gods.

*"But in your hands, Cybele*
*The shield walls hold*
*Stopping steel*
*And saving lives*
*From wild to cozy*
*The gift of safety*
*Blessed by Cybele"*

Fifty Roman youths in new saffron robes accompanied the original priests. The difference was obvious in the faded, older robes of the Galli and the knives slung over their shoulders. The young men were without blades, but just a jubilant.

*"Goddess Cybele*
*Giver of life*
*Guardian and mediator*
*From disorder, from wilderness*
*From uncertainty*
*Guide us from the natural order*
*To harmony, to calm, to shelter*
*To safety*

*Goddess Cybele*
*Protector of society"*

Three of the Senators in the wagon huffed and sneered at the fevered performance.

"Since when do priests carry naked blades?" a Senator asked. "It's unsightly."

"At least our youth have embraced the Goddess," a second offered.

"The knives, Senator, are symbols of their adoration for the Goddess Cybele," Cornelius told him. "Each carries the blade he used to castrate himself."

"What? The priests neutered themselves?"

"Yes, sir. It's a requirement to become a Gallus," Cornelius informed the four Senators.

"Tomorrow," Alerio Sisera proclaimed, "I will introduce a law forbidding Roman citizens from becoming priests of Cybele. We cannot have our youths sterilized. Even in the name of a Goddess."

"Agreed," the other three Senators confirmed.

In the middle of the priests and worshipers, Nasica Scipio sat in the carriage with Quinta Claudia who cradled a black stone. Behind them, Tribune Gordian stood guardian over Rome's best man and most chaste maiden.

"Despite the inappropriate priests of Cybele," one of the four Senators announced, "it was a fine procession."

## Chapter 11 – Politics, Not as Usual

Two days after the procession, Cornelius Scipio hiked up Esquiline Hill. His destination was an old, restored villa.

Angry at being used, he was prepared to dump a wagon load of grievances on the Pontifex Maximus. As he approached the defensive fence, he shoved down the emotions and tried to judge the age of the exposed foundation.

"General Scipio," a guard acknowledged while opening the gate.

Cornelius paused to look at the rocks making up the base of the fence. After a brief inspection, he gave up, strolled to the house, and scanned the stone foundation of the villa. While he was occupied, the door opened, and a servant waved him to the entrance.

"Dominus Scipio, we've been expecting you," the man told him.

Cornelius followed the servant through the house. It was all new construction. They crossed a sitting room and exited the villa onto a rear courtyard. Once outside, Cornelius paused to study the stones in an old piece of wall.

"Every time someone visits my villa," Crassus Dives mentioned as he crossed the patio, "they examine the foundations. It's my secret weapon of negotiations."

"Only because legend says this might be the site of Servius Tullius' palace," Cornelius explained. "Is it?"

"And suddenly, my visitors forget their anger and the reason for their visit," Dives explained. "All the hot emotions are replaced by curiosity."

"Was this the palace of the sixth King of Rome?" Cornelius inquired. "It's reported that he built his palace on Esquiline to increase the hill's popularity."

"If I told you, it wouldn't be a secret, now would it," Dives stated. "But do sit down. We can have refreshments while you deal with your disappointment."

Cornelius dropped into a chair, placed his hand over his eyebrows, and chuckled.

"I left my anger on your old stone foundations," he admitted. "All that remains are simple questions. For example, why?"

"If you're referring to the parade for Cybele," Dives offered. "I needed to get in front of the population. You'd be surprised how many citizens don't know or care about the Pontifex Maximus."

"But to steal…"

"Stop right there," Crassus Dives scolded. "These are negotiations, and you don't want to start with harsh language. Besides, you asked a question. Now, it's my turn."

Cornelius Scipio dropped his hand into his lap and looked Dives in the eyes. He had come to express his displeasure at Dives for taking credit for the procession. But it was quickly devolving into a schoolboy's lessons in arbitration and compromise.

"Seeing as the Galli are undisciplined and offensive, I dare say," Dives inquired. "Can you defend them and Cybele?"

"She was brought to Rome with guidance from the Sibylline Books," Cornelius declared. "Isn't that enough reason?"

"Well done," Dives proposed.

"About the Sibylline Books?" Cornelius inquired.

"No, no. You've already asked the question: Isn't that enough," Dives chided. "You need to wait for your adversary to answer. After a question, the next man to speak loses. Do you understand?"

For the last few years, Cornelius Scipio had been in prayer, asking for blessings, or issuing commands to his Legions. In both cases, he was the last man to speak. Cornelius wanted to inform Crassus Dives of the need for a General to command and not to play games with linguistics.

Before he got the words out, a servant brought a pitcher of wine and a tray of cheese and flat bread to the table. While they were being served, a cloud moved in front of the sun. It floated in the sky for a moment. When it moved off, the bright rays touched and warmed Cornelius' face.

"Does this conversation have anything to do with politics?" Cornelius inquired.

"An astute question, General Scipio," Dives conceded. "Suppose I gave you a different but daring case for the Goddess Cybele. Could you argue it?"

"That would depend, Pontifex Maximus, on when I would be expected to defend the reputation of the Lady."

"Tomorrow in the Senate," Dives answered, "after morning meditations."

\*\*\*

Veturius Philo held sprigs of mint, thyme, and oregano, along with stems of saffron in his hands. He rotated the cupped spices in small circles as he chanted.

"Goddess Victoria, Goddess Vesta," the Consul prayed, "protect our Republic and keep the hearths of Rome burning."

From an upper tier off to his right, a Senator questioned, "What about Cybele?"

Groans from almost half the Senate hinted at their feelings about the new Goddess.

"Cybele, Protective Mother, shelter our homes and families from vile omens, evil Carthaginians, and rampaging barbarians," Consul Philo added. After spreading the spices on the small altar, he faced the Senate. "I have a request from the Pontifex Maximus. He would like to address the Senate. Do I hear any objections?"

"Unless he wants to bang on our ears with another lecture about the Greek Goddess," a contemporary of Fulvius Flaccus disclosed, "let Dives speak."

Accepting the weak endorsement, Philo nodded to the Pontifex Maximus, "Senator Crassus Dives, you have the floor, provided you don't discuss the new Goddess."

"I will not discuss the Goddess Cybele," Dives assured the Senate. He opened his hands and a piece of linen unrolled. Hanging like a yellow orange flag, it matched the bright robes of the Priests of Cybele. The other Senators identified the saffron colored cloth, sagged, and waited for the sermon. But Dives surprised them. "Today, I would like to discuss city finances."

Relief flooded the Senate. Although the Gods were important to every aspect of life, there were other concerns for the Senate of Rome.

"An enormous sum has recently been deposited in the Temple of Saturn," Dives informed the Senate. "I would like to invite the General who returned to our city, bringing victory and wealth to Rome. Cornelius Scipio, General of Iberian Legions, please come forward."

In a formal toga, Cornelius held his arm at chest level to keep his train out from under foot.

"I protest," a Senator objected. "Scipio is not a General or a Pro-consul."

Voices echoed the sentiment and Cornelius almost tripped when his mind conjured up defensive responses. Remembering his purpose, he walked with care. Forgoing his lively campaign gait, Governor Scipio stepped with dignity down the tiers to the center of the chamber.

"Senators. Consul Philo. Pontifex Maximus Dives. Thank you for allowing me to address this honorable body," Cornelius began. Then he pulled a piece of cloth from a fold in his toga, unrolled it, and placed the linen over his shoulder. "You'll no doubt recognize the saffron color of my scarf. It is the same cloth used by the Priests of Cybele."

Moans escaped from an entire section of the Senate.

Ignoring the expressions of displeasure, Cornelius continued, "My return to the city I love coincided with the arrival of a protective Goddess. As proscribed by the Sibylline Oracles, General Valerius Laevinus sailed east to find the Goddess we need. Some question the mannerisms of her worshipers; the bright robes, the personal knives, the driving music, frantic dancing, and loud chanting. Many reject the Galli and the Goddess. Mostly because they don't understand."

"Understand what?" a Senator shouted. "That they are Greek. Disrespectful of our Gods, and our Latin Ways?"

"Yes," Cornelius agreed, "because, all of that."

Confused by the acceptance of their argument, the Latin Way segment began talking among themselves.

"Order. Order in the Senate," Consul Philo insisted. "The floor belongs to General Scipio."

"He's not a General," a couple of Senators called out.

"Then I'll amend my order," Philo said with attitude. "The floor belongs to the Governor of Iberia."

*\*\**

When no one else objected, Cornelius scanned the Senators twice.

"I see men who honor the Gods, both those adopted from other tribes and our original Latin Gods," he revealed. "Men who practice rituals and chants in the proscribed manners."

"The right way, the Latin Way," a voice declared.

"As I just acknowledged," Cornelius confirmed. "But consider this, we've made sacrifices. Implored individual Gods and Goddesses. And still the omens come at us in multiples, Hannibal Barca lurks ready to lay waste to our homes, and barbarians gather preparing to attack. Yet, our Gods do nothing."

"*Asebeia*," a handful of Senators accused. "You should be tried for blasphemy."

"For a statement of fact, you would charge me?" Cornelius challenged. Outwardly, he deflected the accusation. But in his heart, he wanted to flee the chamber and sail back to Iberia. Sticking to his duty, he continued. "The Gods aren't listening to our pleas. At least not in the way we've been praying. Perhaps if we dressed in bright robes, mutilated ourselves with personal knives, performed

115

irritating music, danced as if we were lunatics, and proclaimed at the top of our lungs our loyalty to the Gods, they might hear us."

"Then we'd be like the Galli," a Senator proposed.

Cornelius Scipio pointed at the legislator and dipped his head in agreement.

"Exactly like the Galli," he affirmed. "And that is why the Goddess Cybele was brought here. To awaken the Gods to our plight. You'll no doubt recognize the saffron color of my scarf, the cloth of Cybele."

"Are you going to start leaping and dancing?" Fulvius Flaccus teased.

"No, Senator Flaccus," Cornelius informed him. "I've been at war for many years. I'm not going to dance for anybody. I am going to my villa and be with my family."

The applause started slowly from a section that valued Greek culture. Then it spread to a moderate area. In moments, most of the Senate of Rome stood. They applauded Cornelius Scipio while calling for the Goddess Cybele to help Rome.

## Chapter 12 - To Challenge Heroes

Figuring his part was done, Cornelius collected the end of his long toga, draped it over an arm, and took a step towards the first tier.

"Governor Scipio, kindly remain there," Crassus Dives shouted to be heard over the noise. When the Senators settled back into their seats, Dives reminded the chamber. "I did not discuss the Goddess Cybele."

116

"To your credit, you didn't," a Senator told him. "Yet, you've ended resistance to her and proved you'll make a worthy Consul. Very clever, Pontifex Maximus."

"I assume I'll have your vote," Dives said. "But I did promise to talk about finances."

"More of your ploy to become a Consul?" Titus Crispinus questioned.

"Is it working?" Dives inquired. He waved to his assistant at the back of the chamber. "The Temple of Saturn holds the treasury of our Republic. Unfortunately, over the last several years, the Senate has drained the vault to a dangerous level."

"Consul elect," a Senator called to him, half joking, "you do know, there's a war going on."

Veturius Philo coughed to get everyone's attention then slapped the dais.

"Can I get a second to nominate Pontifex Maximus Dives as the next Consul of Rome?"

Taken by surprise by the early nomination, the Senators took a breath, before a majority replied, "I second the nomination."

Based on the response, Crassus Dives was as good as elected. The Senators believed the choice of Dives' Co-consul would play out months later.

*** 

Through the exit door, Tribune Gordian marched into the chamber, halted at the top tier, right faced, and saluted.

"With your permission, Pontifex Maximus," the staff officer requested.

"Bring them in," Dives instructed.

A moment later, two men entered carrying a heavy load suspended between two poles. They took the steps down to the floor, being careful not to let the covered load swing. Behind them another pair appeared. They also walked with a load slung between two poles. Next, another pair entered the chamber. When the fifth pair of porters started down with a fifth load, Tribune Gordian followed.

***

"General Scipio, good morning," he said.

"Tribune, good to see you," Cornelius replied. "I trust the family reunion went well."

"My mother cried, and my father was stoically proud," Gordian answered. "Until I drew this assignment. Then my father cried, and my mother was stoically proud."

"Just what is the assignment?"

"I was ordered to take a Century of infantrymen in full kit to the Temple of Saturn this morning," Gordian told him. "We met the five pair of porters and were instructed to escort them to the Senate and deliver the loads to the Pontifex Maximus."

"Let me guess," Cornelius ventured. "Your father wants you to be a Senator and your mother wants you to be a priest."

"If you two are finished with the veteran's reunion," Crassus Dives interrupted, "I'd like to get on with the demonstration."

"Yes, sir," Gordian and Scipio acknowledged.

Dives left his seat and walked to the first pair of porters.

"With the city's coffers drained, it was getting difficult to finance civil projects," Dives announced. He jerked the cover off the sling to reveal bars of silver. Then he moved to the next sling and uncovered a load of iron ingots. "And the longer the war went on, the less we had to support our Legions."

A Senator in the back stood and demanded, "Is there a point to this? Or is the Senate of Rome now a coin market?"

"We always have been a coin market," Dives replied. He lifted the cover from a load of copper, then from the sling with lead. "Our docks need to be expanded among other things. And with our low funds, the Senate is limiting the growth of our Republic."

Crassus Dives went to the last sling and jerked the covering to reveal bars of gold.

"What we have here are taxes collected from one citizen," he informed the Senate. He picked up a gold bar and used the shiny metal to point at Cornelius. "A man who cleared Iberia of the Carthaginian threat, settled a Latin city in central Iberia, made peace with Kings and War Lords, and then brought enormous wealth home. Senators of Rome, I give you, Cornelius Scipio."

Whether it was the sight of the metals, the visual of one man's addition to the Republic's treasury, or to salute Cornelius, didn't matter. The Senate erupted in chaos. Dives stood still with the gold bar extended. Only when the chamber settled did he lift the bar overhead.

"Gold is heavy," Dives explained. He dropped the bar. It landed in the sling with a thud. "But not as heavy as the weight on a General when he is commanding eight Legions and twenty-five thousand auxiliary troops."

"If he's such a great field commander and a slayer of Carthaginians," a younger Senator asserted. "Why don't you make Scipio your Co-consul?"

Dives pivoted and smile at Veturius Philo.

"Can I get a second on the nomination of Cornelius Scipio as Co-consul with Crassus Dives?" Philo inquired.

In the pause following the surprise nomination, Gordian offered, "Congratulations, General Scipio."

"Not yet," Cornelius warned. "There are a lot of Senators who don't like me or my tactics."

***

"We had to hunt down Hasdrubal Barca," a Senator complained. "Because Scipio allowed him to escape from Iberia."

Cornelius stepped forward preparing to defend the strategy that allowed Hannibal's brother to evade his Legions. Before he could speak, Veturius Philo made a guttural sound in his throat.

"We? Did you say we?" Consul Philo challenged. "It wasn't anybody in this chamber who found and brought an elusive enemy to battle. Hasdrubal was as slippery as his brother. It took Caecilius Metellus and me to locate the Carthaginian. And two reinforced Legions to beat him. I don't consider him getting away from the Iberian Legions as a fault. General Scipio, from what I've read, had his hands full of traitorous Iberian tribesman."

No one replied or questioned the Consul. Most people were reluctant to challenge heroes. Most people, but a few would try.

"I am not comfortable with Scipio building his personal fortune on the backs of our Legionaries," Quintus Fabius growled. "Or getting them massacred in a campaign destined to fail."

"Can you be clearer, Senator Fabius?" Philo inquired.

"Everyone knows Scipio wants to invade Carthage. Well, fifty-one years ago, Marcus Regulus sailed twenty-six thousand Legionaries and auxiliary troops to Africia," Fabius stated. "In an ill-advised and ill-fated campaign, one my father opposed at the time, Regulus got all twenty-six thousand killed. Dead to the last man."

The crack of a foot stomping on travertine drew the chamber's attention.

"If your father and the Senate had allowed Consul Regulus to come home with his Legions," Alerio Sisera sneered, "they would be alive today. But the Senate got greedy and promoted Regulus to Pro-consul the next year. And while his senior commanders returned to Rome, the General was left in Africa with less experienced Colonels."

"And how would you know all that?" Fabius demanded.

"Because, I was there," Alerio answered with ice in his voice. "We made it to the walls of Carthage before the Carthaginians hired a Spartan to command their army. Then, almost as if the cowards in Rome planned it, we were slaughtered."

"I think we're opening old wounds," Philo suggested.

"The City of Carthage must be destroyed in order to stop Hannibal," Cornelius insisted. "I make no apology for my sworn oath to defeat Hannibal in battle. Do what you

121

will with that information. Make me Consul or not for in my heart I don't care what you think."

The harsh words seemed to end Cornelius' run for Consul. Quintus Fabius laughed, and sat back, figuring his duty to stop the Greek loving Scipio had been successful.

Consul Philo cringed, believing the move to get Dives his preferred Co-consul had slipped away. Despite the belief, Philo asked, "Can I get a second for the nomination of Cornelius Scipio as a Co-consul of Rome for next year?"

Entire sections of Senators, usually opposed to each other, shouted, "I second the nomination."

It appeared that their hatred of Hannibal Barca, and of Carthage, overrode their disputes. Consul Philo relaxed. In the next two months, there would be backroom deals and the trading of favors. But on March fifteenth, Cornelius Scipio and Crassus Dives would be elected as Co-consuls of the Republic.

Then, Fulvius Flaccus stood, stretched as if bored, and announced, "I have a requirement. If Cornelius Scipio remains in Rome for his term, I will vote for him as Consul."

His faction nodded at the ploy to foil Cornelius. Under their directive, Scipio wouldn't gain more fame and popularity, at least for a year. And he'd be at the mercy of political factions and shifting voting blocs.

A pair of hands, clapping in a slow rhythmic manner, greeted the demand.

"Senator Flaccus, you do realize that I am Pontifex Maximus," Dives said while continuing to clap.

"Of course, I know," Flaccus answered. The clapping irritated him because while he could understand the mocking nature of the action, he couldn't pinpoint the sarcasm.

"And you acknowledge at least one Consul should be in the field with his Legions," Crassus Dives probed. Then he inquired. "How do you propose to accomplish that?"

"Well, you go be the General," Flaccus snapped back.

Crassus Dives stopped clapping.

"That's not possible. I am the head of all the Temples of Rome," he stated. "And by law, the Pontifex Maximus cannot travel outside the city of Rome."

## Act 5

## Chapter 13 – Egypt Unbalanced

A string of porters, resembling a line of ants, carried logs from a Phoenician wood transport. They scurried from the deck to the old harbor dock. Then struggling, they made their way up onto the jetty, took the causeway to the Island of Pharos, plodded around to the eastern point of the island, and onto the lighthouse grounds. After stacking the logs under the roof of the lower section, they backtracked, passing workers coming the other way with more hardwood logs.

During the unloading, the sun sank lower over the Mediterranean Sea.

"Pick up your pace," the Ship's Captain shouted. "Hurry up."

But the delay wasn't the speed of the porters. They trekked belly to back or as near as the logs allowed. The hold up of the offloading rested in two points of the operation. At the end, the oak and beech logs were carefully stacked with wedges placed between logs to allow airflow. A foremen of the furnace oversaw that part of the operation. And while he kept a few cedar logs to go with the oak and beech, all the pine and cypress that found its way to the lighthouse were sent back. On the dock at the old harbor, the Ship's Captain caused the other delay.

"That one is for the lighthouse. That one is for the hearths of Alexandria," the Phoenician merchant exclaimed after inspecting each log. "Now that is a fine piece of closed grain wood. Craftsman quality. Show it to the woodworkers."

Furniture and cabinet makers waited on the causeway south of the line of porters. Each quality log got inspected and most were purchased. After buying the cedar, oak, or beech pieces, apprentices carried the logs to the workshops of the craftsmen.

"Pick up the pace," the merchant Captain encouraged.

On the mainland, just off the causeway, the pine, fir, cedar, and cypress logs were stacked for sale to households. Nearby beverage and food vendors set up stalls. Carts hauling wine and beer arrived as the charcoal in iron braziers were lit.

"Clouds," a beer seller declared while peering at the sky. "I may have to order more beer."

"Should be one of the biggest crowds of the year," a meat roaster agreed.

Successfully feeding the people who attended the nightly street party was serious business. It required a fine balance between selling out early and missing sales opportunities or having leftovers when the crowd disbursed late in the night.

*\*\**

Jace Kasia stepped onto the dock with a group of porters. He glided to the front and jostled with a few others, trying to look down into the boat. Once the Archer staked out his position, he peered down and judged what type of wood was coming up from the ship's hold.

Most wanted firewood for the lighthouse. Although a longer trek, the stroll back offered relief from the heavy workload. The second-best route took the porters to the mainland with wood for the households of Alexandria. The walk back to the boat was shorter than from the lighthouse. But neither had the quick turnaround of a trip to the craftsmen's area.

Jace needed to see a certain furniture maker. Rumors held that the entire family had hard feelings about the taxes imposed in the name of Ptolemy IV. Feelings about the Pharaoh weren't of interest to the Cretan Archer. If their desires ended at emotions, they were in the clear. If not, the cedar log he had his eyes on, would provide a means to their executions.

*** 

*Early in his training as an archer, Zarek Mikolas described the differences between wood of the same species.*

*"It's maple," Jace identified a log. "Good for the limbs and the belly of a bow."*

*"What about this one?" the Master Archer question. He rested a hand on a second log.*

*"Another maple. Again, good for the components of a bow."*

*"This maple is early wood and not good for our purposes. Look at the grain on the end of the log," Mikolas instructed. "An*

*open-grain wood is fine for rustic furniture. But for the finish on a bow, we want closed-grain wood."*

*Jace pulled the two logs together and examined the differences between the maple sections.*

***

Using an elbow, Jace shoved a porter aside. Reaching in front of another man, he took the cedar log from a sailor. Seeing it was cedar, none of the porters complained about the shorter trip to the mainland.

Once he had the log on his shoulder, Jace pivoted to the Phoenician and informed him, "Captain. This is fine quality cedar."

"I don't need a porter to tell me my business," the merchant Captain complained. Despite his attitude, he leaned forward and ran a finger down the grain of the log. "Go show it to the craftsmen."

Taking the shortest and the least desirable route, Jace went to the location of the woodworkers.

"Master Amsu," Jace called out to the targeted furniture maker. "This is a choice piece of cedar."

"Let me see that," the carpenter instructed. He put his eyes close to the end, spit on a finger, and moistened the grain. "Put it on the pile behind me."

"Where are your sons?" Jace inquired.

He rested the log on the others the furniture maker had purchased.

"My sons have personal business to attend to before leaving on a trip," Amsu replied. "I'll need a porter later. Interested?"

"Glad for the work, sir," Jace told him.

With a reason in place to see the suspected rebel sympathizers later, Jace hiked back to the dock for another log.

***

"To the lighthouse," the wood merchant directed.

Jace joined the long line. At Pharos, the lighthouse of Alexandria towered over the island. Once under the colonnade at the lower section, Jace handed the log to a furnace man.

"You there, Latian," the foreman signaled out Jace. "Get to the other side and fill a tote. Take it up to the furnace."

The porch surrounding the square base of the lighthouse matched the aesthetics of the structure. To reach the other side of the building, Jace wandered between stacks of wood. Realization came to him that the porch at the lighthouse was more than a design feature. He concluded it might be the world's most expensive woodshed.

***

On the other side, Jace Kasia found piles of dried, split wood. He took a sheet of leather with handles on the ends, placed wood in the sling, folded it and slung the load onto his back. Entering a doorway, the Archer started up a ramp. Overhead the next level of the spiral ramp provided a roof that blocked his view of the higher elevations.

"Master Mikolas, I am in the lighthouse of Alexandria," he whispered to the ghost of his teacher. "In memory of you, I'll see how high they will allow a lowly porter to climb."

After two turns, the ramp ended on a level. Doors to rooms around the structure resembled a second-floor

129

apartment building. When no one stopped him, Jace located the next segment of ramp and started upwards.

***

After the fourth floor, the twisting of the ramp became tighter. Figuring he was in the middle section, Jace watched for an opening. He hoped for a view of the sea and the curvature of the earth. It would be fun to report to Eratosthenes of Cyrene, the head librarian at the Library of Alexandria, that he, Kasia of Crete, had witnessed the bow of the world.

It must have been the heavy load of wood wrapped in the leather tote sack. Because no one he passed questioned his presence on the upper level of the lighthouse. Unimpeded and unescorted, he continued up the steep ramp.

When the ramp hooked a hard right and daylight poured in from above, Jace knew he was near the top. Not too far above him, a granite ceiling ended human access. Yet from the mainland, he knew a statue of Neptune topped the lighthouse. Finally, he stepped onto a level with a granite fire box. From there, he had a view of the Mediterranean.

"Eratosthenes of Cyrene," Jace said, thinking about the librarian, "I can see the curve far out at sea. But for the life of me, I can't imagine it wrapping around the earth."

Conditioned to strenuous physical exertion, Jace stood with the heavy load on his back, gawking at the view.

***

A second load of wood, carried by a middle-aged man came from below. Stooped with his head down, the man stepped around the end of the ramp and slammed into Jace.

130

"What are you doing?" he demanded. The impact jerked the handles from the man's hands and his load of wood spilled onto the level and down the ramp. "Look what you made me do. You know better than to stop there."

"My apologies," Jace said. "I was taken with the view."

"The view," the man repeated. He grabbed a bucket from a ledge above the ramp and a hand full of linen rags. "You've seen clouds before. Now get up there while I pick up the wood."

"I could help with…"

"You wanted the view," the man insisted as he scooped up a piece of wood. "You get the view. Get up there and clean the mirror."

He held up the bucket and rags without straightening. Perhaps years of hauling loads of wood up the ramp had permanently bent his back. Or he was too angry to face the cause of the extra work.

Jace didn't protest. The view had to be better higher up in the lighthouse of Alexandria. He took the bucket of water and the rags, then looked around for a way up to the ceiling.

*** 

Steps chiseled into one of the granite columns gave Jace access to a large sheet of bronze. Canted forward, the metal mirror hung partially over the firepit. Soot tarnished the bottom of the plate and the corners where people had only swiped at the smudges.

With his back against one column and his legs braced against two others, Jace dipped a rag in water, and started to wash the bronze. The water dried leaving a film on the surface while he scrubbed the buildup of soot at the corners. Below him, voices spoke.

"Go and bring up another load of wood," a man ordered.

The one who collided with Jace mumbled something, then several pieces of wood banged into the fire box. A moment later, the footsteps of the stooped man faded as he descended the ramp.

Perched overhead, Jace waited for the voice to order him down. Or to leave. The man did neither.

"Are we alone?" a second voice asked.

"We're at the top of the lighthouse," the first man answered. "Unless Ptolemy commands birds, there's no one around to hear us."

"We're gathering the army at Luxor. In days, the reign of Ptolemy will end, and a man of the people will rule. Long live Pharaoh Horwennefer."

"Long live Pharaoh Horwennefer," the first parroted. Then he clicked his tongue against his teeth and inquired. "If I'm going to send men upriver, how do we identify them. For that matter, how do they recognize brothers in the cause?"

"Use these words," the man instructed. "Have you visited Khufu's tomb? A true brother will reply, Khnum protect me."

"I don't understand why we aren't capturing the lighthouse like we planned," the first complained.

"Because Alexandria is the center of Ptolemy's power. From Luxor, we can catch his army in the open and water the desert sands with the blood of his loyalists."

"Have you visited Khufu's tomb?"

"Khnum protect me," the second man answered before the sounds of his sandals on the ramp receded.

Jace remained suspended over the fire pit. Thoughts flashed through his mind. Should he kill the rebel? There was no way to take him prisoner and get him to the palace. Or wait for the man to leave, then run to Farouk Midhat, and tell the Captain to gather the army of the Pharaoh? Which wasn't likely to happen based solely on a report from a single ring agent.

Before Jace decided on his fate, the man left the furnace level.

"At least he didn't light the signal fire," Jace said as he buffed the bronze mirror to a high shine.

\*\*\*

Before the sun vanished into the sea, and darkness closed in, the last log left the Phoenician ship and smoke came from the top of the lighthouse.

At the first sign of life for the mighty tower, the small crowd cheered.

"Master Amsu, are you ready?" Jace asked the craftsman.

"Yes. My cart is just on the other side of the vendors."

Jace tucked away his coin purse with the day's wages and strolled into the streets created by the booths. As he walked, the Archer glanced around to see if he recognized any other agents. Unfortunately, the ring officer kept the identity of his agents a secret. Not just from the public but from each other.

133

Once at the furniture makers cart, he harnessed the mule and guided the rig to the causeway.

"Have you visited Khufu's tomb?" Jace inquired as he shoved the last log onto the cart.

"No, it's been years since I've had time to traveled to Giza," Amsu replied. "Have you?"

"No sir, I've heard of the great pyramid, and would like to see it," Jace answered. "But like you, I haven't."

Night fell as they walked the mule and the cart with the choice logs away from the harbor. Behind them, hundreds of people had gathered for the street party. A roar of approval rose when light beamed from the lighthouse.

"The overcast will bring out the crowds," Amsu told Jace. "The clouds really show the light. On clear nights, it's hard to tell how far out it shines."

## Chapter 14 – Lunatic Festival

Blocks from the lighthouse and the street party, the illumination on the clouds created a flickering in the distance. Lightning like, except the glow lasted longer and the radiance spread wider.

"That will bring out the lunatics," Amsu proposed after peering at the light.

He walked the mule and cart down the side of his shop. In the rear, the woodworker stopped and addressed the Archer.

"Pull the logs out and leave them," Amsu told Jace. "I'll have my sons deal with them in the morning. Put the mule in the corral and come into the shop and I'll pay you."

For Jace, the phrase I'll pay you satisfied a deeply rooted mandate. And it triggered a connection between the Cretan Archer and his principle.

"Yes, sir," Jace acknowledged.

While he was unloading the logs, Amsu went into his shop. Inside, candles flared to life as the woodworker lit them. Then voices drifted to Jace, meaning someone had come in the front door. Busy with the logs, Jace paid no attention to the discussion until he heard.

"Have you visited Khufu's tomb?" the craftsman inquired.

"Khnum protect me," a male voice replied using the rebel response.

"We all hope for blessings from the Creator," Amsu continued, unaware of the verbal code. "I've been thinking of a trip down south."

"Where did you hear that phrase?" the visitor pressed.

"How dare you come into my shop and be rude to me," Amsu scolded. "You can wait for my sons on the street. Now get out."

Jace rushed, yanking the mule towards the pen. He wanted to head around to the front of the shop and get a look at the rebel. But the mule pulled back and stopped.

"Come on, you," Jace growled at the beast.

Then from inside the shop, he heard Amsu plead, "No. No. Why?"

The woodworker screamed before the sound of his body crashing to the floor reached Jace.

Releasing the mule, the Archer shouted, "Master Amsu, do you need help?"

Jace ran into the shop to catch a fleeting glance of a man fleeing out the front door.

Above average height and dressed in a sand-colored robe, the man sported the Egyptian fashion of the day. His head was shaved. From the back, there were no distinguishing features except for a section on his scalp. A braided tuft of dark hair hung down shoulder length. The braid and location marked him as a warrior. But for who? The only unique things were gold and silver bands woven into the bottom of the braiding.

Jace wanted to catch the rebel and question him. But with his principle injured and the Archer unpaid, Jace dropped to his knees and examined Amsu.

***

If the back braid of the assailant didn't identify the man as a warrior, his knifework did. According to the cut line, in a single move, he delivered a deep stab followed by a gut opening slash.

"Nice technique," Jace remarked.

"What are you saying?" Amsu groaned.

"Nothing. Lay still while I take your apron off," Jace encouraged.

Gently, so as not to further hurt the furniture maker, Jace slipped the heavy leather apron over Amsu's head and dropped it. Then he probed the puncture wound.

"There is one advantage to being stabbed by a sharp knife," Jace commented while squeezing the wound.

"What kind of porter has a philosophy of blades?" Amsu inquired.

Ignoring the question, Jace watched as red blood came out of the wound. Satisfied, the knife missed an artery and the man's bowels, he turned to the apron. The laceration would have opened Amsu's stomach and exposed his intestines. But a woodworking tool in a pouch, where the leather was double thickness, absorbed the killing slash.

"A sharp blade makes a clean cut," Jace declared. "I'll sew you up. You'll hurt for a few days, but you'll live."

"I've never seen him before, but he said he was here to see my sons," Amsu told Jace. "That's the last time I let a stranger into my shop at night."

"Probably a good idea," Jace confirmed. "Where do you keep your vinegar and where can I find a needle and thread?"

"What kind of porter has medical training?"

Jace went to collect the supplies and didn't respond.

Moments later, as Jace stitched the wound closed, he pondered the assailant. Because he acted rashly, the warrior, as most people do, fell back on his early education. A quick attack on a vulnerable area displayed military training. An assassin would have gone for a kill and not be content with disabling a foe and leaving him for dead. And an untrained attacker would have stabbed or slashed, but not used a combination of both.

"A rebel soldier," Jace mumbled as he tied off the suture. "Can I get paid now, sir?"

"How much do I owe you?" Amsu inquired.

"Moving seven logs is," Jace paused. Then he moved towards the rear entrance. "I'll be back after I put the mule in the pen."

From the top of the lighthouse, bright flames danced in the opening of the upper tower. Those same flames, reflected off the bronze mirror, beamed out over the sea. On the mainland, musicians played, and vendors sold drinks and food. The attendees talked, sang, and watched the light reach out in the dark to guide ships to the port of Alexandria.

Jace Kasia roamed the crowd, mostly looking up at the light to hide his purpose. Occasionally, he lowered his head to take a sip of wine and scan the people around him. However, with only a rear braid and small bands of silver and gold to go by, he wasn't actively searching for a specific person. He held the size and shape of the assailant in mind and scrutinized the crowd for a man that fit the mental picture.

As the evening grew long, examples of Amsu's prediction about fanatics coming out appeared in pockets around the street festival. A senseless scream in one area, friends restraining an offended man in another, and someone talking too fast to understand gave truth to the claim of the furniture maker.

Beneath the unstable light, flickering off the clouds, the event was becoming a lunatic festival. Pleased by the chaos, Jace dropped his veneer of disinterest and looked hard at groups of people.

"Now," another madman shouted. "We should go now. He's just down the docks and..."

Sounding as if a butcher punched a side of meat, a fist hit the lunatic on the side of his head with a smack. The madman dropped and the puncher bent down to pick him off the ground.

"Do you need a hand with him?" Jace inquired.

"No, I've got this," the man with the heavy fist brushed off the Archer.

As he got his hands under the unconscious man's arms, a rear braid swung to the other side of his neck. Silver and gold bands flashed in the firelight of a vendor's bonfire.

With his voice pitched just above a whisper, Jace inquired, "Have you visited Khufu's tomb?"

The warrior with the braids had the lunatic halfway to his feet but stopped.

"Why do you ask?"

Jace stepped back as if he'd spoken out of turn. He nodded and pleaded, "It's nothing. Sorry to have bothered you."

Four steps away, the warrior called him back.

"Come here and help me lift him."

Jace took one arm and the warrior leaned over from the other arm and offered, "Khnum protect me."

"That's a relief," Jace confessed. "I was told to be here. But all night I've walked around lost."

"They should have told you to be at the wood transport," the warrior said as they carried the groggy man towards the causeway. "At dawn, we'll row to the Nile and head south."

"I was afraid I'd be stuck in Alexandria. I don't know how much longer I can deal with the loyalists."

"Things will be different under the new Pharaoh."

"That's what I hear," Jace lied.

They reached the dock, went down to the Phoenician ship, crossed the ramp, and boarded the transport. As they rested the dazed man on the deck, Jace glanced around for a place to sit.

*** 

After all the wood had been removed, Jace expected the boat to be empty. Instead, the deck and hold held sleeping men. The scope of the rebel presence put Jace in a quandary. He had planned to join them and see where they went. But arresting a boat load of fighters had its own reward. Now he had to decide. Sneak off, alert Captain Midhat, and have the rebels arrested. Or go for the ride and gather information on their destination.

Picking their way through sleeping men, the warrior and Jace walked to the bow of the ship.

"My name is Ziad, Captain of the Army of the South," the warrior introduced himself.

"Jace Romiliia Kasia, formally of the Roman Republic," Jace replied.

"We don't have many Latians in the cause," Ziad admitted. "How did you come to be in Alexandria?"

"Let's just say, like you, I have a problem with the current state of my government," Jace told the rebel Captain. "I need to learn how to fight and what it takes to overthrow the Senate of Rome."

"Senate. Pharaoh. They get power and grow to love it," Ziad claimed. "Stay in my company, and I'll teach you how to survive and win a war."

"Sounds great, where do I sign up?"

"You just did," Ziad cautioned. "And there are only two ways to leave. Dead, or released by me."

Externally Jace nodded to show acceptance. The movement in the flickering light of the lighthouse made it appear as if his head jerked up and down. Internally, he thought in a smooth flow of the idea, *or I could kill you and just walk away.*

They located empty spots on the foredeck, sat with their legs dangling, and waited for daybreak.

*\*\*\**

By midmorning, the Phoenician ship traveled along the coast of Egypt. The lush Nile River delta filled the shore with greenery. The thin trunks and gnarled branches of tamarisk, acacia and sycamore fig trees gave height to the floodplain. The scent of wet dirt and growing vegetation carried offshore to the transport.

"You have a beautiful country," Jace remarked.

"I have a hard country," Ziad countered. "Beyond the Nile, the land is sand and stone. Like my people, strong and tough, and unfortunately, resistant to change."

"It's why you need a revolution," Jace guessed.

"For a Latian, you are very astute."

"Have you met many Latins?" Jace inquired.

"A few that came to Alexandria on trade missions," Ziad answered. "They were arrogant and rigid."

"Is that anything like tough and resistant to change?" Jace inquired.

Ziad laughed and slapped Jace on the shoulder.

"I like you, Latian," he revealed. "I'm going to keep you close because you entertain me."

Jace smiled even as he considered that almost unprovoked, Ziad stabbed and tried to gut Amsu.

*"Wait until you see my blade work,"* Jace thought. *"Although, I'm not sure you'll find that entertaining, at all."*

\*\*\*

Late in the day, the transport swung north and away from land.

"Hold tight," Ziad urged.

"What's going on?" Jace asked.

"The ship's Captain will turn and line up on the mouth of the Nile," the rebel answered. "He'll ride the air up the river."

"Then why did you say to hang on?"

"Because if the ship gets sideways in the river, it'll get bumpy," Ziad explained. "Can you swim?"

"No," Jace fibbed, "I can't swim. Do you think we'll wreck?"

Once turned on a southern heading, the transport unrolled a foresail to aid the big square sail. At first the ship skimmed over the water creating a breeze across the deck. But as they got closer to the mouth of the Nile, the ship slowed when the hull met the water current.

"The Nile is a powerful river," Ziad told Jace. "You wouldn't believe how much force the water has when it meets the sea."

"I could not imagine," Jace conceded. "How could I? I can't swim."

\*\*\*

The entrance to the river was accompanied by the ship rocking bow to stern and vibrating like a frightened goat.

Yet, the Phoenician was as good a sailor as his people were reputed to be and he proved it by piloting the transport up the center of the river. When the Nile widened, the ship leveled out, and the land glided by faster than if they traveled by horseback.

"I never had a chance to ask our destination," Jace mentioned. "Giza? That's about one hundred and fifty miles up the Nile."

"How did you know that?" Ziad questioned.

"I have a friend in the library," Jace answered. "He showed me a map of the Nile."

"You're right about Giza," Ziad said. "But that's short of our destination by almost four hundred miles. We are heading for the gathering of Pharaoh Horwennefer's army and a new day for Egypt at Luxor."

## Chapter 15 – Old Statues and New Threats

The advantage of traveling by boat, as opposed to horseback or marching, the ship didn't get tired. By mixing the talents of his sailors with rebel volunteers, the ship's Captain kept them heading south, starting from dawn and traveling to sunset.

Nine days after leaving Alexandria, nine mornings of rowing, and nine afternoons of sailing carried the Phoenician ship to the docks at Luxor. Just north of the piers, lines and rows of tall columns identified an ancient but barebones structure.

"Where do we go from here?" Jace inquired when Ziad picked up a bundle.

"I've got to report in at the Temple of Luxor," Ziad told him. "A Sergeant will be along to show you and the other recruits to your quarters."

Ziad jumped from the deck to the dock and marched towards the rows of columns. Ancient cross beams at the top connected the pillars. And the roof, if there ever was one, had long since collapsed. Picture writing that Jace didn't understand adorned the beams.

"Recruits, welcome to the Army of the South," an NCO called from the other end of the dock. "Get on your feet and off that boat. Your easy life is over. Follow me."

Without waiting, the Sergeant marched off the pier, heading in the direction opposite to the Temple of Luxor. On the boat, chaos took over as recruits grabbed bundles and ran to catch up. Jace let himself be carried along in the middle of the mob. It was a choice designed to hide his skills and his purpose for being in the rebel army.

*** 

They walked off the docks and down into the soft mud of the riverbank.

"Watch where you step," the NCO called over his shoulder.

The Sergeant didn't clarify or turn to give advice. Jace remained in the center of the group, taking advantage of the herd defense.

After a long hike, the recruits came to rows of flat-bottomed boats. They were stretched along the bank of the Nile, but having barely any sides, they resembled log rafts more than boats. Weeds and reeds hid most of the rafts.

"While pushing them off the bank be careful where you put your hands," the NCO warned. "Once they're floating, load five men to a vessel. And remember, watch where you put your hands."

Most of the recruits understood, but a few were confused.

"Put our hands, Sergeant?" one asked.

The NCO stomped the wet mud and indicated a small clump of foliage.

"I'm sure there aren't any crocs in those weeds. But there are other things along the riverbank besides Nile crocodiles," he warned. "Mankillers, every one of them."

"Like what else?" a recruit from the city inquired.

"If you see a black dot in the weeds, freeze," the NCO told him. "It's too late to run. While you wait for the black mamba to deliver death, you can either cry or pray."

"Can't we just avoid black snakes?" another questioned.

"You can, except the mamba is deep brown and olive color. Perfect camouflage for the reeds on the riverbank," he told them. "The black dot is inside the snake's mouth along with the venomous fangs. If you see the dot, you're as good as dead. Any more questions?"

Jace did have a couple of questions but didn't think the NCO would appreciate the thinking behind them.

*"Why didn't the Phoenician ship drop the recruits on the other bank? And why did the Army of the South need these awkward rafts?*

He stored the queries in the back of his mind and helped push and launch one of the watercrafts. When it was his turn, Jace made sure to climb onboard fast, and watch that his feet didn't dangle in the water. Although the snakes sounded bad, they couldn't pull you off a flimsy raft. Nile crocodiles could jerk you into the river as easily as a man could harvest bunches of grapes from an arbor.

While five men could balance on the logs, the boats couldn't possibly carry a lot of cargo. They were, in essence, low profile personnel carriers, unsuitable for heavy freight.

Away from shore, the recruits rowed hard with stubby paddles. Rocking and almost throwing the occupants into the river, the raft tilted, forcing the paddlers to reduce their stroke rate. Drifting under minimal paddling, the rafts floated by the docks and the Temple of Luxor, angling towards the far shoreline. For the most part, paddling proved unnecessary. Only when the current began carrying them beyond another NCO, did they employ the paddles to reach the far bank.

"Tote them up the embankment and don't break them," the new Sergeant ordered.

Jace, and the other four from his raft, hauled the flat-bottomed boat to the top of the embankment. As they rested the raft on the ground, Jace chanced a look upstream. A group of lean men with broad shoulders were observing the crossing. Following their eyes, Jace noted more of the low-profiled rafts in the weeds across the river. The blending was so good, if he hadn't known where to look, the vessels would be almost impossible to see.

"Grab your gear and move," the NCO instructed.

Claiming his place in the center, Jace and the recruits marched a half mile before entering a crop of trees.

In the shade of the branches, the coolness offered relief from the heat of midday. But the shelter didn't last and after a hike through the trees, the group emerged on the edge of an army camp.

Tents of various types filled the ground for more than a mile. It resembled a city built of cloth rather than wood and brick. On the other side of the camp, two giant statues dominated the sky. Even at a mile's distance, Jace could tell the structures were tall.

"What are they?" he inquired.

"Just a couple of old statues," a recruit answered. "Luxor is full of them."

The Sergeant guided the recruits into the city of tents. They passed big pavilions, small shepherd lean-tos, ten-man shelters reminiscent of Legion squad tents, plus every conceivable method of holding fabric over a sleeping and sitting area. Some hung heavy from the weight of leather or thick wool. Other tent materials fluttered, the linen being as thin as the wings of a blue dragonfly.

Matching the variety of tents, the streets of the army were just as haphazard. Some narrowed, forcing the recruits to step over guylines, while others spread wide, creating neutral space between tribes.

Jace could tell the ones with bad blood. Sentries glared at each other from opposite sides of the roadway. It was on one of the wide streets where Jace slouched lower and averted his eyes.

The structures were uniform with leather covers, stretched tight over ten-man tents. While the tents told him little, the circular positioning of the structures identified a Company of Cretan Archers. Further identification came from a midsized pavilion in the center for the File Leaders, and several arrow carts.

"Are you ill?" a recruit asked.

"Just a little twitch in my back," Jace lied. In his mind, Jace Kasia recalled the lean men with the broad shoulders on the riverbank. Why were Cretan File Leaders so interested in the rafts crossing the Nile. And he wondered if the presence of Cretan Archers would be a problem for his mission. As he walked, Jace mouthed, "old statues and new threats."

"Did you say something?" another recruit inquired.

"Just wondering if they're going to feed us."

"Or give us leave to hunt," a recruit on Jace's left said. "I'm hungry."

***

They reached an open area near the statues. On the far side of the camp, the ground was sandy and rocky but not crowded. No tent material or food was provided. Each recruit received two blankets and a wooden bowl. For every ten recruits, an NCO presented the squad with an iron pot.

"Take your bowls to the distribution tent and get your rations," he instructed. "Bring it back to your camp and dump your bowls in the cookpot, add water, and you'll have a hot meal."

"What if I don't want to share?" a recruit asked.

"If spending the night chewing dry grain and uncooked goat is more to your liking," the Sergeant said, "be my guest."

A squad of recruits went to collect their rations. The ones waiting stretched out and napped, but several among those in camp began collecting rocks from the desert.

"Why the stones?" Jace inquired.

"Scorpions and camel spiders," he was told. "Both hurt and cause swelling when they bite."

"Why the rocks?" Jace inquired. "Are we using them to crush the bugs?"

"No. We're building up bedding to get us off the sand," the rock collectors replied. "You should get stones for your bedding."

"A waste of time," a reclining recruit claimed. "The bugs can climb. Besides, a rock bed is harder than the ground."

Years of training gave Jace an open mind for new ideas. After weighing the stone bed idea against sleeping on the ground, he strolled away from the camp.

"Why bother?" a ground sleeper called out.

"The bugs will come for us equally," Jace told him. "But to reach me, they will have to make an extra effort and climb."

\*\*\*

Dawn found the recruits without weapons, shields, armor, or helmets. Even without war gear, they were pushed into ranks. Stretching out on both sides, other companies formed up until the combat line extended for a quarter of a mile. A few were armed with sharpened sticks as spears but no iron or bronze, or steel weapons were visible.

*"Captain Farouk Midhat will be very happy,"* Jace considered, *"if this is the best the rebels can do."*

149

"What are we supposed to fight with, our teeth?" a recruit asked.

"I guess they'll issues us poles later today," someone replied after noticing the sharpened shafts of the other companies.

Another recruit added, "we might be hungry this evening, but at least sharpening our poles will take our minds off our bellies."

Jace refrained from laughing. To hold down the ridiculous thought of this rebel force standing against an Army of the Pharaoh, the Archer mentally counted the coins. Selling the information to Captain Midhat would make him rich.

A Sergeant strutted to the front of the company and alerted them, "Pay attention, you lot. I am Jabari. Do what I say when I say it and you'll live. Go against my orders and I may kill you myself."

In the distance, a line of war chariots came at the combat line. With the light horses in full stride, they closed the gap quickly.

"Run," a recruit bellowed.

"Hold," Jabari countered. "Hold your positions."

In a thunder of hooves and a cloud of dust higher than the old statues, the line of chariots bore down on the Army of the South.

"Hold," Jabari and the other NCOs ordered. "Hold."

Then the cloud rolled forward and the recruits lost sight of the chariots. Unseen by each other in the haze, and expecting collisions, several recruits broke ranks and ran.

Their cries of pain from behind the combat line told of the punishment visited on the cowards.

As the dust settled, Captain Ziad appeared in one of the chariots. The rig sat just two lengths from the front rank.

"Chariots don't attack lines," Ziad boomed. "They stop short, turn and let their archers pour arrows into your front ranks."

He mimicked drawing a bow. Up and down the line, other Captains performed the same actions as they gave the same lecture.

"When our return arrows get too thick, or the archer's quill empties, the chariots move off," Ziad explained. "My driver and I will move away. Pay attention to Sergeant Jabari and the others. Because when the chariots return, you'll face actual archers."

The chariots bounced away towards the horizon.

"Identify the spearman at the center of the chariot attack," Sergeant Jabari instructed. "The man closest to the attack needs to alert the three men on either side of him. From there, the ranks behind move to the side or the rear."

He went on to demonstrate the ranks behind the assault line, moving outward between neighboring ranks, or back to create a bowl shape of empty ground. Verbally it sounded reasonable. In practice maneuvers, the sides failed to move outward, and the bowl always held stragglers.

Then the chariots returned.

***

Jace could not fathom what use the formation was to defeat a chariot and an archer. But the NCOs drilled them until the chariots were halfway across the open desert.

"Straighten your lines," Jabari told the recruits. "Who is center of the chariots attack? Identify yourself."

A spearman raised his arm.

"Three to his sides," the NCO shouted. "Shuffle to the side and back."

A moment later, the ranks folded in leaving a wide-open space. The chariot wheeled around, and a Cretan Archer stood on the back of the rig.

"This can't be good," Jace whispered.

"That's a Cretan Archer," a recruit announced.

As if the bowl-shaped formation was big enough to save the spearmen, the archer placed five arrows just shy of the defenders. Jace knew the compound bow was capable of longer distances, but he appreciated the play acting.

From behind the ranks, shouting announced the arrival of new combatants. Egyptian javelin throwers raced forward, tossed their weapons, and ran back to retrieve another. On the second flight of javelins, the Cretan Archer yelled at his driver.

And, as if the javelins had driven off the chariots, the rigs along the line raced away. Not realizing they witnessed a minstrel show, the recruits cheered. Jace did, but only in appreciation of an act well performed.

"Tomorrow, we'll drill the chariot maneuver again," Jabari informed the recruits. "For now, get back to your bivouac and we'll issue you weapons."

They strolled back to their campsite.

Along the way, Jace asked Jabari, "Why are we concentrating on chariots?"

"The mounted archers are a major weapon in a Pharaoh's Army," the NCO answered. "By pulling our spearmen back, we give their archers less targets and open a field for our javelins."

***

At camp, the recruits were issued hardwood shields and iron tipped spears. From bare handed recruits to spearmen, the rebels moved their army a step closer to victory. That afternoon, Jace strolled around the encampments of the Army of the South. Every company had shields and iron spears if not more equipment.

On the eastern edge, he entered the trees. On the far side, Jace jogged to the Nile before dropping down behind a thick bush. From there, he watched Cretan Archers paddle the rafts back and forth across the river. The flatboats were useless for transporting spearmen. But considering the weight of five archers, their bows, and two quivers of arrows each, the flatboats balanced that weight easily.

By sunset, he moved back to his company's area. The report he planned to deliver had changed, and he realized he needed to get back to Alexandria.

"I wonder who they will send after a deserter?" he questioned as he sat on his bed of rocks. "And how long it will take for them to come after me?"

Then in a neighboring company, a spearman screamed.

"Scorpion," an NCO declared. "You won't be training tomorrow."

Jace eased off his bed and went to investigate where the scorpion had stung the man.

Act 6

## Chapter 16 – A Blue Dragonfly

Before dawn, a scream of pain and surprise woke the company. Jace rolled off his stone bed and sat on the ground. In the light of the campfire, the recruits saw Kasia holding his foot.

"Scorpion," he complained, "got me right on the heel of my foot."

A group gathered around and looked at the red area. One noticed the swelling around a lump.

"That looks ugly," he announced. "You won't be walking today,"

"I guess not," Jace agreed.

*** 

By sunup, the company moved to the training area, leaving Jace alone. A number of spearmen remained in the camp, but they were at isolated unit areas. Once sure he was unwatched, Jace took the wrap off his foot, popped the burn blister, and slipped on his sandals. Moments later, he hiked between the stone statures of the sitting giants, heading west into the desert hills.

While a running man might attract attention, a recruit out for a stroll and limping went unobserved. It worked for a mile before the sounds of a chariot team racing from behind caused Jace to turn around. He dropped the spear, the shield, and his bundle.

Dust from the hooves and wheels boiled up and washed over Jace as Ziad reined in the team. The rebel Captain didn't have a driver and that elicited a smile from the Archer.

"Recruit Kasia. I went to the company area to check on you," Ziad told him.

"But I wasn't there," Jace interrupted, finishing the sentence.

Aggravated at being cut off, Ziad stepped down from the rig.

"I thought you were…"

Again, Jace cut him off.

"Do you know we have a mutual friend?" Jace inquired as if Ziad hadn't said anything.

"What has gotten into you?" Ziad demanded.

"Not really a friend. More like a client," Jace corrected. The Archer seemed to favor one foot. He rested it behind his other with just the toe touching the ground. "His name is Amsu."

"I don't know anybody name Amsu," Ziad informed Jace. His hand slipped down to the hilt of his knife as he approached the Archer. "In that case, how could he be a mutual friend?"

Ziad's blade cleared the sheath. During the stab for Jace's chest, the rebel officer leaned forward to put weight behind the thrust. The extra push assured the blade would pass between ribs or cut through the sternum. And the knife

156

would have, if Jace had remained standing down range of the steel tip.

Almost as if a coiled snake, Jace's lower body twisted at the ankles as his torso inclined to the side. The unraveling shot up his knees and his thighs. When the rotation reached his hips, the Archer whipped his upper body around in a half turn.

Most opponents trying to avoid a knife jerked away. And that was fine with Ziad. Even overextended, he could bend his wrist and cut an adversary with a backhanded slash. But Recruit Kasia, to the rebel's surprise, spun towards the knife.

Jace uncoiled, spinning to his left. His wrist caught Ziad's wrist, driving the arm, the blade, and the man to the side. As he continued to spiral, Jace's skinning knife traced a line across Zaid's neck.

"You should have waited for a better opening," Jace lectured as the rebel Captain dropped to his knees. "And you should never attack when angry."

But the lessons were pointless. Ziad fell face first into the dust and died.

Jace examined the body to see if the rebel officer had anything he needed. After relieving Ziad of his coin purse, Jace stepped up into the chariot, snapped the reins, and raced away towards the hills.

***

The chariot navigated dirt streets into what could only be a forgotten city. As if the Gods were raising the structures from the ground up, like growing cotton plants, the crowns of homes and shops defined the streets. The doorways and

windows had yet to appear on the surface. The place
certainly held spirits. While Jace had little religious beliefs,
he possessed a healthy dose of superstition.

Angling northwest, he rushed the horses from the
buried city. After locating a rough trail, Jace allowed the
team to pick their way up into the hills. From a narrow goat
path, he had a view of the Nile and the greenery on both
sides of the river. Also, the enormity of the rebel camp
revealed itself to him. His report changed from caution to a
warning about the size of the Army of the South. Beyond the
river, plants on the banks, and the vast army camp, what
surrounded Jace were mostly rocks. The hot Egyptian sun
having bleached them the color of sand.

Almost two miles from the giant statues and the buried
city, an enormous staircase appeared. Cut into the face of a
mountain, the steps ended at a terrace. Jace reined in and
peered at the monumental structure. He drank and gave the
horses water as he scanned a partially buried second terrace.
On the top tier were twenty-six columns holding up a long
roof. Several of the columns were carved into figures of
giants.

"Were the ancient Egyptians titans?" he asked the
horses. "Or just masters of all they surveyed?"

A realization occurred to him that the entire area might
be as ancient at the dawn of time. And even if not that old, it
was a place for ghosts and Gods. Stepping onto the rig, Jace
urged the team forward.

Not much farther on, they moved down from the hills.
The agile and surefooted horses taking the rough ground
without trouble. With the mountains blocking his progress

to the north, he guided the chariot eastward along a dirt road.

***

If he thought the wonders had ended, a stone structure in the shape of a victory gate came up on his right. Slowing, Jace studied the arch in the center. Expecting it to be a ceremonial entrance, he looked through the arch for a monument or another buried town behind it. Seeing none, the Archer snapped the reins preparing to trot past. But then, he pulled the horses to a stop.

The opening in the structure was not a gateway but an entrance to a staircase leading deep into the earth. Cretan Archers were trained to judge wind and direct arrows to targets. They were also warned about hazards. Jace didn't want to know what spirits or monsters could come up the steps from underground. And he wasn't keen on lingering in the area to find out. The team picked up on his urgency and galloped away from the ascension to the netherworld.

***

The ground leveled at the toe of the mountain and Jace halted the team. He swished a gulp of the remaining water around in his mouth before swallowing.

Both horses stretched their necks to the right, letting Jace know more water was close. He poured out the rest of their water and gave it to the team.

"The Nile would provide," Jace admitted as the horses drank. "But I don't know how much influence the rebels have north of Luxor. We'll move on and see if we can find another source."

159

He headed the chariot north into the flat desert. Looking to evade any pursuit while searching for signs of water, Jace kept watch on their back trail as they moved.

*\*\*\**

Fields of various shades of brown sand filled Jace's vision. Through his squinting eyes, an object waved. But it wasn't that the article made a motion, it was waves of heat off the desert giving the impression of movement.

"We may have found an oasis," Jace said between cracked lips.

With a light touch, he guided the horses towards the movement. In a brief period, the object separated into a cluster of date palm trees with weeds around their base.

"Looks like water," Jace remarked.

They might not have understood the words, but the horses acknowledged their meaning. The team perked up, heading straight for the oasis.

*\*\*\**

As they approached, Jace studied the palm leaves. He wanted to see birds or furry creatures that might eat the dates. And he watched for predators who would use the draw of the water to attract prey. But other than the heat waves, there was no movement in the date palms.

"Not a good sign," he commented while pulling the eager horses to a stop.

The spring was small and situated on the side of the hill where the date palms nested. In the heat, the pool of clear water sparkled. Jace collected the water skins, preparing to dismount.

A dragonfly, Nile blue, flashed down from the sky. After a series of side-to-side lurches, the dragonfly hovered over the spring.

Jace paused to watch the dragonfly.

***

*"They may be brown like that one," Zarek Mikolas had pointed out. "Or red, yellow, or blue. But they all have one thing in common."*

*The master and his student sat beside a tiny, spring fed pond. Insects zoomed around and birds chirped in the trees. One bug rested in front of them on a tall weed. Taut and ready for a quick launch, the creature held its wings straight out from the long body.*

*"They have four wings," Jace answered Master Archer Mikolas.*

*"That they do," Mikolas granted. "But more important for a traveler is dragonflies are hunters."*

*"I can't imagine they're much competition for venison or rabbit meat," Jace remarked.*

*"None at all. But for a lost traveler, a dragonfly is your best tracker," Mikolas informed his student.*

*"I don't understand," Jace admitted. "They aren't big enough to eat our meat. Why would they track our prey?"*

*"Dragonflies hunt bugs," Mikolas stated. "Specifically bugs that favor water. And bugs that favor water aren't present when the water is poisoned. Meaning?"*

*"Dragonflies won't remain around bad water," Jace guessed. "But that doesn't make them trackers."*

*"It does when they fly from poisoned water to fresh water," Mikolas informed Jace. "If you're smart enough to follow a dragonfly."*

161

The blue dragonfly hovered as if a big cat sniffing the air for red deer. Jace didn't know if Greece's red deer lived in the desert, but he recognized a hunter at work.

Holding the waterskins but standing still after his dismount, Jace watched the blue. When it darted off in a westerly direction without landing, he knew the water was bad.

"My best tracker?" Jace questioned the memory of his teacher.

As happened on every occasion when he addressed his deceased teacher, Jace listened for a reply that contradicted the lesson. The Master Archer never reversed his wisdom. And as he often did, Jace followed his training. After hanging the waterskins on the walls of the rig, he snapped the reins and guided the team around the oasis.

Once clear of the hill and the palms, he guided the horses in the direction taken by the blue dragonfly. A direction that would take them deeper into the desert, father from the Nile, and if they didn't locate water, to a destination where a slow death of dehydration waited.

***

Cretan Archers were special because of the years of training. Beyond the ability to deliver uniformed flights of arrows, they were excellent trackers, long distance runners, and deadly hunters.

"I want him back," a rebel Major replied to the question by Cretan Archer Linus. "While I want the chariot and horses back, I really want to get my hands on the recruit who killed Captain Ziad. He will suffer before he dies."

"We can do that, Major," Archer Buckie assured the rebel commander.

"Then get moving," the officer insisted.

"Other Archers have isolated his trail beyond the tombs," Linus reported. "We'll leave when it cools off."

"But he's getting away?" the Major suggested.

"A recruit without training will be exhausted from his escape and in need of sleep," Archer Buckie said. "While he's sleeping, we'll take him in his camp."

"Fine, fine, dismissed," the Major ordered.

Buckie and Linus moved away from the command tent before saying anything.

"Recruit Kasia killed Ziad with a single slash from a small blade," Linus commented. "And he left Captain Ziad's knife and sword behind. What does that tell you?"

"That Recruit Kasia is familiar with blade work and doesn't see value in toting a hunting knife or a heavy sword," Buckie answered. "Here's my idea. We drop him before we find out just how good he is with a knife."

"Sounds like a smart plan," Linus concurred.

The two hunters went to the Cretan compound to consult with their File Leader. Afterwards, they ate and rested. It was going to be a long night. At least, they figured, they would have the two-man chariot for the ride back.

*** 

Late in the afternoon, Jace hopped off the chariot and walked stiff legged to the front of the horses. After getting grips on their bridles, he stepped forward. His position accomplished two things. It kept Jace upright and the horses

163

moving. Both were difficult considering his dizziness and dry throat, and the fatigue and trembling of the team.

"It was a blue dragonfly," he whispered to the horses. Along with other signs of dehydration, his mind couldn't hold a thought. "I think, I remember a blue dragonfly. I'm sure I did."

Step by step, they journeyed deeper into the dry desert. And with each pace, they moved farther from the refreshing water of the Nile River.

***

Cool wasn't an option in the desert. Only a reference to the ability to block the hot sun from one direction. When the shadows grew long, Archers Linus and Buckie slipped the straps of extra waterskins over their heads. After adding a quiver and a bow case, the two adjusted the loads, angled their head coverings to shield them from the sun's rays, and set out from the Cretan camp.

Rather than a run, they settled into a jog. The two Archers would maintain that pace until they caught the recruit. Even if it took all night.

***

Waves of heat coming off the desert floor made everything in the distance dance. Resembling a rolling sea, the horizon distorted into peaks and troughs. Yet the motion had a sameness. A repeating motif in the haze. It was the reason Jace noticed when tall objects with bushy tops broke the pattern. He angled the team towards the palm trees. Without urging, the horses reenergized at the smell of water.

Birds flew into the sky when Jace reached the oasis, and several blue dragonflies darted around, hunting bugs near a

164

deep pool. After tying the horses on the far side of the trees, he took two waterskins to the pond.

Moments later, Jace stood in front of the horses explaining, "Some water for you and you, and some for me. I don't need you to over drink and get sick on me."

In rotations, he poured water into a sack for one horse, then the other before taking a stream from the waterskin for himself. After two trips to the spring, he pinched the skin on the side of the horses' necks. The flesh formed a tent of skin.

"More water?" he asked the beasts. "I agree."

It took two more trips to the spring to fill waterskins before he pinched the flesh of a horse's neck and it immediately sprung back. Then, he unharnessed the chariot and rubbed down the animals with handfuls of leaves.

"Now that we have water and you're comfortable," Jace said as he finished with the second horse, "I have to get ready for our visitors."

He pulled his skinning knife, walked to the hindquarters of one horse, and grabbed its tail.

\*\*\*

Miles away, Buckie and Linus jogged forward, using the tracks of the chariot as a guide.

"He's heading for the oasis," Linus advised.

Far ahead, the tops of palms trees signaled the presence of water.

"If he's camped there, I'll make two offerings to the Goddess," Buckie promised.

"Why two?" Linus inquired. "You usually don't make any."

"If the Goddess Artemis ends this hunt here, I'll make one for a successful hunt," Buckie respond. He slowed to a walk while pulling the bow case off his back. "And a second sacrifice for the aim of my arrow."

"If he is here," Linus reminded his partner.

The archers separated. Walking quickly, Linus moved forward while Buckie warmed up his bow in preparation for covering his partner.

No birds flew out of the tree. No bugs buzzed around. Nothing moved in the oasis.

"Over here," Linus alerted Buckie. "The tracks go off to the west."

Both Cretan Archers examined the straight wheel marks and hoof prints. There seemed to be no hesitation or indecision in the direction chosen by the recruit.

"Kasia is either lost and doesn't know it," Archer Buckie commented, "or he is an expert."

"An expert at what?" Linus inquired.

"That remains to be seen," Buckie stated while unstringing his bow.

The two Cretan Archers jogged away from the poisoned oasis, following the wheel tracks westward.

## Chapter 17 – Pretty Sure

Jace Kasia sat on the back of the chariot, weaving the stands of horsehair into a band. Occasionally, he checked the length against his skull. When it overlapped his head, he set the horsehair strip aside.

Standing and stretching, Jace looked around the oasis to see what he could use to his advantage. Without a doubt, the rebels would send a patrol to bring him back. He wasn't keen on being executed for desertion and the murder of Captain Ziad. And while a shield and a spear were a start, he needed more if he was going to fend off a patrol. While scanning for potential weapons, Jace noticed a collection of palm branches.

Stacked near the cluster of palm trees, palm branches had been gathered by earlier visitors to the oasis. While he could hike in the night, the horses needed the rest. And truth be told, he liked riding on the rig. Because he would burn a portion of the aged branches overnight, Jace started a green pile. Following the custom, he picked up recently fallen branches and placed them on the new stack. Spying more on the other side of the trees, Jace walked to them, bent, and lifted a palm branch.

Black as night, the scorpion froze for a moment with the stinger arched over its back. Longer than a man's hand was wide, and thicker than two fingers, the scorpion wasn't the most terrifying bug. Scarabs were fatter and better armored. Several varieties of centipedes were longer and more fearsome looking. But no other bug had a stinger thick enough to have joints for agility or carried enough venom to incapacitate or kill a man. When nothing attacked it, the scorpion lowered the stinger and scurried to another fallen branch.

Jace squatted and gazed at the shaded underside of the palm branch. He couldn't see much, but the Archer knew the fat-tailed scorpion lurked in the dark. His mind churned as an idea formed. Then he peered at the stack of dried palm branches.

Offering up a rare prayer, Jace Kasai chanted, "Goddess Eris, Goddess of Strife and Discord, bless me in what I'm about to do."

He returned to the rig and his braided band of horsehair. He didn't fit it to his head as he'd done before. This time, he measured it against the rim of the wooden bowl the rebels had issued to the recruits. After pulling his skinning knife, Jace cut a large circle from one of the blankets and fashioned it over the bowl. Once prepared, he cut into a palm branch and fashioned the spine of the branch into a pair of tongs. Next, he went hunting.

*** 

With the fading light, the sun played long shadows against bright streaks from over the horizon. In the twilight of the day, Buckie and Linus halted on a hill. They dropped to a knee to lower their profiles.

"What did you say about him being an expert?" Linus inquired.

"Surely not at hiding from pursuers," Buckie remarked. "Or creating a defensive position."

In the distance, under a bunch of date palm trees, smoke drifted into the evening sky. Flames of a campfire flickered, revealing a sleeping form under a blanket, two horses tied at a bush, and a chariot rig.

"That's just embarrassing," Linus insisted.

An infantry shield rested on the hip of the sleeping man. It appeared as if he was using the shield for cover to protect his body while he slept. Except, the shield covered his torso, leaving the round bulge of his head vulnerable.

"We can't give a knifeman a chance," Buckie declared. He slipped the bow case off his shoulder and added. "If anyone is, he is too stupid to live."

"I'll work my way in close," Linus told the other Cretan Archer. "Keep me covered."

Buckie flexed his war bow, bending life and suppleness into the limbs. Once he bent and strung the bow, the Archer extracted five arrows from his quiver.

"Go," he instructed.

Linus crept forward. Not afraid of a fight, but weary of an unprofitable brawl, the Cretan took small steps. In a circular path, so as not to get between the arrow and the target, Linus got close enough to make out the markings on the shield.

He signaled Buckie the affirmation.

*Zip-Thwack!*

'Crack' came from under the blanket. While a skull was hard and could take a lot of abuse, unless helmeted, it couldn't withstand a steel tipped arrow. Yet, neither the body nor the head rolled. Seeing no blood on the blanket, Linus held up two fingers.

*Zip-Thwack!*

'Crack'

The head, sporting two arrows, didn't change position or bleed.

Buckie waved Linus forward.

***

Long shadows, and dancing flames, gave the campsite a haunting appearance. Adding to the feeling, the body remained in the same position.

Linus came in low with his war hatchet ready to block or attack. Each step closer to the dead man brought a feeling of apprehension. This hunt started with the killing of Captain Kaid, a renowned knifeman. He had been bested by Kasia. Then, the recruit escaped westward into the hills only to have to circle around to get out of the foothills. Tracking the man across the desert, showed two different skill levels. A quality land navigator or a wandering soul who was out of his element. And now the prey used the weak defense of sleeping in the open with a rebel shield for cover.

Archer Linus did not like inconsistencies and Kasia presented too many. Angry at himself for delaying, Linus rushed to the sleeping form.

***

With one hand, he peeled back the blanket up to the limit of the arrow shafts. His hatchet hovered prepared for a chop.

Instead of a man's head, an upside-down wooden bowl created the shape. The two arrows had shattered the bowl. Something moved in the gap between the pieces. The black stinger poked out first, then the fat-tailed scorpion emerged.

In a moment of horror, Linus realized he was bent forward and holding the corner of the blanket over his shoulder. How much trouble he was in came when another scorpion dropped onto his neck and scrambled down the back of his shirt.

The Cretan screamed when the stinger extended over the creature's head and punched into the muscles of his back. Pain and venom dropped Archer Linus to his knees, and then to the ground, where he lay writhing in agony.

*** 

Archer Buckie knew his partner was in some kind of panic and pain. But training took over, and he stepped carefully, rotating his notched arrow searching for a target. Moving slowly, placing each foot to avoid traps, the Archer reached the circle of light from the campfire.

"Linus, what's wrong," he questioned. But the other man whined as he lay curled up on the ground. "Linus. Shake it off and talk to me."

While moving forward, Buckie had been careful. But the one-sided conversation and worry about his partner took all his attention.

*** 

Jace Kasia pushed up slowly. The layer of sand cascaded off his body and he stood just behind the preoccupied Archer.

"Linus. What's wrong…"

"You should have waited for morning."

Jace's arms wrapped around the bowman's throat. As he tightened the pressure on the arteries, cutting off blood flow to the man's brain, Archer Kasia dropped his center of gravity.

Archer Buckie attempted to turn to face his attacker and counter the hold. But the pressure increased and four heartbeats later, the bow and arrows dropped. Jace held his victim all the way to the ground before releasing the bowman.

In a rush, Jace jumped into the firelight. He kicked the broken bowl into the fire, the round from the blanket that trapped the scorpions in the bowl and the horsehair ban that held the cloth in place flared up. Then he tossed in the blanket, and as the items went up in smoke, he used his foot to sweep the camp free of scorpions.

After ripping the shirt off the injured man, he added that to the fire.

"What's your name?" Jace asked.

He rolled the Archer onto his belly.

"Name's Linus. Back hurts."

"Worse than the trials at the agoge?" Jace asked as he cut an X over the site of the sting.

"What would you know about the agoge?" Linus questioned between gasps.

"I know you two came at me like third year Herds," Jace said, comparing Linus and his partner to young students in the academy on Crete. He squeezed the cut trying to drain out the venom. "It's a good thing I recognized you as Cretan Archers or you'd both be dead."

"Are you so sure of that?" Linus challenged.

Even hurt, Cretan Archer pride wouldn't allow him to admit defeat.

Jace used the fingers of his bow hand to press deep into the muscles before crushing the flesh. Blood and venom dribbled out. Linus roared at the pain, before his outburst faded to a whimper.

"Pretty sure you'd be dead," Jace assured Linus. Dumping the Archer on the ground, Jace added. "Let me pull the other Herd into the light before he gets stung. And I get to save his life, as well as yours."

***

Consciousness returned as did an awareness of a woolen blanket under his face. Masking his state, Archer Buckie kept his eyes closed, remained still, and listened for clues to his situation.

Ragged breathing from someone panting in pain. The crackle of palm branches burning in a fire. Warmth from the fire on one side of his body. An aroma of goat meat being roasted. All were clues to the placement of objects, yet frustrating for him was the absence of sounds to identify the location of his assailant.

"Come up for a fast attack," a man advised, "and the result will be disappointing."

The voice came from the other side of the fire, giving Buckie a target.

"You're right," Buckie said in a small, defeated voice, "all the fight has gone out of me."

"I really don't have the inclination for a session in a fighting circle," the man remarked. "It's been a long day and I need to sleep."

"Go ahead," Buckie encouraged.

The man laughed.

***

Jace Kasia pulled the stick out of the fire and blew on the roasted goat. The meat came from Linus and Buckie's

173

pouches, and Jace was glad for the meal. He chewed while contemplating the now awake Cretan Archer.

"Linus is in need of something to deaden the pain, and vinegar to soak the wound," Jace described. "And I can't sleep and guard you. Or treat him without more supplies."

"We have vials of vinegar in our pouches," Buckie told him.

"All used up while you slept," Jace countered. Then with a deep and serious tone, he explained. "I have three options. You die, leaving me free to sleep. If Linus lives through the night, I'll take him to a settlement. Then be on my way north."

"What is the second option?" Buckie inquired.

"Executing Linus and cutting your throat," Jace said. He took a bite and chewed. "Then I'd get some undisturbed rest."

At the dispassionate mention of the brutal acts, and the man's easy familiarity with death, Buckie opened his eyes and attempted to sit up. His ankles were tied, another length of leather bound his arms to his side, and his wrists were lashed together.

"Roll to your knees as you were taught," Jace encouraged.

"How do you know what we were taught?" Buckie asked. He rocked from side to side until the dip of his shoulder and a headbutt to the ground propelled him to his knees. Once upright, the bowman examined his warden. The man was tall, with a fit form, and broad shoulders. "Who are you?"

"File Leader Jace Kasia," Jace said using a title from more than ten years ago.

"Instructor Gergely's Herds?" Buckie questioned.

"When I knew him, it was Lieutenant Gergely's Company," Jace corrected.

Both men fell silent. The whimpering by Linus and the crackling of palm branches in the fire were the only sounds.

Buckie remarked, "You said three options."

Jace took the last bite of goat and tossed the stick in the fire.

"You load Linus on the chariot," Jace offered. He reached to the ground, lifted his hand, and displayed a collection of bowstrings. After throwing them in the fire, he finished. "You return to the Army of the South. I'll get some sleep and Linus gets treatment. By the time you send a patrol, I'll be long gone."

"I take it, those were our bowstrings?" Buckie asked. "Did you get them all?"

"Pretty sure," Jace responded. "But if killing me is more important than taking care of an injured Cretan, option two would be better for me."

Trying to recapture a little pride, Buckie informed Jace, "there's one in my sandal."

File Leader Kasia plucked one more bowstring from the ground.

"I always kept extras in my combat sandals," he said before flicking the string into the fire. "The end of this rests with you. Do we draw a fighting circle and I kill you."

"Are you sure you can?"

"Pretty sure," Jace stated. "Should I draw the circle or harness the horses?"

"Linus is a good friend," Buckie declared. "And there's no profit in fighting you."

"I disagree," Jace mentioned. He stood and pointed at the two helpless Cretan Archers. "We fought a battle and you lost. What are your lives worth?"

## Chapter 18 – A Silver Coin

Not surprising, the boat Jace bought passage on moved down the Nile fasten than any vessel heading upstream. Days from the oasis, he strolled through an armed camp. Tents on either side of the road resembled the Army of the South. They filled the ground for a quarter of a mile to either side of the path, and just like the rebel army, the tents and groups of spearmen were just as mismatched and unarmed.

At the gates to Alexandria, guards barred Jace's way.

"No soldiers in the city," one sentry informed him.

Jace wanted to point out that very few of the men in the camp were soldiers. And based on the absence of spears and bows, fewer still were spearmen or archers. He kept his opinion to himself and answered.

"I'm a resident, and I've been away on business," he told the guard. "Where did all the spearmen come from?"

"Lord King Ptolemy called for a gathering of a Pharaoh's Army," the guard told him. "They began arriving four days ago. Many are fresh off farms and not welcomed by the citizens of Alexandria. To keep peace, we don't allow them in the city."

Jace stopped in the portal to Alexandria and looked back. Although he searched, the Archer couldn't locate the training grounds. In the back of his mind, he considered offering himself as a weapons instructor. The pay should be good and the work plentiful.

"Move along," the guard prompted.

"Where are the training grounds?" he asked the sentry.

"Training for what?" the sentry countered. "It's an Army of the Pharoah. The noblemen already know how to fight, and the Gods will direct the spears and guide the arrows of the soldiers."

"Not likely," Jace mumbled.

He entered Alexandria, his idea of training Ptolemy's army partially dismissed.

*****

Beyond the tomb of Alexander, Jace turned left and went down the block to the house with a blue door. On one side of the stoop, a statue of Zeus as a bearded man stood sentry. On the other side, a statue of a bull with a sun-disk between its horns represented the Egyptian God Apis.

"Very clever," Jace remarked as he knocked on the door. "Zeus protects from the sky and Apis provides grain and the propagation of herds. By reason, they guard the house from top to bottom."

The door opened a little and a brown eye peered out.

"You've been gone for weeks," Nubia scolded. "We thought you were dead. Or taken and forced to row for a pirate crew."

"I'm alive, and truly, the story is more mundane than pirates," Jace lied. "Let me in and I'll tell you about the harvest near Giza."

"That's where the pyramids are," Nubia recalled. She opened the door and stepped back. "We studied the pyramids and the sphinx in lessons. Are they really that large?"

Jace paused halfway over the threshold. He'd never left the ship and had only seen the tops of the pyramids as they rowed by the town of Giza.

"Tell me what you've learned about them," Jace suggested as a cover.

"They say the structures touch the sky," Nubia replied.

"That's a good description," Jace agreed. "What else is there left to say after that."

Onella came from a side room and smiled when she saw Jace. Then the Greek landlady sniffed and pointed towards the rear of the house.

"I want to say, it's nice to have you back Jace Kasia," she announced. "But not so much the odor lingering around you. Perhaps a bath?"

"Yes, ma'am," Jace responded.

"Nubia will fetch clean clothes from your room," Onella offered. "You stay right there. I'll be in the kitchen."

Once he held a stack of desert robes, Jace marched straight to the rear door and out to the bathhouse.

\*\*\*

Uncommon from the last few visits, the harbor entrance to The Pharaoh's Palace was blocked by extra guards. Yet they did little good in securing the fortress.

"I need to see Captain Midhat," Jace explained.

Lines of porters lugging boxes of weapons, shields, and helmets forced the sentry and visitor to the side of the entrance. Jace had seen the war gear in the armory outside Midhat's office. Old and in need of sharpening and polishing, the equipment, while plentiful, showed age, wear, and neglect. Laborers carried the crates of arms to a line of wagons. On the far side of the entrance, porters returning from the transports formed a single file.

"The Ring Captain is busy," the guard remarked. To emphasize the point, he nodded at the crowded entrance.

"He'll want to see me," Jace assured him. "I've just got back from the rebel camp. I have valuable information. It'll be important when the battle starts."

Rather than being impressed, the sentry gave Jace a lopsided grin.

"You do know, we are joining an Army of the Pharaoh," the guard mentioned.

Jace had been in enough fights and battles to know the title of an army had little to do with the outcome. Other than the pride of a Legion to hold their combat line or the Spartans to claw their opponents into submission, few wars were won from the magic of a name.

"And that's why I need to see Captain Midhat," Jace insisted.

"Work your way to the single line," the guard instructed. "But leave your weapons with me."

Considering the boxes were full of knives, swords, and spearheads, it seemed absurd. Jace drew his small skinning knife and offered it to the guard.

179

"Not your dining utensils, your weapons."

"This is the only weapon I have," Jace assured him.

"Keep it and get in line."

Weaving between porters, Jace reached the far side and joined the queue. The sight of the weapons got him thinking again about a position as a weapons instructor. Trying to gage the possibility, Jace remarked to the laborer in front of him.

"I guess the training will start once the spearmen are issued weapons."

"Training?" the man sneered. "That's what fueled the rebellion. After King Ptolemy shaped the Egyptian army into an efficient fighting force, he beat the Seleucid army and forced them into a treaty."

"How did that cause a rebellion" Jace questioned.

Before the laborer answered, an Egyptian officer shoved his way between the lines.

"If I wanted to give you a feast day," he roared. "I would have supplied pig. Do you see any boar around here?"

"No, Lieutenant," the labor force replied.

"Then stop talking and move those supplies."

Jace had been so focused on the movement of the weapons, he didn't notice the footwear of the porters. Every one of them wore heavy sandals. Meaning, the commanders were using professional soldiers to move the gear and not the farmers and fieldhands who needed the weapons the most.

Keeping to himself, Jace shuffled through the entrance and into the long subterranean corridor.

Once in the armory, the line dissolved into work parties. Jace separated from the soldiers and crossed to Midhat's office.

"Captain," Jace announced from the doorway, "I have a report on the Army of the South."

"The army of traitors is more like it," Midhat shot back. "Come in and tell me how they're faring."

Between the soldier's dismissal of training farmers and Midhat's easy rechristening of the rebel army, Jace was puzzled.

"They're growing by the day. Bringing in Cretan Archers, and Nubian spearmen and archers," Jace answered. "In fact, their tents and training grounds cover miles of the west bank. And across the Nile, their headquarters is in the Temple at Luxor. But you don't seem worried."

"And I shouldn't be," Midhat commented. "After building and training his army, Lord King Ptolemy defeated Antiochus the Third. With the Seleucid army broken, our young officers and their seasoned spearmen wanted to continue the war and raid into Seleucid territory."

"Spoils are how a General typically pays his army," Jace suggested. "What happened?"

"Lord King Ptolemy, beyond being a great General like his ancestor, has a merciful and generous nature," Midhat told him. "He granted Antiochus liberal terms and the Seleucid King accepted, ending the war."

"Obviously, it didn't end the fighting," Jace guessed. "It started a rebellion. But how?"

"Many of our young officers took their spearmen and grievances to Horwennefer," Midhat stated. "The rebel leader promised spoils, and plots of rich land for the fieldhands turned spearmen. So, you see, we can't do that again."

"Excuse me, Captain. Can't do what again?"

"Arm and train the peasants to fight."

"But you're going to war to put down a rebellion by a well-trained and well-equipped army," Jace insisted. "How do you propose to defeat the rebels?"

"We are a Pharoh's Army, the Gods are with us," Midhat declared. "When Lord King Ptolemy rides his chariot forward, the rebels will throw down their weapons, drop to their knees, and bow to their Pharaoh."

Jace held a lecture on the tip of his tongue. It told of Cretan Archers not caring for kings or royal traditions if someone was paying them to ignore the ancient customs. But he didn't deliver that talk. Instead, he gave a report on what he'd seen.

"And finally, the rebels have flat boats and can use them to slip across the Nile at will. And those raiders will not bow to the Pharoah," Jace finished the report by asking. "Do you have a silver coin?"

"I owe you more than that," Midhat proposed.

"Yes sir, you do," Jace told him. "But I'll take a silver as payment and will relinquish my claim on the rest. If you'll release me from our contract."

"You're leaving the service of the Pharaoh?" Midhat questioned.

"With your permission, Captain Midhat, and a silver coin."

***

Jace may have lost his position, but he earned a profit, making it a good day. About the next day, Archer Kasia had no idea. To clear his mind and decide on his future, he looked out to sea while walking the docks.

Ships from Athens, the Island of Rhodes, the Island of Crete, the Roman Republic, Carthage, Iberia, Celicia, Cyprus, Pergamon, and a dozen other cities were beached or tied to piers. A hundred accents and languages blanketed the wharf of Alexandria.

"Jace Kasia, Master Kasia," a voice called out.

Turning, he recognized a young man from a seaside restaurant.

"Yes?" Jace answered.

The youth stopped and extended a scroll.

"A ship from Cyprus dropped this last week," the boy told him. "You didn't come by to eat so we held it for you."

Jace gave the youth a bronze coin and tucked the letter into a pouch. Then he continued his stroll. Whatever the letter contained, after taking weeks to arrive, it would wait for a quiet spot to be read.

***

*Cretan Archer Jace Kasia,*

*When last we spoke, you asserted that the capture of the pirate known as Diceärch would require your assistance. At the time, I assured you that my forces in the Cyclades were fully capable of apprehending a single pirate. As well as apprehending his Macedonian protected crew and ship.*

183

*Regrettably, after months of inhuman treatment of priest and clergy, desecration of altars and temples, and theft of cargo from transports and warehouses, I acknowledge my failure. And begrudgingly, I admit to needing your expertise in bringing the renegade to justice.*

*I have stationed my fleet at Kefalos on the Island of Kos and hope you will join me there. As an enticement, wherever your present position, I will double your compensation. And of more importance to a tracker's success, I will advise my fleet to follow your directions.*

*Radames, Admiral of The Cyclades, by the grace of Pharaoh Ptolemy the Fourth. The Lord King, who by the grace of the Gods, commands all the waters of the Nile and the lands of Egypt.*

***

Jace rolled the scroll, tighter than was warranted, and jammed it in the pouch.

"Bad news," the waitress guessed.

"What are the two things you can depend on from a man?" Jace asked.

"He'll claim to have more coins than he possesses," the server answered, "and he'll swear you are the only one for him."

"One out of two isn't bad," Jace told her while holding up his empty glass. "Bring me another."

"You sure are pounding them down tonight," she said in a serious tone. "Which one did I get wrong?"

"A man will tell you, you're the only one, as a last resort. After his first choices have failed," Jace advised. "And he will never give up his power, no matter how persuasive his words."

"Most of the men I know don't have any power," she mentioned. Then holding up the glass the waitress said. "One pomegranate and water, coming up."

She left him at the table deep in thought. Jace Kasia did not want to take the contract. For one, Radames would second guess every direction or order because he was, after all, the Egyptian Admiral in the island chain. Plus, there was an undisclosed problem hinted at in the letter. Both issues screamed at Jace to find another contract.

The pomegranate and water landed on his table with a splash. Looking first at the wet spot and next at the waitress, he inquired. "Why the sloppy job?"

"Because everyone else in here is drunk and has spilled wine or beer on their tabletops and the floor," she explained. "If your table is messy, no one will question your choice in beverages."

"I guess drunk patrons fighting late in the evening can be a problem," Jace allowed.

"Often enough. But I wanted to spill your drink because none of the men I know have power," she emphasized. "All they have is coin and I don't like being told I'm wrong. Especially, when I'm right."

Jace pulled out the silver he received from Captain Midhat.

"As a wise man once said to me," Jace commented, quoting Zarek Mikolas "You take a commander's coin, and you give value. You don't have to like the client, approve of his war, or his personal hygiene. You just have to hold your nose and do the job."

"Are you saying I smell?" the waitress demanded.

185

"No, ma'am," Jace assured the server. He handed her the silver coin. "Here, I'm paying you for the sage advice."

"What advice?"

"Sometimes a sloppy job is not what it appears."

"You don't need beer or wine," she announced as she moved to tend another table. "Your brain is muddled enough without the drink."

"You may be correct," he thought. "Because I'm taking the contract, but I'm not telling Admiral Radames. I can't get much sloppier than that."

## Act 7

### Chapter 19 – Soldier of Moloch

"Stroke. Stroke," the Captain of the transport yelled above the wind. "Put your strength into it. Stroke. Stroke."

Jace Kasia and the three other crewmen bent their knees. Their backs arched over the oars as five humans pitted themselves against the Demi-God Aiolos. Young fir trees trimmed into blades with long handles fought with the wind and the stormy sea in a battle for possession of the ship.

One crewman missed a step when a massive wave washed over the deck. The wave of Aiolos entangled the man, slammed him to the boards, then lifted him on a blanket of sea water. Poets and priests say all things eventually returned to the sea. As they foretold, the sailor, flailing on a cushion of water, slid towards the edge of the transport and his death.

Jace stepped back, mid-stroke, and hammered the toe of his sandal into the sailor's chest. The impact pinned the crewman to the deck while allowing the water to flow around the screaming man. His cries attested to the surprise and pain of the reverse kick. But as the water receded, the screams transitioned to a roar of relief.

187

"Take your oar," the Captain ordered. "Get to your feet and take you oar."

Struggling against the rocking deck and the wind, the sailor grabbed his oar, and used it to regain his balance.

"Stroke. Stroke," the Captain shouted.

***

The merchantman fought throughout the night for survival. All five members of the crew, from the Captain on the rear oar, to the sailors on the port and the starboard sides, rowed in unison. If anyone of them had fallen, like hundreds of transports before, the *Goods of Attica* would have gone to the sea floor and the crew to feed fish. With the rising sun, the clouds moved off, the winds settled into a breeze, and the sailors greeted the new day with gratitude.

"We'll sacrifice to Hermes for the safe passage, later," Captain Thyestes informed the crew. His voice reflected the exhaustion felt by the rest of the men. "Right now, get the sail up."

Jace and the three crewmen heaved on the lines and hoisted the big sail. Once it was tied off, the material puffed up and the ship moved northward.

"Can I relieve you on the rear oar?" Jace asked Thyestes.

"The wind is coming from the southeast," the Athenian Captain told him. Thyestes stepped away from the rear oar. "To counter the wind, push to the west. That'll keep us on course, more or less."

"Shouldn't we be looking for an island?" Jace asked.

"We're a deep bellied transport," Thyestes explained. "Put us in a cove with a shallow bottom, and we'll drag our

188

keel. Add a rock, and we'll be on the beach for a week repairing the hull. Do that, and we won't make a profit."

"I'll keep *Goods of Attica* on a northeast heading," Jace confirmed.

***

After eating, the three sailors and the Captain stretched out to rest. Although the sail limited Jace's view to a slice of sea beyond the foredeck, to the sides of the sail, he saw a broad stretch of the horizon. When a mast and sail appeared in the distance, he noted it right away.

"A ship is coming at us from the port side," Jace announced.

From asleep to fully awake, three if the crew jumped up. The fourth sailor came up slow and holding his chest.

"I can't tell what kind of ship," the sailor remarked. He stood tall and lifted his torso, stretching his height. Then he folded over while grabbing his midsection. "I think you cracked a rib."

"The alternative was letting you get washed overboard," Jace reminded the sailor.

"The ship is definitely coming from the direction of Crete," another crewman offered.

"Is that good or bad?" Jace asked.

"If it's a merchant, we'll be fine," Thyestes answered. "If it's a warship heading for Rhodes, the same."

"And if it's something else?" Jace asked.

"In these waters, off the coast of an island in a civil war," the Athenian stated, "we could be in for a fight. Get your gear."

Jace relinquished the rear oar and went to the storage compartment under the steering deck. From the crawl space, he pulled out an African infantry shield, a Macedonian helmet, an Egyptian short sword with an ivory hilt, and a six-foot Spartan spear.

If they trusted you enough to show you their wares, the merchants at the market in Alexandria had a varied selection.

*"For a spear of this length," Jace commented, "it's front heavy."*

*"It's a Spartan spear," the merchant bragged when he showed Jace the weapon. "Spartan spears range in length from six to nine feet. When the Spartans form phalanxes, they used the longer version. It's shorter than other Greek spears. But Spartans hold their spears with one hand and the nineteen-foot Macedonian spears, no matter how well trained the hoplite, could not be employed with one hand. The shorter Spartan spears double as javelins when not needed for work in a shield wall."*

*"I'll take it," Jace agreed.*

While eyeing Jace's mismatched equipment, the sailors selected clubs.

"Do you know how to use those?" a crewman asked.

Two swung their clubs around warming up for a fight. The third held the club in his arms as if cradling as newborn lamb.

While the crew tested the balance of their blunt instruments, Jace slipped the sword strap over his head. Next, the Archer adjusted the sheath, so it rested behind his hip. With the ivory hilt out of the way, he pushed his arm into the strap of the shield.

"That's not the proper question," Jace commented.

"What is the proper question, Soldier?" Thyestes inquired.

"It's not important if I know how to fight with these weapons," Jace answered. He slipped the helmet over his head. Then with a flourish, he twirled the spear overhead several times before lowering the shaft to the top of the shield. When he answered, his voice resonated from inside the helmet, carrying an edge as sharp as the leaf-shaped blade on the spear. "It's more important, they believe I know how to fight with the equipment."

***

The coastal trader had twelve men in the crew. Four stood in the forward section of the ship, holding spears. While their presence served to intimidate, the other eight rowed the single banker towards the transport.

"What do you think, Captain?" Jace asked.

"They're ragged looking. I say they're nothing but would-be rogues," Thyestes announced. "If they were full grown pirates, the Cretans would have more fighters. What they seek is a soft target to fill their purses and a conquest to build their reputation."

"I meant do we fight?" Jace corrected.

"Most guards I hire for security advise paying a ransom," Thyestes remarked. "But you, Soldier, seem ready to fight and spill blood."

"They're coming on fast," Jace advised. "Their warriors are prepared and their spears at the ready. So, I ask again. Do we fight?"

Thyestes gnawed on his lower lip. Usually, the guards employed to protect the ship and crewmen in ports, and to act as a deterrent while at sea, were older soldiers. Their will to participate in combat long since spent on past battlefields. Yet, their fearsome presence kept unserious marauders and thieves away.

"Maybe we can talk to them," Thyestes suggested. "You know, see if we can come to an agreement."

A majority of men were afraid of being close to death. Plus, a man with a conscience feared the nightmares that came with the killing of another human. This resulted in pirates, both infamous and infantile, being able to easily intimidate a fainthearted merchant.

"They have spears," Jace noted. "Knives we can deal with. But spears allow them to reach out and hurt your crewmen from a distance."

"But what if they kill you," Thyestes worried. "Then they'll take their anger out on the rest of us."

"Retribution is always a possibility," Jace granted. "But so is strengthening your enemies by enabling them. Do we fight or should I get out of your way?"

For as capable and brave as Captain Thyestes was in a rough sea, in his heart, he believed in the sanctity of life. His beliefs would not allow him to order the soldier-for-hire forward to defend the ship and crew.

"Stand back," Thyestes instructed. "The rest of you, put away the clubs. We'll pay a ransom. Roll the sail."

\*\*\*

Four spearmen climbed over the rail at mid-ship. They spread out across the deck and leveled their spears.

"There's no need for violence," Thyestes assured them.

The Captain and three of his crewmen stood on the front of the steering deck. At the rear of the deck, next to the curved keel and rear oar, a man stood in a helmet, holding a shield and a spear.

"What about him," the leader of the pirates mentioned. "He's dressed for violence."

"I've instructed him not to interfere with our negotiations," Thyestes informed the pirate.

"Did you hear that?" the leader declared. Then for the benefit of his spearmen, he mimicked. "I've instructed him not to interfere with our negotiations. Imagine that. The merchant thinks this is a negotiation."

"My good man," Thyestes began.

"I am not a good man," the pirate leader scoffed. "I'm a Cretan Archer and I'd as soon kill you as talk to you."

Inside the helmet, Jace smiled. No Cretan Archer would brag about being an archer while holding a spear. Let alone use the title to intimidate an already submissive Captain.

"But you'll take my silver, wouldn't you?" Thyestes said, cutting out the small talk. "I'll give you twenty to leave my ship."

"That depends on what you have in the cargo hold," the pirate replied.

"Cotton cloth and thread, dates, and grain," Thyestes reported. "Nothing worth your bother. But I will pay you to leave my ship."

*"Acquiesces to an evil man emboldens him,"* Zarek Mikolas had warned Jace. *"It works the same as granting authority to a weak man. They will abuse the power until stopped. Only by then,*

193

*it'll take more strength than if you'd slapped him down at the beginning."*

The words were echoing in Jace's head when the pirate ordered, "Open the hold and let me see."

Thyestes breathed out in exasperation. Picking up on the Captain's attitude, the pirate threatened, "Don't try anything. Or I'll kill you and your crew."

"Remove the deck boards," Thyestes instructed.

***

Two of the sailors hopped off the steering deck, while the third sat and slid off. His sore ribs prevented him from making any jarring or rapid motion.

The first sailors grabbed hooks and went to the sides of the ship. Seeing the iron hooks, the raiders backed away. But when the sailors stuck the hooks in the ends of a deck board and lifted it from over the cargo hold, they relaxed.

The injured crewman stood at the pile making sure the deck boards were evenly stacked. After three boards had been removed, Captain Thyestes indicated the opening.

"Have a look. Cotton cloth and thread. Dates and grain. Nothing easy to offload or valuable enough to delay your departure," he informed the pirates.

"You, by the boards, come here," the pirate invited the injured crewman. "Get down there and move the big bundles around. I want to know what's under them."

Moving cautiously because each step hurt, the sailor inched towards the opening.

"I haven't got all day," the leader of the raiders complained.

Angry, he spun his spear and jammed the butt end into the sailor's side. While attempting to keep the shaft away from his bruised ribs, the crewman grabbed and held the spear.

"He's trying to fight me," the leader screamed.

In response, the pirate next to him ran the tip of his iron spear into the shoulder of the sailor. Blood spattered from the wound and splashed into the leader's eyes.

"My eyes, my eyes," he bellowed while rubbing at his face. "Kill them. Kill them all."

\*\*\*

Jace wanted to murder the leader of the raiders for lying about being a Cretan Archer, and for his weak attempt at being a bully. But other than his mouth, the temporarily blinded weasel wasn't dangerous.

A more appropriate target was the pirate advancing towards the steering platform and Captain Thyestes.

Jace spun the shaft of the spear on the palm of his hand until the tip pointed down the length of *Goods of Attica*. A javelin was just the tool required for the task.

The weapon flashed over Thyestes' shoulder and dipped just enough to spear the advancing pirate in the chest. Another feature of the Spartan spear, the leaf-shaped blade was longer and heavier than other types of spears.

Jace didn't see the tip punch through the back of the pirate's shirt. He was sprinting forward. At the edge of the steering platform, he planted a foot, pushed off, and leaped at another pirate.

\*\*\*

Any group of youths would tell you, to make the biggest splash in a pond from a great height, one needed to tuck in his legs. Jace Kasia wasn't raised with boys his own age. And so, he had no idea of how to make a big splash. Which didn't mean he was unaware of the maneuver. It was just that he learned the technique for a completely different reason.

*"Like a rock, compact and dense, you draw in your legs, rotate forward, and collect your weight behind the shield,"* Zarek Mikolas explained. *"Come down on even the strongest and best armored warrior in that position, and he'll crumble like a three-day old honey cake."*

Jace arched through the air, huddled behind the shield as he'd been taught. His target, far from being a mighty warrior, was the closest raider. As if a boulder had been dropped on his head, the spearman's back and neck snapped.

Jace paid no mind to the crushed pirate. Rolling forward, the Archer came off the limp corpse, while drawing the short sword.

There were still two raiders remaining on the *Goods of Attica*. Archer Kasia pivoted, looking for his next target.

\*\*\*

The bleeding sailor with the cracked ribs shuffled towards the foredeck. Unable to fight, he fled as best he could. But he was quickly running out of deck.

Laughing at the wounded man's feeble attempt to escape, the pirate stalked his prey. In a few more steps, the sailor would run out of ship, stop, and allow the raider to finish the job he started.

Inserting himself in the one-sided duel, Jace cut diagonally across the deck. At a full sprint, he plowed into the spearman.

Off balance and stumbling from the surprise contact, the raider cried out as they reached the rail.

"I can swim," the pirate boasted while toppling over the side. He submerged, resurfaced, and threatened. "I will kill you."

The Archer watched the raider bob to the surface and issue his warning.

"You might want to stop the bleeding first," Jace encouraged.

Around the pirate, the water turned red. Thrashing about, it took the raider a moment to discover the wound. Small, the injury from the short sword seemed to be only a nick on the inside of his thigh. Inverse to the tiny incision, blood pumped out in spurts.

***

A yelp, very close to the sound of a wounded animal, reached Jace. Expecting an attack from the last raider, he swung his shield to clear the blade. But no blade nor spear tip came at him. The yelp carried from midship where two sailors from the *Goods of Attica* were clubbing the pirate leader.

True to his character, Thyestes hopped around just out of club range, begging his crewmen not to hurt the pirate. To his relief, the ship's hired guard, Soldier, shoved the sailors aside.

"I tried to stop them," the Captain stated.

"I know," Jace acknowledged.

Then to Thyestes' horror, Jace stabbed the raider in the heart.

"Clubbing is fine for a fight, but a waste of energy for executing someone," Jace commented.

He cleaned the blade on the pirate's shirt and sheathed the weapon. Then he pulled the raider up on his shoulder and walked the body to the side of the deck. Below him, the coastal trader started to push off, no doubt to escape.

"Stay right there," Jace instructed.

It might have been the streaks of blood running down his chest, or confusion on the part of the rowers, but the trading vessel stop its retreat.

***

"Bring the other two corpses over here," Jace directed the sailors. "Throw them into the boat."

First one dead pirate slapped onto the boards of the trader. Then another but the first body softened the landing. When Jace heaved the leader over, the third corpse made nothing more than the sound of a meaty slap.

To the surprise of the sailors and the terror of the rowers, Jace jumped down into the trader.

"Your other fool is floating on the far side of the transport," Jace informed the rowers. "Be sure to pick up the body before you leave."

"You're letting us go?" a rower inquired.

"After you answer a question," Jace replied. "Where can I find Lieutenant Diceärch?"

The question resulted in several different conversations among the eight rowers. To prevent resistance, Jace called up the transport, "throw me the spear."

Jace caught the Spartan weapon and rested it on the top of the shield. Eight pairs of eyes expanded in awe at the sight of the sharp blade.

"I asked a question," Jace reminded the rowers.

"Diceärch is a Commander of the Macedonian Navy," a rower told him. "I've heard his squadron is based on the Island of Lemnos at Myrina."

The Archer had been right to be cautious. Admiral Radames admitting to needing Jace's help in capturing Diceärch was the first hint that things had gone wrong. And when the Admiral wrote he had his fleet at the Island of Kos, Jace knew for sure. The Egyptian had assumed a defensive posture.

Diceärch must have set an ambush for Radames with his squadrons. Only a mauling of the Egyptian fleet would cause Radames to withdraw and tighten his perimeter.

"Get word to Commander Diceärch, I'm looking for a meeting with him," Jace told the rowers.

"Who are you?" one asked.

"Just call me, a Soldier of Moloch."

Anyone claiming a relationship with the Canaanite God Moloch was, by nature evil, or insane. He would have to be off center to associated with a God who demanded human sacrifice. But then, who else would want to meet with a monster like Diceärch.

**Chapter 20 – Are You a Spartan?**

The *Goods of Attica* rowed out of the harbor with the injured sailor propped up on the rear oar and Captain

Thyestes rowing on the port side. Thyestes having announced he would rather row to Athens than to spend another day on a ship with a Soldier of Moloch.

"I should have lowered my voice when I told the rowers," Jace complained to himself.

The island felt as if he'd come full circle. Not just because a ship dumped him at Karavostasis Harbor without landing, but the circumstances of being uninvited were familiar.

To stress the point, halfway up the beach, four spearmen jogged to block his way.

"State the nature of your business," a spearman demanded.

The port guards eyed Jace's war gear.

"What's your business on Folegandros Island?" another barked.

"That's redundant," Jace remarked in his best imitation of a nobleman. "I prefer to speak with someone in command."

He dropped his bundles and clasped his hands behind his back as if impatient for the answer.

"Lieutenant Rhesus is busy," the third spearman told him.

Jace peered around the harbor at the watch tower, the collection of huts and shops, the awning, and the footprint of the burned-out building. The foundation still showed the scorch marks from the fire. In the small settlement, there were few places the commander of the militia could be located.

"When Lieutenant Rhesus sobers up, have him meet me at the Fisherman's Wife," Jace said. "I'll buy him a bowl of fish stew."

Picking up his bundles, Jace marched by the spearman. His demonstration of confidence overcame their vague set of orders.

"He did answer the question," the fourth spearman offered.

"He did?" asked another. "How did he answer?"

"He's here for the fish stew."

The four shrugged and marched uphill for the shade of the awning. When the Lieutenant woke up, he'd be hungry, and the stranger did offer to buy him a bowl of stew.

***

In the shade of the Fisherman's Wife building, Jace leaned back in a chair and sipped from a mug of vinegar water.

"Why are you on Folegandros Island?" a disheveled Greek officer inquired.

"Wine or beer?" Jace asked.

Moving out of the sun, the Lieutenant sat on the chair across from Jace.

"Beer and a bowl of stew," he answered.

Once Jace ordered the refreshments from the fisherman's wife, he quizzed the officer.

"I hear that Diceärch was a Lieutenant at Karavostasis Harbor. Did you know him?"

"I didn't but I own him," Rhesus disclosed. Jace sat up at the remark until the officer explained. "Because he went rogue from boredom, the Admiral changes the island detachment every six months. And it's a good thing too. This is the end of the world and the death of careers."

"I'm looking to buy some tools and a fishing boat with a sail," Jace told the Lieutenant. "And I need advice on my destination."

"That's very specific and totally random at the same time," Rhesus pointed out. "But nothing is normal at the end of the world. I imagine some of the fishermen will have ideas on your destination."

"I plan to speak with them when the fishing fleet comes in this afternoon."

*\*\**

Later, when the sun sank over the high part of the island and darkness engulfed Folegandros, Jace joined a ring of fishermen. They sat around a roaring fire and the flames illuminated their sunburned faces.

Jace handed the man on his right a wineskin.

"Kasia, I remember you teaching Diceärch when he was a Lieutenant," the fisherman boasted.

He took a stream of wine and passed it to the next fisherman.

"You do too good a job, son," another offered. "I don't know whether to thank you for keeping my wife up all night so I can sleep. Or to stab you because I can't get her to go to bed with me out of fear."

"Your wife hasn't gone to bed with you since you lost your last tooth," one fisherman teased.

"She's more afraid of seeing your face at dawn than she is of that pirate," another added.

Ignoring the banter, the first said, "You made Dicearch a killer. And that's for sure."

Jace started to protest the assertion than changed his mind.

"That's the truth," he admitted. "But Dicearch isn't the only one. I've taught and fought with the Hirpini Tribe against Rome. Battled my way out of a trap by the Boi Tribe. In Iberia, I fought with the Roman Legions. And last month I was with the Pharaoh's army in Egypt."

"That's a powerful lot of fighting for one so young," a fisherman suggested.

"Too much," Jace declared. "I've had enough of battles. What I need is a place where I can look out over the water and figure out the rest of my life."

"I did that twenty some years ago," a middle-aged fisherman informed Jace.

"How did that work out for you," Jace asked.

"He's still here," answered a chorus of three fishermen.

The middle-aged man pulled a coin from a pouch and passed it to Jace. Examining it in the flickering light, The Archer made out a woman's head resting on the body of a lion with wings. In front of the image sat an amphora with a bunch of grapes hanging over the jug.

"A coin from Chios," the fisherman explained. "Besides minting coins, they make spicy wine, cut marble slabs run through with delicate red veins, and they harvest mastic."

"Mastic?" Jace questioned.

"The tears of Chios. Sap drips from branches on special trees. The people of Chios harvest and dry the tear shaped pieces," the fisherman described. "You chew mastic, and it turns white. At first, it tastes bitter. But the longer you chew, the taste changes to something resembling pine or ceder."

"Why?" Jace inquired. "Why chew something bitter."

"Because it tastes good after a while and cleans your breath. And some say, it's good for the stomach," the fisherman told him. Then he observed. "You do need to broaden your horizons."

"I can't argue with you," Jace admitted while handing the coin back. "What I need is a fishing boat."

"Are you going to join us here on Folegandros Island?" the toothless fisherman inquired.

"Not here. I'm thinking about a more interesting place," Jace informed him. He took the wineskin and without drinking, passed it to the first fisherman. "Maybe a place like Chios Island."

\*\*\*

The *Island Princess* left Karavostasis harbor four days later. Towed behind the coastal trader, a yellow four-man fishing boat bobbed in the wake.

"You can buy a fishing boat on most large islands," Captain Yehor mentioned.

Jace and the Captain's two sons rowed from midship.

"I liked that one," Jace called back. "And I'd hate to lose it."

"It's tied securely," Preben Yehor assured him. "I meant you didn't have to bring it with you."

"Let's just say it has sentimental value," Jace said. "Plus, I sealed and painted it myself."

The coastal trader rounded the point of land, turned north, and set sail for Chora Island. It would be the first of many stops.

"I'm not complaining mind you," Yehor stressed as the sail filled. "Since my brother took ill, I'm glad for the extra pair of hands."

Yehor's two sons were boys on their first trading voyage. While they could row, the youths were limited in the cargo they could lift. And were mostly useless against pirates or thieves.

"You going to Chios came at the right time," Jace replied. "I almost set sail myself."

"In your little boat," one of the boys questioned.

"If I had to," Jace told him.

"What's the rush?" the other son inquired.

Jace wanted to tell the youths that he felt guilty about unleashing a monster on the world. But he didn't because, if not for Admiral Radames' offer of employment, the Archer would have ignored Diceärch and got on with his next contract.

"I didn't feel rushed," Jace told him. "It was time to move on."

\*\*\*

The stop at a small trading beach on Chora Island didn't seem worth the trouble.

"Most traders bypass the smaller islands," Yehor discussed his reasoning. "But the *Island Princess* can demand better trades because she does."

"You make the vessel sound like a partner in the business," Jace observed.

"The *Island Princess* is more than a partner," Yehor replied. "She is the business."

***

The Island of Cythera came up on the horizon and Yehor had Jace, and the boys roll the sail and row towards the beach. Before they reached the shoreline an acid aroma of rotting sea life washed over them.

"What's that stink?" the boys asked.

"That is the smell of opportunity," Yehor told them. "They harvest and crush sea snails to produce Tyrian purple. We'll spend the night at Kalantos."

"Isn't purple dye valuable?" Jace questioned.

"To say the least," Yehor assured him.

"Why spend the night on a beach when pirates know you're hauling a high valued commodity?"

"Tomorrow, we'll sail to Azalas on the other coast of the island," Yehor informed him. "And Azalas presents the same issue. So, what's the difference where we spend the night?"

To a trained soldier, the concept of presenting yourself as a target for an enemy without changing your route was a dangerous tactic. Yet the coastal trader didn't seem aware of the flaw in his business practices. But the Archer understood.

All night, Jace napped in the fishing boat, waking at every sound. By sunrise, he was glad to get on with the day. After shoving the small craft into the water, he waited for Yehor and the boys to launch the *Island Princess*.

"We slept on blankets," one of the boys stated as if Jace hadn't noticed the campsite. "You couldn't have been comfortable in that old fishing boat."

"I've slept in worse places," Jace told him.

***

Late the next day, the Island of Cythera fell below the horizon. Jace relaxed his guard once they were away from the beaches. Surely, pirates watched for traders leaving Cythera, knowing they carried purple dye among their cargo. If a crew was lurking, they would have attacked before the trader got that far away.

"Will we be stopping at Dolos," one son asked. "We want to see the shrines."

"The Island of Dolos is certainly a wonder to behold and the home of Temples and the birthplace of Gods," Yehor reported. "And as such, the harbor is full of trading vessels. Meaning what?"

"It means there is too much competition for the *Island Princess*," the other boy whined. "We only trade where we can get the best deals."

"Exactly. To that end, we'll go to Mykonos," Yehor explained. "It's a poor island where the citizens will be grateful for our arrival."

"Are there temples?" the other youth asked. "Or a fort. Or a large town?"

"No. Just a community of fishermen and their families," Yehor told them. "With items to trade and the need to buy goods."

They sailed around two islands, one being Dolos. Not appreciating the day, the boys sulked as the *Island Princess* sailed over the water under a bright sun that warmed the air.

*\*\*\**

Deep into the afternoon, the *Island Princess* beached at Mikonos on the Island of Mykonos. As Yehor described, traders bypassed the poor island to do business at the busy, religious port of Dolos. But also, as he predicted, the villagers came when the coastal trader landed.

"There's nothing here," the boys complained.

"There is trade," Yehor scolded. "And that's all a man can ask in life."

"What is all a man can ask in life?" one of the boys challenged.

"That his customers come out to greet him with trays of goods," he replied.

Although poor, the people of Mikonos were numerous. While Yehor traded, the boys and Jace carried items from the vessel to the beach and goods from the village to the ship.

While Jace worked, he kept his eyes open for trouble. When the trading ended and Yehor and the boys went to the village for dinner, Jace remained behind.

Near dark, a young woman came out with a tray of food and a pitcher of red wine.

"The boys think you're a Spartan," she mentioned while handing him the food and beverage. "They say you are strong, stoic, and like to be alone. And that you don't talk much. Are you a Spartan?"

Her eyes sparkled with curiosity and interest. Jace was tempted to tell her he was a Cretan Archer. In a moment, he

208

could unpack his bow and arrows from the fishing boat and show her a few tricks. Afterwards, it would be nice to spend the evening in conversation on the beach, watching the moon rise. She was lovely and his heart wanted to forget about his mission.

"Strong wine is forbidden," he growled. Taking the pitcher, Jace dumped the wine on the beach. "But I'll take the food. You can go."

Confused by the rude behavior, the young woman ran back to the village, her shoulders jerking as she cried.

*"A disguise is required to create a lore,"* Zarek Mikolas instructed. *"Break the norm of what's expected, and you shatter the illusion. Do anything not in character, and you become vulnerable and will fail at the job. That's the best result. At the worst, you'll die from your weakness."*

The food was delicious. Jace wished he could tell that to the woman and thank her. Instead, when Yehor came out to ask what went wrong, Jace said, "That woman talks too much."

"According to you, I talk too much," Yehor said in a joking manner.

Jace replied, "You do."

His mysterious character protected, Jace sat on the edge of the fishing boat while Captain Yehor stomped back to the village.

Jace's one consolation, he had his weapons and the tools he needed in the fishing boat. It was small comfort when laughter and voices carried from the village.

\*\*\*

In the morning, they shoved the fishing boat and the *Island Princess* free of the beach and paddled out.

"I have a treat for you, boys," Yehor told his sons. "We'll sail all day, but late this afternoon, well beach at Nas on the Island of Ikaria."

"Another fishing village?" one son asked.

"Yes, another trading place," Yehor answered. "But up the hill from the village is a Temple of Artemis."

Surprising Yehor and the boys, Jace spoke up, "The Goddess Artemis is the deity of the hunt. The caretaker of wild animals, wilderness, and childbirth. She is a twin of Apollo and the Goddess of the Bow."

"That's right," Yehor offered, not quite over the shock of Jace giving a long explanation. "You, boys, can visit the temple while we're there."

## Chapter 21 - Dark and Full of Vengeance

As a rocky shoreline came into focus, Yehor announced, "Homer likened the currents and winds around the island to the unpredictability of a crowd. One stirred by desire rather than rational argument. The Poet wrote the gathering of ordinary people was agitated, like the long sea-waves of Ikaria Island. The East Wind or the South Wind had risen, rushing upon them from the clouds of Zeus."

"What does that mean father?" one of the boys asked.

"Simply put, the wind and currents have wrecked many ships on the rocks of Ikaria," Yehor answered. "Both those you can see along the coast and the rocks just under the water. Roll the sail, we'll have more control with the oars."

The ship fought the oars, attempting to ride unseen currents, while winds pushed the hull as if they rowed through a storm. Yet, despite the turmoil, the *Island Princess* moved under a cloudless sky.

"Father, I don't see a beach," the other boy called back. The counter forces on the blade of his oar frayed his nerves and sapped his strength. "Where, if anywhere, can we land?"

"Stay the course," Yehor stated. While his voice was even, he shoved the rear oar back and forth with force, compensating for the undersized oarsmen. And he coached. "One stroke at a time. We'll rest when we reach Nas."

Jace listened silently, admiring the patience and steady strength of Yehor when dealing with his sons. For the Archer, the rowing required attention but didn't prove overly strenuous.

***

As they rowed closer, the rocky face of the island rose from the sea. Above the stone, the land climbed to grassy slopes and higher still, short pines gave bursts of dark green on the hills. And beyond, the mountains displayed a forest veneer. But nowhere along the coast did they see a flat spot or a welcoming stretch of sand.

The afternoon wore on and the boys struggled. Captain Yehor compensated and Jace stroked in a battle with the currents that seemed determined to smash the coastal trader into the rocks. Finally, with the sun three finger's width over the horizon, an outcrop of land forced the *Island Princess* farther out to sea. At the maneuver, the boys moaned in annoyance.

"And as it's been for centuries," Yehor exclaimed, using the rear oar to change direction and head towards the island, "sailors seeking a rest from battling the currents and winds around the Island of Ikaria, are welcomed into the safe harbor of Nas."

The fingers of land jutting out to sea cut the wind and calmed the waters. In the easiest strokes since they rolled the sail, Jace and the boys rowed the *Island Princess* to a broad sandy beach.

"I don't see a temple," one of the boys remarked.

"It's up on the rocks," Yehor told him. "You can usually see part of it from down here."

"When can we go see it?" his other son asked.

"In the morning, after we finish trading with the village."

***

Yehor, Jace, and the boys worked on caulking the sideboards of the *Island Princess*. They melted pine tar, added hemp fiber and cotton fiber. After scooping up a portion of the mixture on the head of a chisel, they pounded the caulking between the hull boards with a hammer.

"Where are the villagers?" one son inquired. He faced inland. A deep creek filled a shallow valley that divided two types of landscape. On the right, rocky heights hid the Temple of Artemis. Across the creek, trees covered the hill, allowing only the roofs of huts and the tops of stone houses to be seen. "Why aren't they coming down to trade?"

"Despite its isolation, Nas is a busy harbor," Yehor answered. "There are no shortages of traders stopping here. In the morning, enough will come that it'll pay for our visit. I hope."

They worked around the hull of the trader. Once they finished, Jace took the remaining caulking and tapped it into the boards of the small boat.

"You fuss over that rowboat, a lot," one boy noted.

"It's my fishing boat," Jace responded between taps with the mallet. Then, in defense of the vessel, he said. "It has a mast."

While the Yehor family settled down around a campfire, Jace sat on the side of the fishing boat. They cooked stew while the Archer gnawed on dried meat. The one difference from previous nights, Jace had his back to the sea. He faced the direction of the Shrine of Artemis. The trader and his boys didn't understand the significance of the Archer's position. Then again, they weren't close enough to hear him praying to Artemis for a successful hunt.

***

Dawn found locals on the beach, looking to trade and buy. With so few customers, Yehor sent the boys off to explore the temple.

"If you don't need me," Jace requested. "I'd like to see the shrine."

"I believe I can manage the multitudes," Yehor joked. "Go. Maybe the Goddess will loosen you up."

"Not likely," Jace stated.

He followed the boys, taking the dirt path that climbed the face of the rocky slope. Partway up the trail, Jace glanced

213

back and examined the beach, next he scanned the sea. A few ships appeared on the horizon, but none seemed to be heading for Nas Harbor. He should have looked again from the top. But he didn't think to reexamine the sea, he let his emotions overcome his training.

At the top of the hill, Jace's stomach sank and the muscles in his jaw flexed in anger. Rather than a shrine to the Goddess Artemis, he found ruins.

***

What remained of the shrine was a field of cut stones. They told the story of an awful event. Scorch marks on the blocks showed where the upper walls had been burned. That detail, in itself, was horrible enough. But the arsonist had waited around for the fire to cool before toppling the stone walls. What the defiler did as the fire raged was best left in the darkest part of the imagination.

The final insult to the Goddess and the reason the shrine had not been rebuilt rested in the pieces of what had once been a fine granite altar.

"Tell me who hammered your altar to pieces? Who violated your sanctuary?" Jace prayed. "Goddess Artemis, who did this to your shrine?"

***

Young voices carried to him. Jace located the boys hopping from stone to stone, playing a game. Seeing as the fire had burned away any real connection to the Goddess, their actions held no disrespect. Even so, Jace felt a bond to the Goddess of the Bow and a sadness at the loss of her shrine.

One of the boys picked up the blade of a broken oar.

"What does *Asebeia* mean?" he asked after reading an inscription carved into the blade of the oar.

The sign was as clear to Jace as if the Goddess spoke directly to the Archer. It wasn't *Asebeia*, meaning blasphemy and sacrilege. Or the other sign that was sure to be in the ruins, proclaiming *Paranomia*, meaning lawlessness and self-delusion. The written messages weren't the evidence as much as the presence of the wooden signs were an answer to the prayer.

Diceärch left signs to claim his victory over the shrine, and most likely, the murder of the Priest of Artemis. What the pirate, now a Commander, didn't know was this set of signs, would lead to his downfall.

Overcome with emotion, Jace spun, putting his back to the shrine. He gazed out to sea to clear his head. But once he looked down at the beach, he dropped flat onto his belly.

\*\*\*

"Boys, get down," he directed while crawling backwards to the edge of the rubble.

"Is this a new game?" one of the Yehor boys asked.

"I need you both to do exactly what I say," Jace emphasized. "Creep to the top of the hill. But stay down and out of sight."

"What next?" the other boy inquired.

"When you see me moving towards the *Princess*. I need you both to stand up and call for your father. Yell as loud as you can and don't stop."

"This is a stupid game," the other offered.

215

"Pirates have a knife at your father's throat," Jace told them after grabbing their shoulders to hold them down. "I'm going to help him."

"Are you going to fight the pirates?"

"With your help," Jace answered. "But I need you to distract them while I sneak up on the men."

"You are a Spartan," the boys said.

Jace didn't correct them. He ran for the side of the hill and began working his way down to the creek.

***

Among the reeds on the bank of the creek, Jace noticed flocks of birds. Many sneak attacks and reconnaissance patrols have been spoiled by flights of frightened birds. While slipping through the water plants, Jace forced air into his lungs. Peering through the reeds, he studied the beach.

Yehor stood between the *Island Princess* and six men with knives. A second ship rested on the beach behind the six men. Its cargo deck was empty. The pirates were obviously planning to take the cargo from the coastal trader. On the far side of the *Princess,* Jace's fishing boat sat out of the way. Five feet from the vessel with his weapons, the creek became a shallow wash through the sand.

Jace gave credit to Yehor. His postured was defiant, even if his armament consisted of a wooden oar. With a final deep breath, Jace slowly dipped below the surface of the water. Easing through the reeds so as not to disturb the birds, the Archer snaked between clumps of underwater roots. Once in midchannel, the obstructions cleared, and the Archer allowed the flow to carry him to the channel at the beach.

There were fat fish, tall fish, and flat fish. The latter was on Jace's mind as he slithered, eel-like, out of the deep water. Hugging the bottom of the channel, he worked his way to the beach area.

Emotionally, he wanted to poke his head above the edge of the channel to see how far he'd come from the creek. But it was a premature, useless, and possibly dangerous urge. Jace had been trained better.

***

*Years before, in a swamp, Jace crawled through slime. With his arms extended, his fingers acted as tiny feet moving his body along the surface. Plowing green algae and leaves, the student archer crept forward, no more obvious than an old log. But his mind lost track of how long he'd been in the putrid water and his brain teased him to just peak.*

*"Take a look," echoed in his thoughts. "Just a little look to see where you are."*

*And so, the boy Jace Kasia lifted his head. As soon as his forehead broke the green algae, startled birds flew into the sky. Frogs, frightened by the birds, leaped into the water. Agitated by the intrusion, a horde of mating dice snakes panicked. They emitted a foul-smelling secretion which coated Jace's body. Then, as if the fates wanted to punish him for his rash behavior, two of the dice water snakes bit him.*

*"At least they aren't poisonous," Zarek Mikolas observed from dry ground. "Seeing as you already stink, how about you go back to the start and try the infiltration drill again."*

***

With the swamp drill fresh in his mind and nothing to fear but a knife in the back, Jace slithered along the bottom of the channel with his eyes closed. Legionaries learn to count steps to estimate miles, and Archers counted paces to judge how far they'd traveled. But neither had a semi-accurate method for how far they traveled when crawling in water that barely covered their backs.

The water around Jace began to flow faster, hinting that he'd ventured far enough. Downhill meant he had reached the crest of the beach. Only then did he lift his head to see his fishing boat and the *Island Princess.*

In a crouch, the Archer came out of the channel and ran to the fishing boat. He lifted a cover, pulled three ties, and freed his war gear.

Out came the African Corps infantry shield, the Macedonian helmet, the Egyptian short sword with the carved ivory hilt, and the wicked six-foot Spartan spear.

Once dressed in his war gear, Jace took a knee and prayed, "Goddess Artemis, forgive this Cretan Archer for what he is about to say and do in the shadow of your shrine."

Next, Jace peered up at the hill and waved to the boys. At first, they hesitated. Only one stood and shouted, "Father. Father."

A single voice was weak and almost swept away by the wind. The diversion held little chance of success, while Yehor stood a chance of dying. But when the second boy jumped up, waved his arms, and added his voice, the call reached the beach.

\*\*\*

"Father. Father," the boys screamed from the top of the hill.

"Are those your brats," a pirate asked. "Maybe we'll kill you, take your boat, and the boys. They'll fetch a good price in the market."

"No. No. Take the cargo but leave me my boat and my boys," Yehor pleaded.

"You should have thought of that before you picked up the oar and challenged us," another sneered.

"Father. Father."

Yehor turned to the hill with tears in his eyes. Everything he loved stood waving their arms and yelling the same word over and over. Adding to the heartbreak, his livelihood and possibly his life were going to be taken on this beach.

"What do you think?" the fifth pirate asked his companions. "We keep the boys and raise them to join our crew. I'd like a personal slave."

The five men turned their backs to the sea and peered at the boys high on the hill.

"Father. Father."

In a rage, built from holding himself in character, Jace Kasia came for the pirates. Only it wasn't a Cretan Archer charging up the beach. It was something evil, dark, and full of vengeance.

blank page

# Act 8

## Chapter 22 - An Unholy God

Balanced steps on sand created the sound of a broom lightly sweeping a stone floor. With no more noise than a breeze disturbing grains of sand, Jace Kasia crossed the beach.

"...I'd like a personal slave."

The sixth pirate folded over to his left. Jace pulled the Spartan spear from the man's side and knocked him over with a hip swing. Using the momentum from the hip contact, the angry Archer jerked the spear over his head. The sharp tip spiraled upward while the butt end smacked the fifth pirate in the head. Dropping to the sand, the pirate sat confused, and blinded by the lightning that flashed before his eyes.

While the spear tip and shaft spun to his right, Jace plowed the fourth pirate into the third with the African Corps shield. Although caught by surprise, being knocked down wouldn't keep them out of the fight. Jace accomplished that with kicks combined with churning knees that beat, dazed, and then disoriented the men. Acting as a vengeful spirit, the Archer walked through them, heading for the last two.

\*\*\*

Realizing there was a disturbance behind them, the final two pirates pivoted to the attacker. They came face to face with a Spartan spear. Held just above a shield, the steel tip, as if a viper coiled to strike, floated. Targeting one pirate than gliding to threaten the other, before moving back to the first, the weapon seemed to be deciding which man to strike and kill.

A Macedonian helmet hid the features of the warrior controlling the spear and the shield.

"Hold on there, friend," one of the pirates said in a sickeningly sweet tone. "We should talk this over. We're both men of strength. You know, we take what we want."

"You have interrupted my voyage," Jace growled.

The helmet gave a metallic sound to his voice.

"Look, we didn't know this was your ship," the second pirate assured him. "If we had…"

"If the fifth man stands," Jace warned, "I'll decide."

The fifth pirate, partially recovered, held his knife in one hand and slowly placed the other on the ground. Prepared to spring up and fight, he hesitated at the declaration.

"Decide what?" the first questioned.

"Who will be sacrificed for the interruption of the voyage?" Jace answered. Tense moments later, he continued. "The God protector is a harsh master. Human sacrifice is demanded for any infraction of his laws."

"Wait, a human sacrifice?" the second pirate repeated. "Who does human sacrifices anymore?"

The fifth man's head cleared, he leaned forward, and braced.

"If he moves again, I'll offer you to the God. And maybe a second man just to demonstrate my adherence to the laws," Jace mentioned as if discussing the price of grain.

"There are six of us and one of you," the second pirate pointed out.

Jace crossed his ankles and lowered his torso. Twirling, he extended the shaft, and allowed the tip of the spear to slice open the first pirate's leg. In a heartbeat, the move was completed. Jace Kasia returned to his original position, with the spear hovering over the shield.

Screaming in pain, the pirate fell to the ground. Pulling a cloth, he applied it to the wound.

"What was that?" the pirate demanded between moans.

"Now you are four able to fight," Jace commented. "Are you willing to die for your cause?"

"We have no cause," the second pirate informed him.

"A man without a cause is weak," Jace exclaimed. "I am strong from the God's laws. Who is chosen to die?"

"Look. We don't want to fight," the second pirate begged. "Let us collect our wounded and leave. Accept our apologies."

From the ground, the first asked, "Who are you?"

Jace hesitated. For all the tricks, lies, and deceptions a Cretan Archer might use during a mission, he always honored the Goddess of the Bow. To pledge anything else, especially near a shrine of Artemis, was an insult to the Goddess.

"A Soldier of Moloch," Jace boasted, wincing a little inside at the assertion. "A keeper of his laws and his shrine."

"What shrine?" the second pirate asked. "Moloch is a Babylonian God. He has no shrine on any of the islands."

"I will build an altar on the northern tip of Chios," Jace proposed. "The light of Moloch will burn each night for those who seek his protection."

At the mention of a new shrine, the pirates glanced around to see if their companions understood the benefit. No doubt, Commander Diceärch would pay a fat purse for the information.

While the pirates thought of coins, Jace craved a more personal payoff. He hoped the rogue Commander would salivate over the opportunity to destroy a new shrine and to torture a priest, a holy man arrogant enough to build a temple on the coast of Chios.

"You may leave the beach," Jace granted. Yet, in a smooth and powerful throw, he launched the spear at the fifth man. The spearhead punched through the man's midsection, throwing the pirate back, and pinning the body to the ground. Jace announced. "Since you failed, a Soldier of Moloch decided."

The second pirate took a step forward but stopped. He stared down a length of Egyptian steel extended over the shield.

"And leave my spear," Jace insisted.

***

Fearing the Soldier of Moloch would pick another man to sacrifice, the three healthy pirates loaded their wounded companions and the body of the dead one. Rushing, they pushed the boat off the beach. In moments, the ship vanished around the northern point of the harbor.

Jace and Yehor stood watching long after the pirate ship was out of sight. While the Cretan Archer was sure Dicëarch would get the message, the trader Captain felt conflicted.

"Call your boys down," Jace instructed. "I want to speak with them."

"You murdered that man?" Yehor accused. "Without giving him a chance to defend himself. I don't know if I want you around my sons."

"You don't have a choice," Jace informed him. "Not that you're in danger from me. But you need my arms to row through the Ikaria currents. And I need you to get me to Chios. Face facts, we're stuck with each other. Now call down the boys."

***

Jace sat on the edge of the fishing boat. His helmet rested on his thigh, held in place by an arm. The sword remained at his hip, while the spear and shield were propped against the hull. Timid and afraid, yet excited after witnessing the fight, the boys shuffled their feet as they approached.

"You are lucky," Jace told them. "I'm an orphan and grew up with a hard master as a teacher. He taught me about war and weapons. You have a kind and caring father. A man who knows business and poets. Cherish him, for all your days. Do you understand?"

Both boys nodded their understanding.

"Good," Jace announced. "Go and prepare the *Island Princess*."

Once the boys were on the coastal trader, Yehor admitted, "that's not what I expected from you."

"You thought I might recruit them for the unholy God?" Jace inquired. "No Captain. I attempted to calm them. After witnessing violence, some boys want to learn to fight. You don't want that in a son. Other boys have nightmares. Now that they have a portion of my story to explain my abilities, they can talk to each other about what they saw."

"You do know those pirates will come for you," Yehor cautioned. "Or they'll tell that blasphemous, animal Diceärch where you plan to build the shrine."

"They will," Jace agreed.

The Archer turned and began stowing his war gear. The abrupt end of the conversation left Yehor standing on the beach. For a moment, his mouth hung open in surprise at the reply. After a few moments, the trader turned around, and went to check on his boys.

*** 

They caught a strong wind. Taking advantage, Yehor steered them away from the island, the underwater rocks, and allowed the sail to carry the ship north. As they rode the wind, the boys talked in whispers and occasionally glanced at Jace.

By midafternoon, the trader waved Jace to the steering platform.

"Where do you want me to take you?" Yehor asked.

He pointed ahead to a sliver of land in the distance.

"You need to be rid of me as soon as possible," Jace informed him. "Anywhere on Chios will do. I'll sail from there."

"In the fishing boat?"

"It's not a coastal trader," Jace noted. "But it's small and slow enough so I'm not likely to sail by a good beach."

"You are an odd man," Yehor offered. "I can't figure out if you're a kind and caring protector, or a raving madman."

Jace watched as more of Chios emerged on the horizon.

"Perhaps, Captain Yehor," Jace told him, "I'm a little of both."

*** 

The boys stood beside their father as the *Island Princess* sailed away from the beach at Chios. While Yehor faced forward, guiding the ship along the east coast, his sons faced aft, watching Jace rig the mast on the fishing boat.

The trader would sail along one coast of the island. To avoid pirates seeing Yehor and the boys with the Soldier of Moloch, Jace headed up the west coast.

Near dark, a layer of clouds moved in, forcing Jace to locate a beach. He sailed to shore and hauled the boat out of the water. Before sunset, the clouds grew darker and fat drops of rain began to fall. For shelter, he partially overturned the boat. Once he crawled under the hull, the Archer questioned his chosen profession.

He wasn't afraid of hunting a murderous pirate. That was the easy part. Being lonely, that was hard.

As water dripped from the hull, he pondered returning to Crete and being a farmer with Neysa Kasia. His stepmother would like it. Or he could sail to Rome. He was sure a letter to Cornelius Scipio in Iberia would get him a position as a Centurion in a Legion. At least, he'd have a roof over his head, hot food, and steady work. After drawing up

227

his legs, Jace Kasia wrapping his arms around his knees, and listened to the rain pound on the hull.

***

Two days later, Jace guided the boat to a beach of gray gravel. After pulling the boat out of the water, he went to a fisherman sitting on a rock. As he approached, he noted the man was sewing a fishing net.

Squatting to put him at eye level with the man, Jace asked, "Is this Paralia Keramos?"

"Depends on who is asking," the fisherman replied.

Jace needed to know his location but didn't want to leave stories of a lost man in a fishing boat stumbling around the coast of Chios. It wasn't a good look for a Soldier of Moloch and his plan.

"Who would I need to be to get a straight answer?" Jace questioned.

"A trader, which you aren't," the man replied. As he pulled a needle through the hemp netting, he scanned the fishing boat. Then he studied Jace's hands and said. "You aren't a fisherman, or a stone mason. Or a member of Chios militia. Which you aren't because they don't have any Latians in this region."

There were people who could be fooled by lying and by putting up a pleasing front. Then there were keen eyed tradesmen, who knew a fisherman had scars on his hands from throwing and pulling fishing nets, and that masons exhibited deep calluses from working granite. The man had easily cut Jace off from any effortless lies.

*"When in doubt," Zarek Mikolas said during training sessions, "rather than telling the truth, go for the most outrageous*

228

*lie you can think of. The one that changes the subject of questioning you to a statement of disbelief or a value judgement by them."*

"You aren't wrong," Jace admitted using the fisherman's manner of speech. "I'm a priest."

"Holy men have soft bellies and smooth skin," the man stated. He added the chuckle of a man who uncovered a lie. Next, he described. "Priests don't have scars on their arms from blade practice like you do. Or enough strength to drag a four-man fishing boat out of the surf, by himself. You aren't a priest. But I'll tell you where you are because I haven't had a laugh in days. This is Paralia Keramos. Now, be on your way."

Jace stood, faced left down the beach, and pointed to a hill.

"The high ground is about eleven hundred paces from here," he guessed.

"If you're a bird or a mountain goat," the man cautioned without looking up from his work. "From here, it's a long meandering trail."

"Is there a beach near there?" Jace inquired.

"A small cove on the other side. You can land a fishing boat there if the navigator is careful," the man told Jace. "But only a fool would take a transport or a warship in too close."

The Archer studied the distant hill. In his mind, he planned and schemed.

"You aren't a priest," the man concluded. "What's your profession?"

"I'm the priest who will build a shrine up there," Jace answered.

"Are you unaware?" the fisherman asked. "Look out there, to the north. Not two days sailing from here is the Island of Lemnos. And on Lemnos is the harbor of Myrina and docked at Myrina are pirate warships. And those pirate warships are commanded by a pirate named Diceärch. And Diceärch murders priests."

"Is that a fact?" Jace commented.

"You must be a martyr. Priests typically have enough sense to avoid situations that lead to certain death."

"A typical priest wouldn't have knife scars on his arms," Jace pointed out. "Or a hard belly, and enough strength to build a shrine on the high ground."

"You might as well light a fire every night to guide Diceärch to you," the fisherman offered in exasperation.

"The unholy God Moloch would approve," Jace proposed. "I will build the fires."

"You aren't a priest or a martyr," the fisherman concluded. "You are a madman touched by the Goddess Manea. In short, you're insane."

## Chapter 23 – From the Crest

Better than a signal tower, a flat spot on the slope offered an unobstructed view of the Aegean. Jace dropped an armload of wood and faced north. After a slight adjustment to the northeast, he strained to see land. He couldn't of course, but the charts he reviewed at Karavostasis Harbor assured him there was a big island out there.

"The fisherman was right," he said to the wind, "Lemnos Island is two days from here. But the Island of Lesvos should be a day. And beyond Lesvos, if I make it that far, is the home port of the Pergamon Navy."

The perfect plan did not exist. And the bolder the strategy, the more chances there were for a breakdown at each step. Especially when dealing with a sadistic heretic like Diceärch, failure meant a painful death. Yet, to separate the Commander from his protection of warships and pirates, Jace needed to isolate Diceärch. And that required a multipart plan.

With those unhappy thoughts in mind, Jace Kasia turned from the sea, crossed the flat area, and started uphill. He'd located a rockslide in the forest higher up from the level ground. And his plan required loads and loads of rocks and wood to build a proper façade.

*\*\**

By the second day, Jace had become a beast of burden. There were loose rocks closer and more plentiful. But pulling them on a sled downslope was preferable to hauling them up from the beach. Jace dropped the leather reins and wiped the sweat from his forehead.

During the rest-period, the Archer counted stones, estimating the number of trips needed to build a curved front wall.

"Four loads," he thought, before dumping the sled. Afterward, he harnessed himself in and headed up the grade for another load of rocks.

*\*\**

At dusk, four days after he first climbed to the crest, Jace stood on the east side of the site. He peered down into the ravine and out to the water of the rocky bay. Satisfied that he couldn't see his fishing boat or where he stashed the sled, the archer marched to the opposite side of the flat area. On the west side, he peered over the winding trail, and beyond the lower hill at the village of Paralia Keramos. The fishing fleet was returning from a day of casting and hauling nets. Although Jace searched, he couldn't locate the man he spoke with from among the other fishermen.

"When they come, don't be brave," Jace offered to the fishermen. They couldn't hear, or even know about, his advice. But he gave it anyway. "Simply point them to this hill."

After surveying the number of rocks, the piles of dirt, and the stacks of firewood, Jace strolled to a hole in the soil and lit a small cookfire. The trap was almost ready. It required a little more construction before he invited guests over to consecrate the Shrine of Moloch with their blood.

For the evening meal, he kept the fire low and the smoke to a minimum. Once his camp stew boiled, Jace lifted the iron pot off the tripod, leaned against the rocks, and ate dinner. It would be the last full night of sleep until this part of the mission ended. Or he died. In either case, rest would come later.

\*\*\*

Broader than the foredeck of a two banker, the fake shrine glowed in the midday sun. Resembling a parapet, or a fighting position, the curved wall presented a wide stone face to ships at sea and those approaching the beach at the village. What the sailors missed were the abrupt ends of the wall. The illusion further deteriorated when one saw the dirt packed behind the single course of stones. The dirt supported the row of rocks and created a platform, perfect for holding an inspirational fire.

Jace piled wood on the dirt platform to make the fire appear bigger. The structure and the height of the hill allowed the flames to be visible far out to sea.

With the steel and flint held above the tender, Jace paused. Once he struck the spark and declared the presence of the God Moloch, the fates controlled the plan. After a final glance at the empty sea, Jace snapped the flint against the steel. A spark hit the dry tender and a flame sprang to life. Conversely, as the fire grew, the days dwindled for the pirate known as Dicëarch. Or if the plan went wrong, the final days of Cretan Archer Jace Kasia.

*** 

They rowed in during the darkest period of the night. Two triremes, Jace judged. Their black shapes carved ripples on the moonlit sea. When they backed to the beach, shadowy crewmen scurried over the sides, dropped to the water, and were lost in the night. Moments later, the hulls glided from the water and came to rest on the shoreline.

From the fork in a tree, Jace watched the pirates move in the direction of the village. The Archer could do nothing about it, except offer a prayer of protection to the fishermen and their families.

His perch grew on the slope of the first hill. It gave him a view of the beach and the start of the trail that led to the

Shrine of Moloch. It was his second sleepless night and possible his last of standing vigil in the tree.

On the hill behind Jace, the fire of Moloch burned. The light beckoning anyone in need of protection who was willing to pay the terrible price. Or someone like Diceärch, who attempted to wash away bitter memories with the blood of priests.

Jace climbed down, untied a case, and extracted his war bow.

"The visitor better be Diceärch," the Archer complained as he flexed the limbs, warming the wood in preparation for stringing the bow. "I'd hate to have wasted all this work for nothing."

He bent the bow behind his leg and slipped the bowstring over one end. Down at the beach, pirates were making different types of arrangements.

\*\*\*

On one of the beached triremes, Commander Diceärch paced the steering deck.

"From here, the shrine looks inviting," he remarked. "But I'm leery of a trap."

Footsteps on the ramp alerted Diceärch to the arrival of a sleepy fisherman. Sergeant Sarpedon accompanied the man. The pair boarded the ship and crossed to the pirate leader.

"What have we here?" Diceärch asked his top NCO.

"Before the shrine was built, this fisherman spoke to the priests," Sarpedon advised.

"You actually talked with the priests?" Diceärch questioned. He took the fisherman's arm and pulled him close. After prying the man's fingers apart, the Commander pressed coins into the scarred hand. Next, he pressed the fingers closed around the metal. "How many clerics and men-at-arms where there? Can you describe them?"

The man rolled the coins between his fingers.

"Well sir, there was only one cleric and no spearmen," the fisherman described. "You know priests, soft bellies, smooth skin, and weak backs."

The Commander scrunched up his eyes and peered into the shadowy face. The fisherman stared back in his best tradesman's gaze. Heartbeats later, Diceärch looked away.

"If the priest is so soft," he inquired. "How did he build a shrine?"

"How does a shark defeat a fisherman's net? He keeps working at it until he gnaws a hole in the weave. Then he rests before chewing some more. Just like the priest built the shrine. A little at a time."

"Have you been up to the shrine?"

"A Shrine of Moloch?" the fisherman gasped. "Sometimes my grandchildren don't obey me. But I would never give them over to the unholy God. No, sir. I have not, and I have no desire to go to that altar."

Diceärch stepped away from the fisherman.

"Sergeant Sarpedon, get my coins back from him and raid the village," the Commander ordered. "I want all the mastic and grain they have stashed under their floorboards."

"Here, take the coins," the fisherman offered. "I would do better if I learned to read men."

"It's a gift, you don't have," Diceärch assured the fisherman. Then to his Corporal he instructed. "Split your

235

guard detail. I want half around the ships and the rest behind the village."

The Corporal saluted and headed for the other ship-of-war.

"And Ambrus. You have control of our stay," Dicearch confided in him. "Sound the alarm and we'll leave. If we can't go, set a shield wall until I return."

"Yes, Commander," Ambrus acknowledged. "Where will you be, sir?"

"Up there confessing my transgressions to the Priest of Moloch."

The Corporal allowed his eyes to land on the fire for a moment. Then he marched down the ramp. The sight of the fire on the crest was soon forgotten by the Corporal but not by his Commander.

***

Dicearch clapped his hands together and a pair of big sailors responded.

"Are you ready, Commander?" one of the crewmen inquired.

"As soon as the assault on the village begins," Dicearch answered. "Rule number one. When facing a superior force, intimidate with violence. It gives pause to your enemies and makes them question their commitment to the fight."

"Superior force?" the second sailor asked.

"There are more villagers than I have men," Dicearch told him. "I won't leave the ship until Sergeant Sarpedon has control of the hamlet."

"After that sir, the shrine?" the first proposed.

"Yes. Once it's safe for us, we'll go and fulfill my destiny."

"You say that before every shrine," said one of the sailors. "And sir, it gives me a thrill each time."

*\*\*\**

Diceärch and his two companions marched down to the beach and headed east towards the trail, the bonfire, and the shrine. Streaks of light touched the sky, but daybreak was a long way off. Moonlight remained the dominant illumination.

When the pirate Commander reached the start of the path, ten armored pirates greeted him.

"Crewman Calais, I require privacy while I worship," Diceärch protested.

"Yes, sir, we'll wait at the toe of the hill while you climb to the crest," Calais explained. "Corporal Ambrus said if you protested to remind you of rule number five."

"Plan your escape route before engaging with an enemy," Diceärch remarked. "I take it you are my escape route."

"I don't know about escape, sir," Crewman Calais mentioned. "But if you yell for help, we'll be there."

"Fair enough. Walk with us to the base of the hill."

*\*\*\**

Thirteen pirates strolled the winding trail, sometimes walking in darkness, and other times in moonlight. Just flickering shadows, it was difficult to separate man from bush or natural object from target.

Outnumbered, Archer Kasia scrambled up a rougher, steeper, and quicker route to the crest of the hill. Jace hadn't expected a crowd. Murdering priests and desecrating shrines required a callousness most men lacked. Even heartless killers and otherwise depraved individuals, deep in their souls, feared the Gods.

When he topped the hill, Jace peered at the sky. Fast running out of night, he couldn't delay, the plan required more specific light. Racing to the fake shrine, Jace placed logs on the fire before doubling back to watch the trail.

Having Diceärch and his crew backlit by a roaring fire would give Jace an advantage.

***

From the crest of the hill, Diceärch waved for his sailors to cover his flanks.

"The holy man is mine," the Commander reminded his two collaborators in evil.

To let him know they understood, each Sailor slapped the head of a club into the palm of his hand. The three stalked forward towards the shrine, a tent, and what they thought was a sleeping priest of Moloch. While dancing shadows stretched out behind them, their bodies, from the rear, were solid black silhouettes.

***

One of the tests to become a Cretan Archer required hundreds of arrows placed in targets with no misses. Putting arrows in two targets wasn't a concern. Jace's challenge came from the center target. He needed Diceärch alive. Preferably unhurt, or if injured at least mobile. Crippled added complications. The worst case was having to hunt the pirate commander in the dark, and possibly losing him to the reinforcements.

Wounding two silhouettes, who walked fifteen feet apart, did not present a problem for Jace. But there were choices for the first arrow. A head shot would make noise when the arrow impacted the skull. And more disturbance when the body fell. Piercing the throat left the victim stumbling around, which would draw attention to the attack.

Jace drew the bow until the feathers of the fletching tickled his ear. After targeting the man on the far right, the archer swung the shaft to the left and selected the other sailor.

*Zip-Thwack!*

The arrowhead smashed through the floating rib near the man's spine. Penetrating flesh, the steel tip entered the large organ just below the diaphragm. A strike, kick, punch, or an arrow to the liver vibrated throughout the body. Sharp pains radiated outward. Spasming, the lungs couldn't expand, the diaphragm locked in place, and the throat had no ability to send a cry of distress to the sailor's mouth.

Believing the man had tripped in the dark, Diceärch looked with disgust at the sailor on his hands and knees.

"Get up," he scolded.

*Zip-Thwack!*

The second arrow appeared in the chest of the man on the far right. Higher than the first release, Jace's arrowhead split ribs. Entering the sailor's right side, the shaft caused the man to inhale quickly and drop to a knee. It took several heartbeats for the pain to normalize. Although he couldn't stand with an arrow through a lung, the sailor managed to croak out a single word.

Diceärch spun from the man on his hands and knees to his other henchman. On his right, that man was on one knee, his voice rasping low.

"Ambush," the sailor muttered.

"Calais," Diceärch called for his backup, "I..."

The knee hit him between his shoulders driving the pirate commander to the ground. Stunned for a moment, he tasted dirt, collected his wits, and pushed up. Preparing to fight, his hand reached for the knife at his waist.

"It's not there," a metallic voice informed him.

The wood was smooth, finely sanded, and coated with a hard substance. When the war bow slipped over Diceärch's head and pressed against his throat, the pirate Commander attempted to shift away. But the bowstring trapped his head between the string and the wood of the riser. Hands jerked his arms backwards and tied his wrists together.

"You're a fool," Diceärch accused his assailant. "You didn't have sense enough to silence me. My men will be here before you can run away."

No sound came from the attacker as the bow was removed. A leather noose replaced it. Hands jerked him to his feet and the metallic voice instructed, "March."

Diceärch attempted to move his hands but found the leather line ran from his neck to his arms. When he lifted his arms, the strap tightened around his throat.

"You don't understand who I am, do you?" the pirate Commander questioned.

Higher on the hill, as Diceärch and his attacker approached the tree line, Diceärch's two sailors found their voices.

"Calais. Calais, come quick. Ambush. Ambush."

On the slope below, Crewman Calais and his nine oarsmen sprinted up the hill. At the crest, the wounded sailors pointed to the forest.

"Never mind us," they exclaimed to the reinforcements. "He took the Commander into the hills. Go after them. Hurry."

***

Sunlight from over the horizon painted the tops of the tallest trees in amber. But the light of the coming day had yet to penetrate the deep forest.

"That's far enough," Jace said. His voice through the opening in the helmet gave him a metallic tone. "Do me a favor. Yell for your men."

"Calais. I'm up here."

Jace shoved a piece of linen into the pirate's mouth.

"That's enough," Jace told him while wrapping another piece of cloth around Diceärch's head.

Below them, Calais and his men searched the woods.

"Commander Diceärch, call out," they shouted. "Sing out."

After checking the gag to be sure it was secure, Jace shoved a cloth sack over the pirate's head.

"This way Commander," he said while pulling Diceärch to the east, towards the edge of the hill.

"Commander Diceärch, sing out," the hunters called, their voices getting closer.

At the crest of the hill, overlooking the dark ravine, Jace stopped his prisoner.

"Don't move or you'll fall off the cliff," he warned.

With Diceärch unsure of his location and afraid to move, Jace unstrung his bow and stowed it in the case. Then he took off the Macedonian helmet and hid it under a bush. Finally, he moved a pile of dead branches, exposing the rock sled.

"Step forward and drop to your knees," he instructed. Once Diceärch was flat on the sled, Jace shoved it from the crest, pushed it downhill for a couple of steps, then jumped on.

Behind them, voices higher on the hill, bellowed, "Commander. We're close. Call out and we'll come to you."

Rays of sunlight split the hill. At higher elevations, the trees glowed in the morning light, while below the rays, the lower half of the hill turned grey. With better visibility, the searchers moved faster and covered more ground. Surely, they would overtake Diceärch and his attacker in the next clearing, or the one after that.

## Chapter 24 – Rule Number Five

Streaks of grey and green flashed by, branches slapped Jace, and tree trunks less than an arm's length away threatened to crash the sled. Down into the ravine they plunged, the runners gliding on a blanket of leaves. Held only in shallow tracks by the weight of two men, the rock-sled bounced, twisted, and turned. At the bottom of the steep slope, they jerked and headed in a new direction. Now racing alongside a shallow stream bed, the sled slowed as mud gripped the runners. When the runners sank into the wet soil, the sled jolted to a halt.

Jace pulled a confused pirate Commander off the sled and pushed him forward. While Diceärch stumbled blindly ahead, the Archer kicked leaves over the sled to hide it from view.

*** 

A little closer to the rocky bay, Jace stopped the pirate. Stepping away from his prisoner, he yanked leafy branches off the yellow fishing boat.

"Step high," he instructed. Despite lifting his foot, Diceärch tripped and fell into the small boat. Jace told him. "Stay down."

Squatting beside the boat, Jace watched the shadows in the ravine. Above him, the shrine was too far back from the crest to be seen. With his heart pounding, the Archer attempted to control his breathing. Instinct encouraged him to row away from Chios as quickly as possible. Only years of training allowed him to ignore his own nature and stay with the plan. After a long wait, the ravine brightened, informing Jace that full daylight lay over the island.

Bending his legs, Archer Kasia put his shoulder to the fishing boat and pushed it onto the rocky shore. After more powerful shoves, the boat floated free. Hopping in, Jace tossed an old fishing net over Diceärch, settled a pair of oars in the oarlocks, and began rowing for open water.

***

Crewman Calais vibrated with anger. They had a fix on the Commander's location, yet when they searched the forest, he had gone. Where? The section leader had no idea. He and his nine oarsmen walked to the fake shrine.

On the mound beside the hot embers, Calais watched as a yellow fishing boat lifted a sail and caught the wind. Then twenty more came into view, and the yellow boat became just one of many boats in the fishing fleet out of Paralia Keramos.

"This will not sit well with Ambrus," Calais complained. He indicated the wounded sailors. "Help them. We're going to the beach. The Corporal and Sergeant Sarpedon are not going to be happy."

"What about the *Asebeia* and *Paranomia* signs," a rower inquired.

"Feed them to the fire," Calais suggested. "For all we know, the Commander was taken by the God Moloch. We don't need to be the target of revenge by the unholy God."

Calais watched the fire flair up to consume the sign for blasphemy and then the one proclaiming self-delusion. After a final glance out to sea, where the yellow fishing boat was barely ahead of the fleet, the section leader guided his crew down from the shrine. It had been a long and disappointing night. And he did not look forward to the morning.

*\*\*\**

Far from the Island of Chios, Jace yanked Diceärch to a sitting position and pulled the cloth sack from his head.

"Hello Lieutenant," Jace greeted him.

Dicearch's eyes widened in recognition. After staring at Jace for long moments, he jerked his head, looking around at the open sea. Then he growled unintelligibly.

"Rule number five," Jace explained. "Plan your escape route before engaging the enemy."

Dicearch worked his jaw, chewing on the linen cloth.

"Your ships-of-war aren't looking for you."

The pirate bobbed his head as if having a serious conversation.

"We're headed for Behram. I know the Pergamons would like to execute the defiler pirate. But the Egyptians are paying me," Jace described. "You may be wondering how I plan to keep the Pergamon Navy from cutting your throat. Truth is, I'm wondering that myself."

Dicearch shook his shoulders as if trying to throw off the bindings. In his struggles, he exaggerated the movement of his arms which caused the noose to tighten around his throat.

"The knots and style of tying you, I learned as a boy," Jace informed the pirate. "They're good for keeping control of a prisoner. Relax and the line will loosen, and you can breathe. Or you can struggle and take a nap."

Eyes related a lot of emotion. And the bulging eyes of Dicearch were easy to read once his throat opened.

"That's not very nice, Lieutenant," Jace proposed, guessing at the meaning of the harsh look. "Speaking of not nice, prepare yourself for what's coming. Over the next two days, I will not feed you or give you water. Weaken a prisoner and like the bindings, it makes them, or in this case, you, easier to handle."

Being careful to keep his wrist pressed to the small of his back, Diceärch bounced up and down on the bench of the fishing boat. The fit lasted until the pirate grew weary of the silent outburst.

"I would conserve my energy, Lieutenant Diceärch," Jace advised. "Because you don't know when you'll eat again."

***

Late in the day, the island of Lesvos came up on the horizon. Jace bypassed villages, choosing instead a secluded beach for landing. Once the fishing boat was on shore and stashed behind a line of bushes, he walked Diceärch to a tree. Jace sat the pirate down and tied him to the trunk.

Murmurs emitted from the gag.

"Food? Water?" Jace asked. "I don't think so, Lieutenant. There's still too much fight in you."

Jace fixed a stew of fish and vegetables, yawing as he waited for the food to cook. He'd been up for three days and nights. If he was going to get the pirate to Admiral Radames, the Archer would need to navigate Diceärch's greedy friends, and keep the pirate's safe from avowed enemies. For that, Jace needed a clear head. After a glance at his prisoner to be sure he was secured to the tree, Jace closed his eyes.

While the Archer napped, a two-banker rowed just offshore. The pirate ship moved by without stopping after scanning the beach for signs of the missing Commander Diceärch. It traveled north along the coast of Lesvos.

***

Near dawn, Jace shook the pirate's shoulder to wake him.

246

"I'm going to remove the gag and give you a drink," Jace explained. "If you try to bite me, the next few days will not be pleasant for you."

Dicearch nodded his understanding. Untying the linen from around the pirate's head freed his mouth and gave Jace access to the ball of linen.

"Oh, but that is nasty," the Archer announced.

He threw the wet and crusty cloth to the ground and lifted a waterskin over Dicearch's head. As if a baby bird, the pirate strained his neck to get a sip. Drops wet the pirate's cracked and dry lips.

"More," he croaked. "Please, more."

Jace started to feel sorry for the broken man. Bound, hungry, and thirsty to the point of begging, Dicearch seemed anything except a monster.

***

*"Pity is not a virtue for a Cretan Archer," Zarek Mikolas taught. "Your purpose is to earn a profit. Whether it's putting an arrow in a target, tracking a man, lying to a widow, or cutting a throat to protect your identity, you do it without remorse."*

*"But what about killing this rabbit?" Jace asked. "I'm afraid I'll have nightmares."*

*The Kasia boy stroked the animal in his arms. It appeared as if the creature could awaken, ruffle its fur, and hop away. The body felt warm against his chest.*

*"Philosophers argue the workings of our minds," the Master Archer answered. "Scholars study the meaning of our actions. And priests are concerned with the influence of the Gods on our lives."*

*"But we aren't philosophers, scholars, or priests," Jace pointed out.*

"No, we aren't," Zarek Mikolas agreed. "We are Cretan mercenaries. The rabbit will eat our crops, breed, then bring his brood to the farm so they all dine on our labor and toil. Our job is to protect the food from predators. Just because the rabbit is soft, furry, and cute doesn't mean it's not dangerous."

"But deep in the night, my mind troubles me," Jace informed his teacher.

"I will never tell you to not dream or have nightmares. They are nature's outlets for our fears and problems," Archer Mikolas described to his young student. "I do ask that you remember you are strong, well-trained, and have a reason for everything you do."

\*\*\*

Jace allowed a few drops to moisten Diceärch's lips.

"More, please," the pirate begged.

"I remember," Jace said as he capped the waterskin.

From a wounded man, Diceärch changed to a vicious creature.

"If my hands were free, I'd kill you and take all the water I want," the pirate threatened while baring his teeth. In a moment of clarity, he inquired. "You remember what?"

"If I hadn't got out of the building you set on fire," Jace replied. "I remember, I'd be dead."

Jace loaded the fishing boat, pushed it into the water, and sat Diceärch on a bench. Next, he rowed away from the beach, heading north along the coast of Lesvos towards Behram on the coast of the Pergamon Kingdom.

\*\*\*

Midday, when the sun rested high in the sky, they noted the sail of a ship coming from the north.

"If you say anything or signal for help," Jace warned, "you'll be the first to die."

"I have no wish to die," Diceärch told him. "To kill you, yes. But not to die."

The ship turned out to be a big transport. Following that, another merchant ship appeared.

When a third long range vessel came into view, Jace questioned, "Where are they coming from?"

The pirate laughed.

"You don't know where you are, do you, Archer?" Diceärch challenged. "Give me a stream from the waterskin and I'll tell you."

In battle, during missions, and on jobs, momentum shifted, and priorities changed. The pirate had been sailing the northern Aegean Sea for a period of time. He knew the islands better than Jace who only studied charts.

"It's reported that a person can last three days without water," Jace mentioned. "Lie to me and you'll test the theory."

"Make that, two streams," the pirate requested. "My information is that valuable."

*** 

By early afternoon, the yellow fishing boat sailed into the south harbor of Mitilini. For fishing boats and two-bankers, the harbor offered beaches on two sides. Warships, large transports, and coastal traders had access to piers and docks. In the middle of the harbor, between a set of piers, the islanders had dug a canal. The ninety-foot-wide channel ran through the heart of Mitilini.

Jace pulled down the sail and allowed the boat to drift.

"Where does the canal lead?" he inquired.

"To the north harbor," Diceärch told him. "There's enough traffic here that you don't need to sail to Behram."

"You really are afraid of the Pergamon Navy," Jace suggested.

"You said it yourself," the pirate clarified. "You have no idea how to protect me from being murdered by them."

Jace noted white granite bridges spanning the canal. As he gawked at the construction, a trireme came down the center of the waterway. All three tiers of oars were rowing, and no blade touched the side of the wide channel. And while the ship's officers ducked a little, the upper deck of the warship passed easily under the bridges.

Jace sat mesmerized by the sight of the white spans over the canal.

"Archer. Archer Kasia," Diceärch shouted. "You know I fear the Pergamon Navy. Under these circumstances, perhaps you should as well."

***

The Pergamon warship spanned sixty feet from the tips of the oars on one side to the ends of the blades on the other side. At the center rode the bronze ram, and it was plowing rapidly down the center of the canal.

Large ships would be damaged from contact with the business end of the bronze weapon. While midsized vessels would be split in half by the ram, giving some sailors a chance to swim to shore. But a fishing boat would simply splinter into fragments while the passengers were ground to fish food.

Jace snapped the oars into the oarlocks and began rowing.

Stroke. The margin of safety shrunk from thirty-one feet to twenty-eight feet. Stroke. Twenty-five feet to twenty-two. Stroke. While the boat surged on the stroke, Jace pulled his knife, and stepped to Dicearch.

Fearing for his life, the pirate jerked away. But rather than stabbing him, Jace grabbed Dicearch's wrists.

"If you live, I'll find you," the Archer notified the pirate.

After cutting the bindings, Jace grabbed his bow case and the quiver of arrows. The steep dive from the gunwales, even with the buoyancy of the waterproof cases, carried Jace deep underwater.

Sounding as if a thousand waterfowl were thrashing the surface with their wings, the oars of the trireme beat a deadly rhythm. Compared to the din of the oar blades, the crunch that marked the destruction of the yellow fishing boat was quick.

*\*\**

Jace bobbed to the surface behind the splash of the last oar. On the wake created by the moving hull, he floated towards the east side of the harbor. Twisting as the wave took him, the Archer scanned the harbor.

At first, he was saddened by the loss of coins from the death of the pirate. Then, Jace saw Dicearch swimming to the west bank of the harbor. And his attitude revived a little.

Searching hundreds of ships across two harbors would not be an easy task. But Jace had one element on his side. The reward for Dicearch from Pergamon, Rhodes, Athens, and from Egypt limited who the pirate could trust. Yet there numerous greedy sailors who would take Diceärch's coins and spirit him away from Mitilini.

***

Sloshing to shore, the Archer jogged up the beach and located a hard road. On the street, he ran for the nearest bridge. A sign announcing Ermou Bridge flashed by. Then the white marble of the arched span came into view. Slowing slightly, Jace rounded the corner and lined up with the bridge. And to his surprise, he spotted Diceärch standing at the approach on the far side.

"Why not flee when you had the chance?" the Archer asked. Next, ten seamen stepped around the pirate Commander, protecting him. And Jace mouthed his answer. "Because you found one of your boat crews."

There were instances where retreat was warranted. And others where the lack of common-sense pushed one to attack against overwhelming odds. Exhausted from hauling rocks, shoveling dirt, and chopping firewood, Archer Kasia slowed but continued to march forward. His anger at failing the mission drove him to recklessness.

Rule number five or any thought of an escape route before engaging, fled his mind, along with his training and rationale. Jace just wanted to get his hands around Diceärch's throat. Apparently, the feeling was mutual as across the bridge the pirate Commander stood his ground.

## Act 9

## Chapter 25 – You'd Be Dead

Ten targets presented an opportunity. If the Archer could get his bow out of the case, the arrows from the quiver, and a string on the war bow. Ill-advisedly, he marched forward while the pirate crew moved towards him. Rapidly, their knives and short swords were becoming the more deadly of the weapons present on the bridge.

Jace had trained to battle one, two, or even three opponents in hand-to-hand combat. But ten, presented a problem. Realization, as well as his clothes drying, and coming to his senses caused Jace to hesitate. Halted in the center of the bridge, he contemplated running.

On the far side of the white marble span, Diceärch screamed in triumph while shaking his fists in the air. In that instant, Jace knew the pirate was absolutely touched with madness. Had he rowed away, the duel between the Archer and the Lieutenant would have been over, and most likely, never repeated.

When the Archer taught Lieutenant Diceärch the five rules of warfare, helped the inexperienced Lieutenant build up the harbor's defenses, and install discipline in his squad, Jace assumed the training would be appreciated. The lessons were embraced and applied. Yet, in his black soul, the pirate turned the instructions into a deep resentment of the teacher. Until this moment, Jace hadn't realized the depth of Dicearch's twisted sense of reality.

Up on the balls of his feet, Jace braced for a pivot and a sprint to safety. Then, the line of pirates stopped. Jace paused as well, curious about the strange behavior of the superior force.

***

A shout of *"Non est magnum quod,"* came from behind Jace.

"Who would call out, isn't that great?" Jace thought. Then he answered his own question. "A Legion NCO spoiling for a fight."

Jace looked back to see ten armored Roman Marines jogging up the street. With shields smaller than infantry shields, but spears just as sharp, he could tell by the set of their jaws, they intended to unleash violence on the pirates.

The Marines rushed by and an Optio stopped beside Jace.

"Isn't that great," the Legion NCO exclaimed. "We've been chasing that crew for days. And here we are clearing the canal for the passage of our squadron, and the pirates come marching across the bridge, right onto the tips of our spears."

"The Gods are good," Jace stated. "I'm after the one standing by himself on the far side. Do you mind?"

"There's more than enough pirate gristle for everyone to have a chew," the Optio stated.

On the bridge, the Marines took the pirates off their feet then stabbed the prostrated forms, staining the white marble with red smears. Jace ran between the small battles, chasing Dicearch off the bridge and down to the beach.

*** 

Dicearch sprinted in the direction of a liburna while fanatically signaling for the navigator to launch from the beach. Unlike a disciplined crew, the pirates responded at their leisure.

"Get us off the beach," Dicearch bellowed. "Now. We have to go, now."

Jace was close enough to hear the words. Still, he knew a quick shove on the hull would put the nimble two-banker in the water. And once afloat, in two strokes, it would be out of reach.

Taking stock of his load, Jace considered dropping the bow. But that left him defenseless, and with the empty case and the quiver of arrows flopping around on his back. Footraces were best performed without extra gear. Before Jace decided, the race ended.

Dicearch scampered aboard and issued orders to launch. Jace slowed to a saunter, angry at himself for his inattention and allowing the Lieutenant to get away. The Archer walked forward with no hope of getting paid by the Egyptians.

*** 

Yet, where there were Roman Marines, there would be the Legion Navy. And two of the Navy's triremes raced from the channel. Rowing hard, they blocked the escape route of the pirate vessel. A third warship took up a station in the center of the harbor watching for allies of the pirates.

Marines dropped from the upper deck, splashed into the water, and soon had the liburna surrounded. A combat officer joined the assault force. He eyed Jace with suspicion.

"You're Latin," the officer remarked.

"I'm not with the pirates," Jace assured him.

"Do you have business here?" the Centurion questioned.

There were times to be a mercenary, and on occasion, a Legion staff officer.

"I'm Tribune Jace Kasia Romiliia of Scipio's Iberian Legions. And I'm on a special mission," Jace replied with a partial lie.

"You're a long way from Iberia, Tribune."

"Don't I know it," Jace commented. Then he inquired. "You wouldn't happen to be sailing south, would you?"

"After Lesvos we're scheduled to pay a courtesy call on the Isle of Rhodes," the Legion officer answered. "Is there something you need, sir?"

Considering that Rome didn't have a bounty on Diceärch, traveling on a Legion warship had to be the safest way to transport the blasphemous pirate.

"I need to speak to your squadron commander," Jace said. "After I've secured my prisoner."

\*\*\*

Jace Romiliia stood next to Senior Tribune Gaius Centho. The other two triremes in the squadron traveled behind them. At midship, the big sail bellowed in the breeze, propelling the vessel. Below the sail and strapped to the mast, Diceärch attempted to engage Roman sailors in conversation.

"Is your crew susceptible to bribes?" Jace inquired. "Because the Greek will offer a man's weight in coins to be free."

"My Centurions have been with me for four years and the other ship's officers almost as long," Centho answered. "They have good relations with the crew. If any were going to mutiny, it would be over bad food or mistreatment. It wouldn't be over the promise of a bag of pirate silver."

"Good to hear," Jace admitted. "Tell me, I've been away from General Scipio's staff for over a year. Any word on the Iberian campaign?"

"I've been patrolling off the east coast. Far from Rome and news of happenings in the west," Centho explained. "Since we pushed Philip of Macedonia out of Illyrian territory, General Galba has his squadrons venturing farther out into the Aegean. We protect Republic shipping lanes and occasionally get to hunt pirates. Like that pirate of yours."

"Diceärch is more than a pirate," Jace told the senior staff officer. "The former Greek Lieutenant has risen far above his station. He's wanted by none other than Pharaoh Ptolemy IV of Egypt."

"What did he do to earn that honor?" Centho asked.

"You know, I'm not sure," Jace lied. If he told the noble Roman officer the pirate desecrated shrines and butchered priests, Diceärch would die right then, no question. Maintaining his ignorance, Jace offered. "But it had to be something big, like stealing from the royal treasury."

"That's probably where he got the coins he's using for the bribes."

"You may have solved the riddle, Senior Tribune," Jace complimented him.

*** 

Five days later, a slice of green rose from the sea. The three Roman warships headed for the point of land.

"That's the Island of Kos," Centho informed Jace. "I assume we'll be parting ways soon. You to Alexandia and me to the Island of Rhodes."

"The Egyptian fleet is docked at the Port of Kefalos," Jace said. "You should meet Admiral Radames. He's a trustworthy man."

"Part of my duties is diplomacy with other countries," Centho reported. "I'd like to meet the Admiral, if you can arrange the introductions."

Unknown to Jace, he spoke too soon, "I don't see why not, Senior Tribune."

*** 

They approached the point of land but didn't see any Egyptian picket ships. Even as they rounded the piece of land and sailed south along the coast of Kos, no warships challenged them.

"Ship's Centurion, get the rowers seated," Centho ordered, "and the Marines armored."

"Is there a problem, sir?" the Centurion questioned.

"There should be a fleet here," the Senior Tribune answered. "Until I know why the Egyptians haven't posted lookout ships, I expect a problem."

"Yes, sir," the Ship's officer answered. He addressed the First Principale, the Centurion of Marines, and his signalman. Then he spoke to Centho. "Preparations are underway, Senior Tribune. Anything else?"

"Maintain our course," Centho replied.

***

By late afternoon, the squadron sailed into a bay. On the far side of the inlet, the town of Kefalos perched on the hills above the port.

"Take us in for a look at the harbor," Centho advised. "Leave one of our warships in the bay to watch for unwelcomed visitors."

From midship, Dicearch gave a shriek and bellowed before collapsing against his restraints, "Rule number four, always keep lookouts." Heartbeats later, he repeated. "Rule number four, you ignorant pup."

While the pirate laughed, a navigator declared, "that one is double touched by the Goddess Manea. He's both insane and mad."

"And dangerous," Jace warned. "He'll cut you with a blade and laugh just as hard at your pain."

The prisoner was half the length of the trireme away. Yet, the rear oarsmen leaned back as if trying to put extra distance between themselves and Dicearch.

***

The port of Kefalos had two docks flanked by flat beaches. Warehouses backed up the port, while the village itself sat in the hills above the beach. From all appearances, while the harbor town wasn't crowded, the village didn't seem to be in distress or danger.

"There's no wreckage. I don't think the Egyptians fought here," Centho proposed. He directed his combat officer. "Take two squads and find out where the Egyptians went."

"Yes, sir," the Centurion acknowledged.

While the combat officer selected his squads, two of Centho's three triremes rowed to the beach, cut half circles in the water, and backstroked until the keels touched sand.

Twenty Legionaries, an Optio, and the Centurion dropped over the side and waded to shore. A handful of dock workers greeted the shore party when they splashed out of the water.

"Has the port been attacked?" the combat officer demanded.

"No, Latian," a porter assured him. "It's been pretty calm since the Egyptians left."

"Where did their fleet go?" the officer questioned.

"Something big happened in Alexandria," another dock worker said. "Not sure what. But a messenger ship arrived and early the next morning, the entire Egyptian fleet rowed away. Every last ship and oarsmen."

"For Alexandria?" the Centurion inquired.

"I guess so," a third porter offered.

The combat officer waded out, climbed the side of the three-banker with the aid of a rope and reported to Centho.

"Senior Tribune, the fleet, from as much as I can tell, sailed for Alexandria," the Centurion described. "A messenger ship arrived with news, and they left in a hurry."

"What could have happened to get the fleet recalled?" Centho said puzzling over the action of the Egyptians.

Jace swallowed hard and kept his mouth shut. He had an idea about the recall. But it ran a distant second to his worries about the current situation. Going to the Island of Rhodes with the Roman squadron was out of the question. In Rhodes, Diceärch would be recognized and probably stabbed as soon as he left the trireme.

"Senior Tribune," Jace announced. "The prisoner and I will wait at Kefalos. There's sure to be transports heading to Alexandria from here."

"You're welcome to travel to Rhodes with us," Centho informed Jace.

"I do appreciate the offer. But I need to fulfill my obligation to Admiral Radames quickly. And get back to Rome to find transportation to Iberia," Jace said using any excuse he could to avoid Rhodes. "If I don't report to General Scipio soon, he'll think I've gone barbarian."

The lie satisfied the Senior Tribune as he said, "I must admit, I enjoyed your company. As for your prisoner. No one in the crew will miss him. But I understand, duty is duty."

"That should be the code of every General's Tribune," Jace remarked.

***

At dawn, the three warships rowed to the south, heading for Rhodes. Jace and Diceärch stood on the beach.

"That was close," the pirate commented.

"What was close?" Jace asked.

"If the Senior Tribune had insisted on you going to Rhodes. I'd be dead."

"I don't expect gratitude?" Jace questioned.

"Tribune Kasia, why would I offer you gratitude."

"Because without the Roman Marines guarding you, you'd have a chance to escape. Now if one of your pirate crews shows up at Kefalos, you think you'd be free."

"Wouldn't I be?" Diceärch countered.

"No, Lieutenant," Jace assured him, "you'd be dead."

## Chapter 26 – About a Girl

In response to the absence of the Egyptian fleet, the town repaired gates blocking the paths up to the homes and businesses in the hills. According to the dockworkers, the news had already spread to the other islands in the Cyclades.

"Right now, brigands backed by Macedonia, Spartan pirates, and Cilician bandits," the cargo handlers assured Jace, "are rowing for our undefended island."

Diceärch bent sideways as if sharing secrets with a confident.

"You wouldn't murder a man just because a few of his friends dropped in for a visit," Diceärch probed for the hundredth time. "Would you?"

Something in his insane brain made him believe if Jace agreed to a specific condition, then the crimes of the former Lieutenant would be excused. They might have been for a fat purse, except a couple of years ago the pirate had blocked the door to Jace's room, set fire to the building, and left the Archer to die in the fire. For that, before Diceärch went free, Jace would take his life.

"No deal," Jace told him.

The pair stood on the dock watching the broad arc of the entrance to the bay. In the two days since the Roman's dropped them on Kos, no ships heading south had docked at the harbor. At the warning from the cargo handlers, desperation set in and Jace considered paying for passage on the next transport. Whether the ship traveled east or west, as long as it was away from the island, Jace wanted to be on it.

"Inbound vessel," a dockworker shouted. With his coworkers, he ran to the top of the beach, stopping at the bottom of a winding path that stretched to the hills and the town above. "You might want to get up here, Archer. At least until we know if the ship is a dishonest trader or an honest pirate."

"Don't you mean an honest trader, and a dishonest pirate?" Jace questioned.

He tugged on the rope to get Diceärch moving away from the dock.

"A coastal trader will lie, cheat, and steal to get a better deal," the cargo handler pushed back. "A pirate will kill you straight away if you put up a fight. Which action is more honest?"

"Your argument has merit," Jace proposed. Looking at the entrance to the bay, he inquired. "Can you tell the trustworthiness of the ship, yet?"

"From the bent mast, I'd say he's as big a scoundrel as any of the king's tax collectors," another dockworker described. "He's Cretan and has a bad attitude."

They strolled back to the dock to await the coastal trader.

"Might be due to the missing section of his thumb," another handler offered, "and the missing sections from a finger on his right hand."

Jace smiled. Not at the plight of the inbound trader. But at the fates that sent him a crippled Captain from Crete.

"One question about the trader," Jace asked. "Does he have a reputation for delivering once the deal is done?"

"Every time," the handler assured Jace. "No matter the weather, even if he gets a better offer. He honors the contract."

Better than a Captain out of Crete, the Gods had sent Jace a man with a code. While thinking if he could afford the passage, Jace jiggled his coin purse.

***

The shoulders, although no longer used for pulling a bowstring, had the width to attest to his earlier life. He walked with purpose, his eyes took in the surroundings searching for traps and dangers. Past middle age, he leaped to the dock as spry as a deer.

"Captain Rodas," Jace asked, "are you acquainted with Acis Gergely?"

"You mean Instructor Gergely," the coastal trader replied, "the crippled teacher at the agoge."

"No, sir. I meant Lieutenant Acis Gergely, the commander of Archers," Jace insisted.

Rodas cocked his head and squinted through the creases around his eyes.

"Acis hasn't been on a contract since his mutilation?"

The words held more meaning than the recognition of Gergely's missing hands. They hinted at Rodas' own amputation.

"Since he commanded an expedition to the Roman Republic where his company fought against Hannibal Barca," Jace reported. "I missed the battle of Cannae. Lieutenant Gergely sent me north as a scout."

"You are a Latian," Rodas pointed out. "How did you come to work with archers?"

"Zarek Mikolas trained me," Jace stated.

"So far, in this brief conversation, you've identified yourself with two legendary Cretan Archers," Rodas concluded. "Is there something you're trying to tell me?"

"No, Captain, I'm trying to lower the cost," Jace responded.

"The cost of what?"

"The cost of leasing your ship for a voyage to Alexandria, Egypt," Jace answered. "I'm fairly sure, you can make a profit every day, and I can afford it, if the price is right."

"How do you know I won't take your coins and dump you in the sea?" Rodas inquired.

Jace held out a hand. Between two fingers, he held a silver coin.

"Take the coin, Cretan Archer," Jace invited, "and accept the contract."

"You know a lot about the Archer's code," Rodas mentioned.

"Would you feel better about accepting me as a client if we went a few rounds in a fighting circle?" Jace questioned.

Rodas took the coin and asked, "Where are your bundles? How many? I'll have my deckhands fetch them."

"Just three," Jace informed him. "The case with my war bow, and my quiver of arrows are by the tree with my prisoner."

As Jace expected, Rodas didn't even blink at the mention of a prisoner. He had taken a contract and would adhere to the deal for as long as the client required his services.

*** 

The trading vessel had low freeboards and high rails to allow taller stacks of cargo. And while the single-banker boasted a larger steering platform, the rest of the ship kept the standard two oarsmen to a side arrangement. Without a hold, the cargo rested between narrow walkways. And towering above the deck, the mast curved back as of it was from a tree grown on a windswept island.

With the arrival of the sun, *Thanatos' Chariot* slipped away from Kefalos, leaving the Island of Kos in the ship's wake. On a southern bearing, the sail caught the wind and drove the vessel across the sea.

"You said war bow," Rodas commented while guiding the vessel with the rear oar. "I'd like to see what you call a war bow."

"I can string it for you," Jace proposed. He untied the laces and added, "and I can afford to donate a few shafts to the sea Gods, if you want to test the pull."

Rodas held out his right hand. Only the first joint remained of his thumb and his forefinger. With the shortened digits, the trader could grip the rear oar, haul a rope, or grab onto a rail. Conversely, he could not pick up a coin, hold thread and needle or draw a bowstring.

"Forty-five years ago, I would have taken you up on the offer," Rodas advised. He held up his right hand and tapped the stumps together. "But happily, I am no longer able."

Jace extracted the bow from the waterproof case. If he had any doubt of Rodas' previous occupation, the deep breath at the sight of a Cretan war bow resolved the confusion.

"Fine craftsmanship," the trader noted. "Who built that?"

"I did," Jace assured him while flexing and warming the wood. Moments later, he strung the war bow and held it out to Rodas.

"What am I supposed to do with that?" the trader challenged.

"In your third year as a Herd, you practiced left-handed archery," Jace reminded him.

"I did terrible left-handed," Rodas admitted.

Jace waved one of the two sailors to the rear.

"Captain Rodas needs a break," Jace informed the deckhand.

\*\*\*

Shaking from nerves, or from struggling against the strength of the bow, Rodas drew the shaft back to his ear, and released the string.

*Zip-Thwack!*

In a flight that carried the arrow out of sight, the shaft climbed into the blue sky.

"Have a go at another, Cretan Archer," Jace encouraged.

With a sly smile, the old skipper selected a shaft, notched it on the bowstring, and sent it after its companion.

*Zip-Thwack!*

A lightness graced his face while watching the feathers of the fletching vanish and the arrow disappear. Then, he handed the bow to Jace.

"You've done a service for an old man," Rodas vowed. He rotated his left arm to loosen the muscles in his shoulder. With a grimace, he clarified. "It's rare to come across a friendly Cretan Archer and rarer still to experience the power of a war bow."

"I'm glad you feel that way," Jace said.

"As much as I appreciate the experience, I am not lowering my fee."

"We have a deal, and I would never ask you to change it," Jace told him. "But I do want to know what happened to your thumb and forefinger."

"Let's just say, I lost them over a girl," Rodas deflected.

"Your vessel is named for the God who carries humans to the underworld when the Fates cut their threads," Jace listed. "*Thanatos' Chariot* is not a normal name for a trading vessel. Nor is the name Rodas. You don't appear to be the type of man who'd retire to tend a rose garden."

"Zarek Mikolas was always the curious type," Rodas stated. At the mention of his teacher and mentor, Jace faced the trader. "Zarek graduated a couple of years after I arrived at the agoge. I didn't know him well. But it's not surprising that he'd teach his own Herd to have a questioning mind."

"He did that. Which leads me to the item that begs for an explanation about the amputations," Jace insisted. "You said, but happily I'm no longer able to pull a bowstring."

"Perhaps, I meant my age," Rodas suggested.

"About a girl, forty-five years ago?" Jace pointed out the error. "You wouldn't have been too old for love or to be an archer."

"Forty-five years ago, I had my finger, my thumb, and my youth," Rodas boasted as he extended and contracted the fingers on his right hand. "I was both a prodigious lover and a master of the bow."

"Can I assume the loss of your finger and thumb was about a girl?" Jace guessed.

"Actually, about two girls," Rodas corrected.

"We have nothing to do for the rest of the day, tell me the story," Jace encouraged. With the sail puffed up from the wind, the sea calm, and the hull cutting through the water, the sailing was easy. "Let's start with your name, Rose Garden."

"Rose Garden, Cretan Archer, is the end of the story," Rodas said. "The start of the tale begins when a Company of Cretan Archers was hired by the King of Cyrene to guard his eastern border from an invasion by Ptolemy II of Egypt."

They sat on the edge of the steering platform and Rodas pulled a wineskin from under the deck.

"No thanks," Jace said refusing the wine.

"Water," Rodas corrected. "I never developed a taste for strong drink."

As Jace took a stream of bitter water, Rodas pointed to his heart and confessed, "In Cyrene, they call me Rodas of Haîma."

From the title and its meaning, Jace choked on the vinegar water.

## Chapter 27 – Rodas of Haîma

"Cyrene sits on top of an easily defended hill," Rodas described. "Seven miles to the north is the sea, a stretch of beach, and a port. While the west, south, and east offer hard days of travel over rough desert. In short, our patrols started at the palace in Cyrene, looped far into the desert, and ended where we started, at the palace. I was the youngest File Leader, and my Captain took advantage of my lack of seniority."

"Most young leaders get the worst details," Jace commiserated.

"The springs around Cyrene flow into pools where citizens fill their water vessels. Before the excess water flows down to the flatland and eventually to the sea, it collects in ponds. The ponds are where the citizens bathe and wash," Rodas told Jace. "After long patrols, most Files rested in the shade of our barracks. But I was junior, and my File drew the duty of guarding a pond on the far side of the city."

"At least you could cool off in the water," Jace suggested.

"I don't think our Captain ever visited the pond in the west," Rodas said, ignoring Jace's comment. "As a matter of fact, three days a week, citizens weren't allowed to bathe in the water."

"That's an odd occurrence," Jace observed. "Wait, what was the reason no one bathed in the western pond?"

"I didn't say no one bathed there. You see, three days a week, Princess Berenice and her attendants came to the pond. It was a good choice. A natural grotto, the rocks protected the Princess and her ladies from prying eyes," Rodas described with a slight smile on his lips. "The first day of our duty, Commander Tymek of the palace guard and four old, fat guardsmen accompanied the royal party. Seeing us, Tymek ordered my archers away. But I was young, and stubborn. Contract or not, I dropped my long pack preparing to fight him. My archers were exhausted, and I was angry. There was no way I was crossing the city to tell my Captain I failed a simple assignment."

"You fought with the commander of the palace guard?" Jace asked in horror.

"I would have except one of the Princess' ladies came up for the pond," Rodas eyes grew misty. "Aello marched between my balled-up fists and his undrawn sword. Small, like a bird, with raven hair, and piercing brown eyes, the lady informed Tymek that the Princess preferred young archers to obese men loyal to her mother."

"The Princess requested your protection and expelled her own royal guards?" Jace questioned.

"At the time, I didn't realize there were problems in the court," Rodas admitted. "Commander Tymek told her, they are mercenaries and can't be trusted. He added Cretan Archers fight for coins and have no honor. Yet, no matter

271

how much he bristled and maligned us, Aello stood like a statue with one graceful arm pointing to the path that led back to the palace."

"The Queen will hear of this, the Commander shouted to be heard around the rocks and down to the pool. Barely audible, a small voice responded. And Commander, the King will hear of your insolence."

"Contention between a King and a Queen," Jace summed up. "Not a situation a File of Archers wants to get in the middle of."

"If those were the only points of view, I could have avoided them, and things might have turned out differently," Rodas proposed. "Princess Berenice was sixteen and betrothed to Prince Ptolemy III of Egypt. According to Aello, the Princess was happy and excited about becoming the Queen of Egypt."

"Queen of the Nile is a good position if you can get it," Jace teased.

"Princess Berenice was well situated to get the job," Rodas insisted. "But the next month, King Magnas died. When we got back from a desert patrol, the royal party came to the pond and Princess Berenice was crying. I offered my condolences to her through Aello. It's not that her father died, although she loved him, the lady told me. The Princess is crying because her mother, Queen Apama, decided that for the good of Cyrene, Berenice should marry someone else. Queen Apama had sent for a Macedonian Prince who was a half-brother to the King of the Seleucid Empire."

"The Queen broke a deal with Egypt, and invited in an enemy of the Pharaoh?" Jace gasped. But after consideration, he proposed. "On a good note, having Egypt threatening Cyrene had to be good for you archers."

"It did extend our contract," Rodas confirmed. "Months later, Prince Demetrius the Fair landed at Cyrene. And I have to admit, he was a handsome man. And nice to the Archers, soldiers, and the citizens. Nothing personal against the man, but Aello said the Princess dreaded the marriage. But for the good of her people, she was facing the inevitable with a positive attitude."

"One has to respect people who suffer difficult duty without making a fuss," Jace theorized. "When Prince Demetrius married Princess Berenice, he would be a Prince of Cyrene and of Macedonia. A double title. That is impressive."

"But that's not how it works in Cyrene," Rodas corrected Jace. "Demetrius the Fair was elevated to King of Cyrene, making Berenice his Queen. The former Queen Apama became Queen Dowager. And that should have settled the palace intrigue."

"I've a feeling something went wrong?" Jace projected.

"A few weeks later, when we returned from a patrol through the desert, Queen Berenice and her ladies came to the grotto," Rodas said in a low threatening voice "In the Cretan Academy, we all carried bruises. And we hide the pain out of fear of being seen as weak. Yet, we grew to recognize the yellowing of the skin on the outskirts of a bruise, the puffiness that surrounds a shallow cut from a fist, and how we held ourselves stiffly to keep from aggravating the soreness in our bones and the muscles around our wounds. Despite her hat with the low brim, and the high collar of her robe, I knew. Someone had used their fists on Queen Berenice. When I mentioned it to Aello, she denied any such thing. But I knew because I'd hidden my injuries during training."

"There's only one man who could beat a Queen," Jace warned. Noting the emotion rising in the trader, he added. "A Cretan Archer doesn't want to get in the middle of a squabble between a King and a Queen."

Rodas twisted his neck around to look into Jace's eyes. After a moment, he returned to gazing down the length of his ship, and out to the horizon.

"One day, a servant arrived at the pond. I didn't think he knew what to make of ten Archer's sitting guard around the grotto," Rodas reported. "But I stood up to greet him. Clear the pond, by order of the Queen, he insisted. I told him it wasn't Berenice's day, but we would be happy to comply. It's not for Queen Berenice, he informed me. The pond is for Queen Apama. I sent my File down to clear the pond."

"At the time, how old a woman was Queen Apama?" Jace questioned.

"Around forty-three and as lusty as a nanny-goat in season," Rodas gave the surprising answer. "Queen Apama and King Demetrius strolled down the path from the palace with their hands wandering all over their bodies. They never looked at me or any of the Archers. They only had eyes, fingers, hands, and arms for each other."

"I hope you went to your Captain and requested a different assignment," Jace begged.

"I was twenty-two and as tough as a weathered oak board. There was no way I'd extract myself from the situation," Rodas told him. "Queen Apama and the King were in the water, splashing, and laughing when Queen Berenice ran from the palace. Aello stopped by me while Berenice raced down to the pond. How could you do this to me? Berenice screamed. Shut your mouth child. This is the way of the world, Queen Apama scolded. Get used to not getting your way. Then Demetrius the Fair invited, come in and join us. A scream and a laugh reached us. A moment later, Berenice appeared at the top of the grotto with tears streaming down her cheeks. Aello grabbed my arm and clung to me for a moment. Then she released my forearm and ran to escort Queen Berenice back to the palace. To this day, I can feel Aello's fingers around my arm, holding on as if the earth would swallow her up without my support."

***

"The palace feared the Egyptians would march into Cyrene, so they ordered an increase in patrols. We joined the Company for a week of patrolling in the desert. We saw no Egyptians and for our troubles we collected snake skins, sunburns, thirsty throats, and sore feet. It was so hot that when we got back, I strung my war bow to check the joints."

"After exposing a bow to extreme weather, it's always a good idea to check the bonds of the hide glue," Jace agreed.

"My File set up a target, and although it was near sundown, I put a trio of shafts down range. All three arrows hit, center-mass," Rodas boasted. "I was accepting congratulations from my File, when Aello ran from the direction of the palace. Come quick, she begged. Oh, please Archer, please come with me. What could I do? With her two soft hands gripping my writs, I was powerless to keep

275

the little bird from pulling me, my war bow, and five arrows up the path. I warned her, the palace guard wouldn't allow me to pass. But she insisted she knew a way in."

"A pretty girl, sundown, and a secret summons," Jace remarked. "I've seen that written as a cautionary tale too many times to mention."

"Add another one to the stories," Rodas sighed. Then he explained. "Before we reached the guard, Aello guided me off the path and into a rose garden. The flowers were in bloom and the scent hung heavy in the evening air. We squeezed between two rose bushes, a pair of columns, and through an open portal. Once inside the palace, I heard a woman crying. Then a slap and the woman whimpered like a wounded animal."

Rodas paused to take a stream of water. After swallowing and biting his lip, he continued.

"Aello urged me through a curtain and into a bedroom," the coastal trader related. "In the light of two burning braziers I noted a pair of palace guards. They faced the hallway. With their backs to me, they didn't present an immediate threat. The problem came from beside the bed. King Demetrius held Queen Berenice by the neck and slapped her. I can put arrows in targets all day, hunt all night, and take down three men in a fighting circle. But for a domestic dispute, I had no training. A sick feeling bubbled up from the pit of my stomach. When the King loosened the grip, Berenice whimpered, making a pitiful sound. And then I realized I was witnessing something sick and vile. Because, from the bed, Queen Apama laughed. The hairs on my neck stood on ends, and I started to back out of the room. My heel touched the curtain, just as Aello screamed."

"You still had time to escape, didn't you?" Jace inquired.

"Maybe I did. Maybe not. I don't remember if I even thought of it," Rodas admitted. "The guards spun, leveling their spears at me. The years of archery took over and I put an arrow in the gut of one and a shaft through the throat of the other guardsman. Aello screamed a second time and I turned to the King as I notched the third arrow. He held a dagger against the neck of Queen Berenice and glared at me. Is that mad dog yours, Demetrius asked her? A lesson flashed through my brain from years earlier. Always protect the client until he pays off the contract. I started to lower my bow. But then, I remembered we were hired by King Magnas, Berenice's father. Zip-Thwack! The arrow slipped under Demetrius' arms, threading the meat of his chest. By reflex, he jerked his arms back and away from Berenice's throat. He fell onto the bed and into the arms of Queen Apama. The dagger landed on the floor."

"That was a good defensive arrow," Jace allowed. "He might have been injured, but at least you didn't kill a King."

"You assume too much, Jace Kasia," Rodas warned. The former Archer inhaled and pushed air out from between pursed lips. When it became obvious, he was delaying, Rodas told more of the tale. "I snapped out of battle mode and turned to run. But Aello wrapped her arms around my hips, buried her face in my chest, and said thank you. Thank you. I smelled roses, felt her warmth, and wanted to stay like that forever. Forever lasted until Commander Tymek and two guardsmen lifted me in the air and slammed me onto my back. Hold his arm out, the Commander ordered a guardsman. I knew what he wanted. Every soldier who ever had a comrade fall to an archer's arrow wanted it. Either I sacrificed a thumb and a finger, or he would chop off the entire hand. I turned my hand over, extended my thumb and forefinger, and braced. The steel was sharp and the cut clean. Then Tymek declared, for murdering my King, I sentence you to death."

"But an arrow across the chest is only a flesh wound," Jace advised. "You didn't kill the King."

"From the corner of my eyes I noticed Queen Berenice standing over the King and her mother with the dagger posed for another stab," Rodas reported. "But then I returned to the immediate danger, the Commander's sword hovering over my neck. My thumb and finger hurt, and my arm lay in a wet spot of my own blood. And I smelled roses. To this day, I hate the smell of roses."

"What happened next?" Jace demanded.

"Queen Apama began sobbing while cuddling Demetrius' body in her arms. The sound drew Tymek's attention, and he paused in mid chop. Queen Berenice looked at the Commander of the Palace Guard and asked him, allegiance to me or exile? Choose. Now. Tymek stepped away from me and bowed. Your order's my Queen, he said. In Berenice's first directive as the sole ruler of Cyrene, she pointed the blade at Queen Apama and said. Until I give you permission to speak shut your mouth mother. And get used to not getting your way. Commander Tymek, release the archer for he is my Rodas of Haîma."

Jace stared at the mutilated thumb and forefinger before studying the man.

"You kept the title Rose Garden of Bloodshed?"

"I couldn't be an archer any longer," Rodas replied. "And Rodas of Haîma seemed to be as good a name as any for the new me."

"What happened to Queen Berenice?" Jace inquired.

"A couple of years after that night, she took Apama and moved to Egypt," Rodas answered. "Queen Berenice married Prince Ptolemy III."

"That would make her the mother of Ptolemy IV the current Pharaoh of Egypt," Jace concluded.

"He was the ruler of Egypt," Rodas of Haîma said, "the last time I checked."

blank page

# Act 10

## Chapter 28 – On the Menu

Ring Commander Farouk Midhat stormed between the guards, ignoring their salutes. Before reaching the Major's tent, he kicked a divot of sand and grass into the air. Without pausing, Captain Midhat crashed through the shower of soil, reached the pavilion, and pushed aside the tent flap.

"Major, there must be a mistake," Farouk complained.

He crossed the floor while gesturing with a piece of papyrus. Waving the reed paper in front of him gave the appearance that Farouk Midhat was attempting to ward off evil spirits or to dissipate a bad smell. Either or both fit Farouk's mood.

He halted at the desk of the Commander of the Palace Guard. With controlled fury, the Captain gathered enough patience to salute.

"How could there be a mistake?" Major Glaucus questioned. He leaned forward and snatched the papyrus from Farouk's hand. After reading the message, the Major declared. "The instructions came directly from Colonel Kyros. Everything seems to be in order."

"For the last week, my command has withstood attack after attack while the palace guards and the Pharaoh's personal guards retreated in an orderly fashion," Farouk explained. "My losses have been heavy, and our equipment is in shambles. Sir, the outer ring is barely an effective blocking force. And now this?"

"Because you've been so effective against the rebels, Colonel Kyros and I felt that you should have the honor of covering the Pharoah's final battle maneuver. For that, you've been elevated to a Major in the Army of the Pharoah," Major Glaucus advised. "Lord Ptolemy will board a barge at Giza. Once he departs, you'll be free to disengage from combat and march the Army of the Pharoah to Alexandria."

"But Major, the nobles have already pulled their chariots, soldiers, and peasants from the front line," Captain Midhat informed the Commander of the Palace Guards. "They've gone home."

"That doesn't sound right," Major Glaucus said. But he didn't pursue the line of reasoning. Instead, he bragged. "Look Captain, we're moving out before first light. As a decoy, we'll leave the pavilions and tents in place. That's sure to give the rebels pause. The deception was Colonel Kyros's idea. A clever ruse, don't you think?"

For a week, the noblemen, their surviving chariots, soldiers, and farmworkers, had coordinated with mercenary Companies to fight along a broad front. At the center, Captain Midhat's band of fighters held the middle, protecting the palace guards and the Pharoah's personal guards as the army retreated.

At times, units lost control of the moving combat line. Only through the grace of Ra and extra effort were they able to close the gaps. From Luxor, the defeated and embarrassed Army of the Pharoah fought their way north for three hundred miles. And for every mile, they guarded against rebel forces coming at them from the western desert and from Cretan Archers rafting across the Nile.

"But sir, now that we're between the Nile and the Faiyum Oasis, we can consolidate our positions and stop the rebels," Farouk told the Major. "Listen, sir. We can still turn this battle to victory."

"It's twenty-three miles between the Nile and the oasis," Glaucus pointed out. "That's too far to hold. Besides, think of the future. We're thirty-three miles south of Giza and in the middle of nowhere. There's nothing here for historians to write poetry about. No Captain, or should I say Major, you listen. Follow orders. And you'll be handsomely rewarded for your loyalty when we get back to Alexandria."

Disrespectful words reverberated through Captain Midhat's mind. Along with the insubordination, he also thought, *"If I get back to Alexandria?"*

"Yes, sir," he acknowledged while taking back the papyrus.

With his death warrant in hand, Farouk Midhat marched from the Major's pavilion. Beyond the calm of the Pharoah's compound, survivors of the retreat cooked, sewed up wounds from the day's fighting, and repaired damaged gear for the next day's battle.

Shaking off the sense of impending doom, Midhat cleared his mind and focused on solutions. Halfway across the compound, the Captain stopped and faced the cluster of supply tents.

"Just what could a Major of the army requisition from the stores of the palace guards?" he whispered before strolling to the supply tents.

***

At dusk, a mule drawn supply wagon entered the camp of the Outer Ring's command center. Lieutenant Masuda pushed off the ground and limped to the wagon.

"What have we here?" he asked.

As one of the last remaining combat officers in Ring Command, Masuda had proven to be tough and reliable. The men respected him and not just for his treatment of them and wise decisions on the battlefield. They responded to the Lieutenant for his uncanny ability to stay alive during the retreat.

"Major Midhat sent helmets, armor, and spears," the teamster answered.

"And where is 'Major' Midhat, now?" Lieutenant Masuda inquired.

"He said something about getting supply wagons of meat and grain."

"Let's see what you've brought us," Masuda remarked.

He pulled a wrap off the load. In the light of the setting sun, the bronze armor, helmets, and steel tipped spears glowed blood red.

***

More luxurious than the typical display of stars in the desert, on the night Pharaoh Ptolemy IV left the compound, the stars glowed and shimmered with additional luster.

"A sign from the Gods," one of Ptolemy's priests commented.

283

Watching over the loading of the royal wagons, Chief Minister, General Sosibius had his chariot parked beside Colonel Kyros' chariot.

Another priest, struck by the brilliance as he emerged from a pavilion, threw his arms in the air, and exclaimed, "Surely a good omen for Egypt and the Pharaoh."

"Keep your voice down, priest," Colonel Kyros whispered.

Standing beside his driver, the Commander of the Pharaoh's Personal Guard stood slightly bent. The fighting had stripped him of flesh and suppressed the authority in his voice. Guarding the Pharaoh, when the living God was just ranks away from savage rebels, had taken a toll.

"A lack of appreciation for the Gods is what brought on this disaster of incompetence," the priest shot back. "One should glory in the Gods and show reverence with passion."

"That's a fine speech if you were in Alexandria surrounded by walls and wealthy benefactors," the Colonel scolded. "But here, a mile from a rebel horde, during a night operation, your voice only serves to alert spies and scouts. Be silent and keep moving to the wagons."

What Colonel Kyros didn't add and General Sosibius knew too well, Kyros' speech was an attempt at avoiding a mutiny. If the remainder of the army witnessed the command staff fleeing, they would desert before the Pharaoh reached safety.

*\*\**

Lord Ptolemy and his entourage of priests, politicians, and supplicants boarded the wagons. Around them, the personal guards formed a circle. Kyros' men would maintain that tight perimeter all the way to Alexandria. Around the personal guards, Major Glaucus' palace guards created a circle of protection further from the Pharoah. Both officers remained above the fighting during the running battle. Although worry kept their nerves on edge, being elevated and isolated from the clash of shields and spears left them with a belief in their individual importance.

Missing in the defensive formation was Captain Midhat's outer ring. In the rapid escape from the rebels, no one thought of Ring Command as anything other than a unit easily sacrificed for the good of the whole. Days later, that egotistical thinking would lead to a tragedy and a death in Alexandria.

***

Once the Pharoah, his entourage, and followers were loaded, the teamsters nudged the mules forward.

As the wheels crunched and the shapes moved in the night, General Sosibius instructed, "Colonel Kyros, you have responsibility for the Pharoah."

"Aren't you coming with us to Giza, Chief Minister?" Kyros asked.

"I've been a General for the Pharoah for sixteen years," Sosibius reminisced. "I fought with him at Raphia. And I'm honored to say, I played a part in Ptolemy's victory when he defeated Antiochus III and his Seleucid army."

"This is but a setback, General," Kyros assured him. "My spies tell me the rebel supply lines are stretched thin and they're hungry. Two armies have trampled the crops and stripped this land of food. They can't pursue us much farther north."

"Nor can we survive as an army much longer without supplies," Chief Minister Sosibius admitted. "As for your spies, I know your information came from Captain Midhat's network. While you accompany the wagons, I'm off to find Midhat. Let's see if the newly promoted Major can come up with an idea on how to slow the advance of the rebel army."

***

Along the defensive line, hundreds of cookfires glowed in the predawn. Although more stirring to the senses were the aromas wafting from roasting meats on spits and pans of spicy mixtures boiling over flames.

"The condemned men ate hearty meals?" Sosibius commented.

He couldn't blame Midhat for the extravagance. His men and all the survivors along the Egyptian front had fought well during the retreat. In the sky, the first rays of dawn touched the high clouds.

The Pharaoh would only be a third of the way to Giza and the barge. Sosibius worried the rebels would break through and catch Lord Ptolemy before he reached safety.

Stepping down from the chariot, the Chief Minister glanced around the headquarters of Ring Command. Despite the variety of delicious food, the soldiers nibbled on hard biscuits and dried meats. Confused by their restraint, he walked to a fire. Drippings from a roasting lamb caused pops and bursts of flames when the fat hit the burning wood.

"Is something wrong with the meat or the grain?" Sosibius asked the servant turning the spit.

"No, General," the cook assured him. "Cut a piece, it's delicious."

Nervous about being poisoned, Sosibius declined and faced the camp. Every soldier possessed two shields, two helmets, and at least four spears. One set clearly came from the stores of the palace guard. The other set of war gear displayed repairs and patches from hard use.

Before Sosibius could locate an officer or a senior leader to question, Major Midhat and a limping junior officer marched out of the deep shadows.

"General Sosibius?" Farouk Midhat questioned. "Sir. What are you doing here?"

"I thought my presence would boost morale," Sosibius replied. "But you're feast, I dare say, will do a better job."

"Major, excuse my interruption," the junior officer advised, "but we are running out of night."

"Good point, Lieutenant Masuda," Farouk acknowledged. "Get them up. And get them moving."

Masuda left and Sosibius studied the shadowy face of the Ring Commander.

"Moving where?" the General inquired. "You aren't thinking of an attack, are you?"

On either side of them officers of the mercenary units encouraged their spearmen to get up. Around the two senior officers, the Ring soldiers folded blankets, gathered bundles, and prepared to leave the bivouac.

"Set them up," Lieutenant Masuda instructed. "Make it look good."

In ones and twos, soldiers walked out beyond the cookfires and set up their old shields. Using broken spear shafts, they propped up the shields until a continuous string of them stretched along the defensive line. Then, they placed old spears, so the tips pointed towards the enemy.

"Good job," Masuda declared. "Now, go."

In the first light of day, Sosibius gasped as the soldiers jogged away from the fight.

"What is the meaning of this, Major Midhat?" he demanded. "I remained behind to help you fight. Not to stand by and watch you run away like cowards."

"General, twelve miles north of here, the ground rises," Farouk informed the Chief Minister. "I need the high ground to stop the ones who make it through."

"Make it through what? An empty camp, a false barrier of shields?" Sosibius protested. "Just what will slow the rebel advance. And keep them from over taking you as you run away?"

Across the empty ground between the two armies, the voices of officers shouting orders and calling their men to formations carried to Farouk.

"General, we should go," Midhat suggested. "I'll see you on the hill."

Frustrated because he allowed a junior officer to gain the upper hand, Sosibius moved quickly to his chariot.

"Apparently, we're regrouping on the high ground," the General told his driver. "Twelve miles north of here."

"Sir, I know the area," his driver reported. "The high ground is no more than a gentle rocky grade and a few sand hills."

"That's what I was afraid of," Sosibius whined. "Drive."

As the General's chariot rolled away, Major Midhat peered over the line of shields to see movement across the field.

"Make some smoke," he shouted to the men at the cookfires. "Then get out of here."

With his order given, Farouk Midhat ran to his horse, mounted, and rode away from the site of the battle.

***

Chief Minister Sosibius gazed at the platform of the moving chariot. His head rocked as he balanced and fought through levels of negative emotions. By restricting his view, the General cut out the landscape and focused on finding a solution. While he wanted to blame Major Midhat for the loss, in reality, the defeat of the Army of the Pharaoh landed on his shoulders.

"Chief Minister," his driver called. When Sosibius failed to reply, he suggested. "Chief Minister, you want to see this."

The driver had been his man for years and knew better than to interrupt the General during a session of meditation. Curious more than irritated, Sosibius gazed over the heads of the horses.

"Where did they come from?" he whispered before realizing the truth. A glimpse back showed one rider, trotting for the low hills. On either side of Major Midhat, groups of cooks jogged towards the high ground. Then the General raised his eyes and strained to see the line of rebel warriors he assured were following. Yet, no matter how much he studied the horizon, he couldn't locate the enemy.

Wondering what Midhat planned, he addressed the driver. "Get me to the top of that hill, fast."

When the chariot passed through the stacked ranks, he understood the illusion. Only two lines of men occupied the crest of the hill. But they were staggered, making it appear that rows of spearmen stretched behind them. Plus, the front rank wore the bronze armor of palace guards, giving them a formidable appearance.

***

When Farouk Midhat reached the crest, the Major slowed just long enough to say, "General, please get your chariot off the crest of the hill. You're ruining the illusion."

Farouk walked his horse down the backside of the hill. In a moment, he was dismounted and out of sight from anyone approaching the battle line. Mercenary Captains rushed to consult with the Major as did the wounded Lieutenant.

"You heard the Major," Sosibius instructed his drive. "Apparently, we're ruining the illusion."

"Yes, sir," the driver responded.

He snapped the reins and a moment later, the rig vanished behind the hills.

***

Sosibius stepped off his chariot and walked towards Major Midhat. Seeing the Chief Minister approaching, Farouk stopped talking with the five commanders and Lieutenant Masuda.

"Continue, Major," Sosibius encouraged.

"Thank you, sir," Farouk answered before returning to the unit Captains. "If we get a breach, pull your second line,

290

and seal the gap. The rebels shouldn't get here until late today or late tomorrow."

"I bet not at all," an Athenian ventured.

"How so, Captain?" Sosibius inquired.

"General, a man with a full belly after being hungry wants to relax and allow the food to digest," he replied. "Add a healthy dose of wine and he'll sleep for two days. None of that, General, makes a man want to shake off the luxury and charge into battle."

"You really think this is over?" Sosibius asked.

"Sir, with as much food as we left the rebels, most will stop the attack to eat," Farouk described. "And while they eat, they'll begin finding the wineskins and beer tubs I left in the pavilions. I don't know a spearman alive who would rather fight than eat and drink."

"Neither do I, Major Midhat," Sosibius agreed. "How long before, we're sure?"

"I have scouts posted and watching them," Farouk stated. "If they come, we'll fight. If they retreat south, we'll rejoice."

"That's the best plan I've heard all week," Chief Minister Sosibius announced. "When do we eat?"

Lieutenant Masuda pulled a hard biscuit and a strip of dried meat from a pouch. He offered them to the General with an explanation, "With apologies, sir. But they are the only things on the menu."

### Chapter 29 – A Red Legion Cape

*Thanatos' Chariot* rowed into the harbor of Alexandria.

"I can't see an empty segment of beach," Rodas complained.

Typically, middays provided an abundance of landing sites. The outgoing merchant ships having already left for their next port of call, and those transports inbound were still far out at sea. The problem revolved around the recall of the Egyptian fleets. Warships filled the beaches, making dry landing places a rarity.

"Cruise around," Jace suggested. "We're looking for *Ra's Brightness*."

"Will they give me a landing site?" Rodas asked.

"I don't know for sure," Jace told him, "but they might."

They rowed some and drifted, then rowed some more, and drifted a few lengths.

"Maybe over in the Great Harbor," Jace recommended.

"That's home to the Pharoah's fleet and it's always crowded," Rodas warned. "Besides, it's a long sail and another long row into the harbor."

"I could go over the side with Diceärch," Jace offered. "We could wade to shore."

"Or I could swallow my pride and dock at the temple area," Rodas proposed.

"Hold on," Jace inquired. "You can dock at the temple beach?"

As soon as Rodas said it, Jace looked at Diceärch. From a temple area the situation could go in several directions. The mad pirate could have an episode where he condemns temples and priests, which would lead to him being taken from Jace and arrested by temple guards. Or the insane pirate could scream to priests that he was a free man being held against his will by the Archer. Which would lead to Jace being separated from Diceärch, allowing the pirate to escape into the busiest seaport in the world. Or...Jace stopped considering alternatives.

*"The best solution to any problem is the simplest,"* Master Archer Zarek Mikolas taught. *"Look for the answer in repeated words or actions as you explore different outcomes."*

"Thank you, Master Mikolas," Jace whispered. Next, he addressed the coastal trader. "If you can get access to a temple beach, do it."

Rodas turned *Thanatos' Chariot,* and they rowed for a small beach where the causeway from the lighthouse met the mainland. Two priests attempted to wave them away.

"In the name of the Benefactor Goddess Berenice," Rodas called to them as the ship backed towards the beach. "I claim a visit with the Prize-Bearer, Priestess of Berenice."

"By what right?" one of the priests asked.

"I am Rodas of Haîma, by her named, by her blessed," the trader answered.

One priest ran down and waded into the tide to help push the ship onto the beach. The other ran for a temple complex.

"Very convenient," Jace remarked.

"For you, Archer. Now I have to sit through ceremonies and eat with priestesses and priests for the next two days," Rodas complained. "I hope you appreciate my sacrifice."

"Indeed, I do," Jace confirmed. He wrapped a cloth around Diceärch's head and tied the gag. After that, he dropped a cloth pouch over the pirate's head and announced. "Sometimes he spits and bites. He is quite insane."

"Precautions are required," Rodas said validating the claim.

The theme that repeated while Jace considered the situation all boiled down to keeping Diceärch from talking. Muffled and blinded, the pirate wouldn't be causing any trouble for the Archer. Trouble would come from a different direction.

*** 

Two men, lashed together with a rope, one with a bag over his head and the other guiding them both, struggled through the crowd. Between rowers, sailors, soldiers, and spearmen, Alexandria appeared to be a city under siege. Yet for all the weapons and manpower, no enemy camped outside the gates. Nor did a foreign fleet lurk over the horizon.

It was a relief for the Archer when they reached the palace. The Pharaoh's Palace radiated the power of the ruler of Egypt for all who witnessed the stonework. They took the narrow walkway towards the harbor with the water on one side and the massive wall on the other.

At the end, near the harbor, Jace approached the entrance and addressed a pair of palace guards, "I'm here to see Captain Midhat."

"The ring officer hasn't returned," one of the guards told Jace. "And neither have any of his officers."

People passed them and entered the palace without being challenged. Jace ignored the civilians, figuring they had business in the palace.

"He hasn't returned from lunch or an engagement?" Jace asked.

"From Giza," the other guard informed him. "The last anyone heard, Captain Midhat and Chief Minister Sosibius were south of Giza, commanding the rear defense."

"When was that?" Jace inquired. He needed somewhere to stash Dicearch while he searched for Admiral Radames. Then he remembered the man who cared for the Ring Commander's weapons. "I need to speak to the Ring armorer."

"If you know where the armory is located," the first guard instructed, "go ahead."

Jace pulled the rope to get Dicearch moving. After a pace, Jace put out a hand and stopped the pirate.

"Hold," he ordered before asking the guards. "Aren't you going to check with an officer before letting me in the palace."

"No more than we do with them," the guard said, referring to four men who strolled through the portal. "The city is an armed encampment. We have thousands of soldiers, spearmen, and sailors in the streets. What rebel would want to face them?"

"You act like the Ring is still in effect?" Jace suggested to the guards.

The job of combing out threats before they reached the palace happened mostly in secret. One issue with unheralded success, few appreciated the dangers and subversive plots stopped in their infancies. The guard confirmed the idea with his next words.

"Who needs the ring," he bragged. "If anyone gets in and causes trouble, one of us will give him a taste of our steel."

Jace tugged the rope, and the Archer and pirate took a step.

"Six days," the guard stated.

"Six days what?" Jace asked.

"It's been six days since the retreating command staff saw Captain Midhat and Chief Minister Sosibius," the guard informed Jace. "The last report by the scouts told us they were outnumbered by rebel spearman."

The palace, Jace pondered, was missing the lowest level of protection from the outer ring and the very pinnacle of the Pharoah's security in the person of the Chief Minister. Did the middle levels, the palace guards, and the personal guards, realize the danger?"

Having no answer, the Archer pulled the pirate forward, and they walked into the palace of Lord Ptolemy IV.

***

As they strolled down the corridor, Jace recalled his earlier impression. The long entrance was a kill zone for invaders. But what if the invaders weren't an army but an assassin or two?

"No one is paying you to review their security procedures," the Archer reminded himself.

Disregarding the mental exercise, he located the doorway and pushed Diceärch through. In the outer office of the Ring officer, Jace located the armorer.

"Agent Kasia. You were right," the armorer admitted. "The Pharoah's expedition failed to stomp out the rebellion. And I'm sad to tell you, Captain Midhat hasn't returned, yet. But I hold out hope."

"I take no joy in being right," Jace told him. "This prisoner has to be kept isolated. And I need to stash him somewhere for the night."

The armorer eyed the hood and leaned back.

"He's not sick," Jace assured the armorer. "But he spits, and I find the hood spares me from the nasty habit."

"There's a small closet in Captain Midhat's office," the armorer suggested. "It's where he kept the funds for Ring Command."

"How small?"

"You can duck and walk in, but you can't stretch out on the floor," the armorer answered. "But you can sit."

Jace urged Diceärch forward. They entered Midhat's office and Jace located the small door. He opened it, untied the pirate's arms, and pulled off the hood.

"Looks solid enough," he told the pirate. "If you behave, I'll feed you a meal of beef with wine for breakfast."

"Suppose you don't return?" Diceärch sneered.

"Then someone in a week," Jace proposed while shoving the pirate into the space, "will locate your body by the smell."

After closing and barring the closet door, Jace moved to the exit. He stepped into the doorway, paused, and looked across the armory at a familiar face. Then smoothly, so as not to draw attention to himself, the Archer slipped to the side.

Gently, as if a leaf blown by a breeze, he moved out of Sergeant Jabari's field of vision.

***

The rebel Sergeant looked different in the cape of an Egyptian officer. But the effect of him being a nobleman was spoiled by the posture of a brawler. Then again, few would question the Captain as war saw the promotion of rough men to elevated positions. Sergeant Jabari had the look of that kind of wartime leader. Now dressed as an Egyptian Captain, Jabari spoke with the Armorer.

If Jace carried a blade bigger he might have confronted Jabari. But a long-bladed sword gave all the advantages to the swordsman when dueling against a thin-bladed skinning knife. Jace waited until the exterior door closed before rushing to the Armorer.

"Who was that?" he inquired, not willing to give away the reason for asking. "Is he a Ring agent?"

"I've never seen the man before," the Armorer told Jace. "He was looking for the office of Major Glaucus. He claimed to be assigned to the palace guards, but that's not possible."

"Why?" Jace questioned.

"Because the palace guards are chosen for their looks and height more than their fighting ability. And that Captain doesn't meet the first requirement."

"Where is Major Glaucus' officer," Jace asked. Then he looked down at his woolen workman's clothing. "Do you have something more formal I can wear?"

"Agent Kasia, I have just the gear for a Latian like yourself," the Armorer assured Jace.

***

For all the appearance of security, the hallways of the palace were crowded: Vendors delivering goods, porters hauling items, plus relatives and friends of the Ptolemies visiting. As well, people begging favors from the government, and foreign dignitaries were there to court Ministers of Egypt. They walked the corridors of the fortified building traveling from one area to another in random patterns. In that cluster of bodies, an Egyptian Captain, even a false one, went unnoticed.

Real security for the royal family came from a personal guard positioned in front of every private suite. While the guard prevented unwanted intrusion into the family's area, his presence also identified the rooms of important people.

Jace Kasia quick-marched down the hallway, his red Legion cape billowing behind him. The breast plate was tight across his archer's chest and because of that, he passed on the back plate. But the front armor, the Centurion helmet tucked under his left arm, the red cape, the gladius at his hip, and the hobnailed boots on his feet completed the illusion of a military diplomat from the Roman Republic.

Jace paused at an intersection. The carved beams of the interior structure displayed brilliant colors. He admired the craftsmanship of the woodwork while deciding if he should follow the crowd deeper into the third floor or take a side corridor.

"What are you doing here, Sergeant Jabari?" the Archer whispered. "Spy or assassin, what are you today?"

A spy would stay in the crowded hallway as cover, while an assassin would seek his victim in an empty environment. For Jace, the most profitable outcome would be from stopping an assassination. Following the code to make a profit, the Archer stepped out of the crowd and made his way to the empty corridor.

*** 

The answer hit him before he noticed the boots and legs of a downed man. As Jace raced to the body, the sharp aroma of burning wood heightened. The personal guard had fallen on the shaft of his spear and Jabari left it there. It didn't explain the rebel Sergeant's mission, but leaving the weapon let Jace know the man didn't intend to fight.

Smoke poured out from under the closed door. Farther along the corridor, smoke drifted from under another door. No smoke came from the door at the end of the corridor. Thinking he'd catch up with the assassin at the end of the hallway, Jace stepped over the dead guard.

"Help. Help us," a voice creaking with age called from inside the room. Coughing interrupted the plea before the man restated. "Help us."

Smoke billowing from under the door let Jace know the room lacked air. Also, he had no doubt flames crawled over the ceiling and walls and possibly covered the floor. To open the door and enter the room meant death.

Except, the man calling for help happened to be Eratosthenes of Cyrene. The head librarian for the Library of Alexandria, tutor to the Pharoh's children, and a man who covered for Jace after the Archer killed two Cilician pirates in an alleyway.

"Help us," came weaker as Eratosthenes' voice dissolved into a fit of coughing.

"Debts come in many forms," Jace said while unsnapping the catch on the cape. Next, he whipped the red cloth in the air and let it settle over his head. "Let's hope this works and we don't meet on the road to Hades."

***

Jace Kasia flung the door open and raced into the smokey room. Flames roared over his head. As if a bug had absentmindedly crawled under a pyramid of firewood, the heat radiated downward. Taking the hint, Jace stooped.

A burning couch and three flaming chairs blocked his way. The thick sole of his hobnailed boot protected Jace's foot when he kicked a path through the flaming barrier. He moved deeper into the room.

"Help. Help," drifted through the crackling of burning timber. Nearly spent, the man's strength ebbed from the coughing and the panic. And most telling, his will to fight drained away with a loss of faith in being rescued.

Through the smoke, Jace located a dark shape. Moving fast, he came upon Eratosthenes.

Huddled against the wall, and crying, Eratosthenes of Cyrene cradled a boy of five or six. His arms protected the small body from the flames.

"Librarian, we should go," Jace said.

Eratosthenes didn't know someone spoke to him or he no longer believed in salvation. He remained tucked around the boy. His breaths came in the quick, sharp intakes of an injured animal about to expire.

Squatting, Jace placed an arm over the shoulders of the scholar.

"We should go," Jace urged.

301

With tears rolling down his cheeks, the head Librarian lifted his face to Jace. After blinking away the moisture, he sighed, "Kasia of Crete, what are you doing here?"

"About to burn up, if we don't hurry," Jace answered. "Is there any water nearby?"

"For washing or for drinking?" Eratosthenes inquired.

When faced with a crisis, the mind of an inexperienced person would revert to a routine and a place where they were most comfortable. A priest might pray when attacked by a robber rather than fight. A vender would attempt to bargain with a vicious gang instead of handing over his coin purse. And a philosopher of geography, who created the first globe of the world, would require precision in his speech.

"Water for both drinking and for washing, please," Jace said as calmly as the situation warranted.

"In the corner," Eratosthenes directed.

The Archer dashed to the corner and found two amphorae of water. After dumping his chest plate, Jace snapped the cape from over his head. He tipped the vessel and soaked the cloth in water. Although the top of the fabric steamed, underneath it remained cool.

Back at Eratosthenes, the Archer squatted, slid his arms under the Librarian and lifted both the man and the boy. When Jace curled them against his chest, they benefited from his years of pulling a bowstring.

From under the wet cape, Jace ordered, "Hold on."

"With all of my might," Eratosthenes promised.

Jace ducked, placing his head over the Librarian, and powered through the smoke, the burning timbers, and the falling embers. At the door, he staggered under the load. Hands reached out and took the man and the boy from his arms.

*** 

Throwing off the hot, steaming red Legion cape, Jace glanced around. He expected to be the center of attention. Humbled but glad to help, he looked for recognition. But no one paid attention to Eratosthenes of Cyrene or to Jace Kasia. Everyone was fawning over the boy.

"Who is he?" Jace asked the Librarian.

"That boy, Kasia of Crete," Eratosthenes explained, "is Ptolemy Epiphanes, the next Pharoah of Egypt. After, of course, the passing of his father, Lord Ptolemy IV."

## Chapter 30 – To the Republic Bound

There were rumors, then again, there were always rumors.

"Lord Ptolemy is dead," one crowd whispered, while others were more specific. "He died in the fire."

Jace didn't know and he didn't care. What interested the Archer was the procession. First came the priests of the great King Alexander, then priests of the Ptolemy Cult, followed by young unmarried women to honor Arsinoe III, an older Queen. Next the Gift-Bearer, representing Berenice the last Queen Mother, marched beside Rodas of Haîma.

From beside the Priestess of Berenice, Rodas smiled and saluted Jace. His ordeal of dining with priests and priestesses didn't seem to dampen the old Archer's spirits.

Behind the first four elements, a cart surrounded by city guardsmen rolled by. On the bed of the cart, they'd placed a cage. In the cage, Dicearch hissed and spit out curses towards priests, priestesses, shrines, temples, and every God or Goddess he could think to insult. From the man's energetic condemnations, his belly was full and his anger at the Gods in full boil. Jace had advised the Temple of Alexander not to overfeed Dicearch.

The reason for the extra guards had to do with the tirades. But the guardsmen weren't there to protect the public from a single pirate. They were on duty to protect Dicearch from an outraged public. Worried about the prisoner's safety, the temples wanted to extract the revenge, and not leave it up to a mob.

After the prisoner cart went by, priests from minor temples walked up the boulevard. The ceremonial parade stretched four blocks and moved slowly. Boredom settled in after the cart went by.

"Will you be staying in Alexandria?" Farouk Midhat asked from behind.

"I don't think so, Colonel Midhat," Jace answered. "Too many people dying. Even for a Cretan Archer."

When Major Midhat and Chief Minister Sosibius arrived in Alexandria, they found the royal living quarters burned and charred, and the bodies of servants being embalmed.

At midday, Major Glaucus and Colonel Kyros were weighed down with rocks, rowed out to the deepest part of the harbor, and shoved overboard. That afternoon, Farouk

Midhat received a promotion and accepted responsibility for the defense of the palace.

"Will you at least stay for the execution?" Midhat inquired. "You did capture Diceärch."

"Not all of it," Jace said. "Senior Tribune Centho is rowing out with his squadron at midday."

"Then let's get you to an area where you can watch and still make an escape unobserved."

***

They hiked to an open area by a canal fed from the Nile. In the center of the field, two posts had been sunk into the earth. Midhat guided Jace to three wagons placed on one side.

"The temples voted, and they decided on the manner of execution," Midhat explained. He pulled out a coin pouch and balanced it on the palm of his hand. "Climb up on a wagon and watch. When you're ready, jump off the backside and go. Take this purse of gold coins as our gratitude for saving Pharoah Ptolemy IV, and Prince Ptolemy V from the fire."

Jace had only saved the Prince and the Librarian. He started to correct the Colonel, when Midhat grabbed the Archer's hand. Farouk pressed the purse into his palm. At that moment, Jace realized the rumors of the Pharaoh's death were true.

"Perhaps, you were overcome by smoke and don't recall all the details," Colonel Midhat suggested.

Jace closed his hand on the coins and swallowed. In hindsight, leaving Alexandria turned out to be a grand idea.

If he stayed, someone might decide a dead Archer was preferable to a bribed one for keeping a state secret.

"It's been an honor serving you, Colonel," Jace stated. "I'll pray to the Gods for a quick recovery for the Pharoah and his son."

"I'm sure he'll appreciate the sentiment," Farouk Midhat affirmed. "Pay attention to what happens to an enemy of Egypt, Archer Kasia. I think you'll find it instructional."

Colonel Midhat turned and marched towards the palace. As the officer walked away, in his heart, Jace reconfirmed his plans to leave the city.

"Let's see what lesson I need to learn," Jace remarked.

He leaped onto the wagon and found piles of a substance covered by linen sheets. The same linen sheets covered the same type of load in the other two wagons.

*\*\*

The cart rolled to the center of the field and the crowd gathered around the perimeter. City guardsmen pulled Diceärch from the cage and guided him to the posts.

"The Gods are a lie," he screamed. "You are fooling yourself if you think the priests speak for them. Vile men of temples lie. The Gods lie. And you like sheep follow their rituals."

A young priest climbed to the wagon bed and Jace asked, "Why do you allow him to spew his blasphemy?"

"He'll stop soon," the priest assured Jace.

The priest looked to the other wagons, waiting. In the field, Diceärch was stripped naked, and his arms spread and tied to the posts. What form of punishment Jace had no idea. But he knew humiliation wouldn't work on the pirate.

To prove it, the crowd hissed, snickered, and jeered at the pirate. Dicearch laughed at their collective opinion of him. Then he returned to his sermon.

"You give and the priests take," he bellowed. "Do they ever give back. Do the Gods ever deliver anything except misery?"

While he prattled on, Agathocles, Head Priest of the cult of the Great King Alexander, strutted to the doomed man.

"Gag him," Agathocles ordered a guardsman. Once only mumbles came from Dicearch, the Head Priest raised his arms and exclaimed. "I allowed the filthy pirate to speak. I let his own words condemn him for his crimes against men, priests, and the Gods. Is there anyone who will stand and defend the sacrilege? The wickedness? His desecration of shrines and temples? Speak now. But if you will save this creature, you must speak louder than the pirate's own words."

The crowd grew silent. Most were afraid to speak lest they be singled out as a defender of the pirate.

Moments later, Agathocles pointed to the wagons and snapped his fingers.

"Scour him to death," he ordered.

The linen sheets were removed to expose hand sized pieces of pumice. Priests from every temple walked up, grabbed a piece of the rough mineral, and in a procession, glided to the prisoner.

Then, one at a time, they scraped skin from his body with the pumice stone. At first, the scratches resembled claw marks from a kitten. But as the line of priests circled for another pass, the wounds grew deeper and more painful.

"Ungag him," Agathocles instructed. "Let's hear his blasphemy now."

Having seen enough of what happens to a person who drew the wrath of Egypt, Jace leaped from the back of the wagon. As he hurried towards the harbor, behind him, the gag was pulled, and in a voice as raw as his flesh, Diceärch of Aetolia screamed.

***

With the hot Egyptian sun directly overhead, the three Roman warships rowed out of the harbor of Alexandria. On the steering deck of the led ship, Jace stood beside Senior Tribune Centho.

"What's our route, sir?" Jace inquired.

"We'll sail along the coast than head north to Crete," Centho answered. "From there, we'll sail to Aetolia. Farther up the Greek coast, we'll track west to the Republic. We should be home in sixteen days. You can catch a ship to Ostia and from there one to Iberia."

Jace marveled at the Senior Tribune's ability to judge the travel time over such a great distance. Two weeks seemed both a long duration, and yet, a relatively short number of days to make the passage.

"Senior Tribune, is there a chance to make port at Phalasarna on Crete?" Jace inquired. "I know people at the Archers' Academy and can make introductions."

"You certainly came through in Alexandria," Centho granted. "Although it would have been good to meet the Pharoah, having dinner with Colonel Midhat and Chief Minister Sosibius will lend authority to my report."

"It was my pleasure, sir," Jace acknowledged.

\*\*\*

The stop at the Cretan Agoge was more than a social call. In his bundles and under his tunic, Jace had stashed a considerable number of coins. Weight alone demanded that the Archer put some of them in a safe place. And to pay a fee to the Archon of Phalasarna for the safe keeping of the rest was a cheap solution.

"I don't see any problem with a diplomatic stop at Phalasarna," Centho agreed. "After that, we'll be to the Republic bound without delay."

"It'll be good to be home," Jace said.

Home meant many things to different people. For some it was a destination and for others a place to touch before moving onward. Tribune Kasia referred to visiting Crete as being home while Senior Tribune Centho understood Jace's remark to be an anticipation of returning to the Roman Republic. Both were right in their own way.

\*\*\*

After a layover at Phalasarna, the squadron of three-bankers sailed for Aetolia. As the ships voyaged northward, Jace unrolled a scroll and re-read the letter from his cousin.

*Lucius Jace Romiliia Otacilia Kasia*

*Citizen of the Roman Republic, Legion Officer, Prince of the Hirpini Tribe, Citizen of the Isla of Crete, and Cretan Archer,*

*When you receive this letter, travel as soon as possible to Rome. Cornelius Scipio is leaving Iberia and returning to the Capital. He has no idea how, but after the limitations of being an Iberian General, he swears he will find a way to become a General of the Republic.*

*After leaving behind or retiring his Iberian Legions, the General will recruit and build new Legions. He needs an expert trainer. Especially someone who can untangle the mystery of how to defeat war elephants. For this contract, he will give you any position needed and any pay scale you require.*

*Looking forward to seeing you,*

*Bodyguard and confidante for Cornelius Scipio, Optio of Legions, War Chief of the Hirpini Tribe, and your cousin, Sidia Decimia*

"I'm on the way Sidia," Jace whispered before rolling the scroll.

He was glad Senior Tribune Centho was occupied with the navigators. The last thing Jace wanted was to spend the rest of the voyage explaining all his names and affiliations.

*\*\*\**

Despite a storm, they reached the mainland and tracked northward along the coast. Two days into their sail around Aetolia they encountered another trio of Roman triremes. The six warships beached to share a meal, stories, and for Centho to get news from the Republic.

"Something big is happening on Silicia," the Senior Tribune from the other squadron mentioned.

"How so?" Centho inquired.

"Consul Dives is battling in the Senate for Legions and funding for an expedition to Africia," the naval staff officer answered. "His Co-consul has sent out recruiters to enlist Legionaries to fill four Legions."

"It sounds like an invasion of Carthage," Centho offered.

"We're not sure. It could be war against the Numidians," the Senior Tribune countered. "They turned down Consul Scipio when he asked for a treaty."

"Excuse me, sir," Jace interrupted. "Consul Scipio?"

"Yes, Cornelius Scipio was elected Consul when he returned from Iberia," the naval officer replied.

"I guess you won't be traveling to Iberia, Tribune Romiliia," Centho ventured. "But you might be out of a job. If so, we can always use a good officer in the eastern fleet."

"I don't know about my previous position," Jace admitted. "But I know this. It is Consul Scipio's sworn oath to drive Hannibal from the Republic. With General Cornelius Scipio in charge, sirs, you can be assured, the Legions will march on Carthage."

"How can you be so sure?" Centho inquired.

"Because, I am the General's Tribune," Jace replied.

## Chapter 31 – Elephant Hunters

The Legionary stumbled as the staff officer walked him sideways.

"Don't cross your legs," the Tribune instructed. "Don't cross your legs and your legs won't cross you up. Take wide side steps."

After crabbing past three men in the front rank, the officer released the shield and ran back to face another Legionary.

"Move with me," he directed while grabbing the shield.

"Get off my scutum," the Legionary declared. He rocked the shield, trying to dislodge the staff officer's hands. "I already know how to walk."

From the corner of his eye, the Tribune noticed the Centurion. The combat officer was heading their way, probably to discipline the Legionary for insubordination.

"Centurion. You take care of that side and I'll handle this one."

"Yes, sir," the combat officer acknowledged, although he didn't sound convinced.

"The details of this movement require coordinated and choreographed steps," Tribune Kasia told the infantryman. "If anyone is out of position, it ruins the dance."

"We're fighters, not entertainers," the Legionary scoffed. "Who cares about a dance?"

Tribune Kasia ducked and flowed around the shield. Once behind the scutum, he wrapped his arms around the infantryman's hips and settled a shoulder into the man's midsection. Driving with his legs, Jace Kasia lifted. As if throwing a sack of grain, he tossed the Legionary up and over his shoulder. Flipping in the air, the Legionary landed on his back. Tribune Kasia spun and kicked the infantryman between the legs.

\*\*\*

Curled up on his side, the obstinate Legionary howled in pain.

312

"You didn't need to do that, sir," an Optio informed Jace. "I could have handled him."

"In Crete, where I trained," Jace explained, "a dance meant a coordinated movement or a fight. Seeing as the Legionary chose not to move, that left fighting."

"How was I supposed to know that sir?" the injured infantryman asked.

"You can't know your enemy's every move," Jace exclaimed so the nearby squads could hear. "But you can know your movements well enough to counter any surprises the enemy throws at you."

"Like fighting instead of walking, sir?" another infantryman inquired.

"Exactly," Jace confirmed.

"Century, get into your Maniple ranks," the Optio ordered. "This time, everyone does the drill. Or I will assign you the dirtiest and nastiest detail I can think of. Perhaps, I'll have you dig our latrines deeper, overnight. Rah?"

"Rah, Optio," the eighty heavy infantrymen answered.

\*\*\*

Tribune Kasia marched to the front of the three-row Maniple formation.

"Let me restate," he proposed, "you can tell always tell where along your combat line a war elephant will hit your shields."

"How can we tell, Tribune?" the Corporal of the Century asked.

"The fact is no warrior or soldier runs in front of a charging war elephant," Jace told him. "A trip would end

313

badly. That leaves you with a clear view of the bronze tusks. Elephant fighting is the name of this drill."

"We can't fight an elephant," a Legionary suggested. "Not ten or even fifteen of us, sir."

"You're correct," Jace confirmed. "But we can get out of the elephant's way and let the animal pass. Then close the door before the enemy's assault force turns the battle into a melee. Let's imagine a war elephant coming at your Maniple."

Jace moved to the hurting Legionary and put his hand on the man's shield. This time, the infantryman didn't resist. Jace's other hand rested on the adjacent shield.

The Tribune instructed, "You in the center will hold your positions. On the right, two of you angle backwards, and move in behind the second row. And on my left, you two do the same but to your left. On the second row, you two fall back to your left and the other pair to the right. Third row, where do you go?"

"We angle back and tuck in behind the fifth row," the two pairs answered.

Only six infantrymen remained in the path of the imaginary elephant. Jace used a hand to indicate the rear of the formation.

"You six are my elephant fighters. Raise up your shields, scream, and draw the attention of the elephant and its rider. Once the elephant sees you, jog to the back. That will lure the beast down the center of our kill zone," Jace stated. The injured Legionary grunted in pain as he ran for the back of the formation. Once the six elephant fighters were clear, Jace directed. "Men at the ends of each row, face inward, and brace."

The walk-through ended with a fifteen-foot hole in the Legion formation, secured by interlocking shields on both sides.

***

On the third demonstration of elephant fighting, an entourage trotted up to the Century.

Jace saluted, and greeted Cornelius, "Good morning, Consul Scipio."

"Some of the advisers are puzzled by the exercise," Cornelius mentioned. "What's the philosophy behind the drill?"

"Sir, it should allow our Legions to defend against war elephants," Jace replied. "In Egypt, they used a version of the drill to defeat war chariots. But we're still working out a few problems."

"Then we don't know if all this training will accomplish anything," a Senate advisor suggested. "Beyond getting good Latin men killed."

"For sure, sir, both good and bad men will die," Jace confirmed. "After all, it is war."

A breeze blew inland from the sea, bringing coolness to the late morning. By evening, the air from the mountains would rush down from the heights, reversing the air current.

Resembling the changing winds on the Island of Sicilia, the Senate advisor huffed his displeasure, shifted from Kasia, and addressed Scipio, "Planning to lose is a bit harsh, don't you think?"

"Harsh, adviser, is an uncontrolled breach in our Maniple," Cornelius cautioned, "and dead Legionaries hanging on the tusks of Carthaginian war elephants."

"If you can't stop his elephants," the advisor pushed back, "how do you plan to defeat Hannibal?"

Consul/General Scipio looked in the direction of Jace Kasia and declared, "I'm confident that my Tribune will figure it out."

**The End**

Sample of the next book in the series:

## When War Gods Battle

*A Legion Legacy* series
Book #9

## Chapter 000 - An Unsatisfactory Victory

The flap on the tent unsealed and the storm slapped it
back where the flap and the wet goat hide stuck together.
For a moment, the inside of the tent took the full impact of
the tempest. Junior staff officers bent to collect fallen pieces
of parchment, while one rushed to close the errant flap. But
he stopped at the entrance when along with the wind and
the rain, King Masinissa stomped in. Leaving muddy
footprints across the General's floor, the ruler and
commander of the light cavalry pointed back at the splatters
of wet dirt.

"That," the King of Western Numidia shouted, "is
what's left of the defenders of Carthage."

"Can you be a little more exact in your exuberance?"
Cornelius requested.

He eyed the mud on his polished wooden flooring. It
would have to be scrubbed before the servants loaded the
pieces in a wagon. For all the big issues Cornelius delt with
on the expedition, he found himself irritated by little things,
like mud on his floor. But he needed the Numidia cavalry
and didn't say anything.

"You've beaten them, General Scipio," Masinissa exclaimed. "We've beaten them. Carthage will come begging to you for a treaty."

"I'm not sure I can accept a treaty," Cornelius admitted. "Hannibal is still on Republic soil."

"But now he'll be a man without a country," Masinissa stated. "One by one, his allies will desert him, until his army crumbles, and he's forced into exile."

Cornelius lifted his chin and stared at the ceiling of the tent. As if he watched a sail at sea, the tent material rippled with the wind.

"I'll reserve judgement until I see the offer from Carthage," he stated.

Then General Cornelius Scipio, commander of Roman Legions in Africia and Sicilia, and from all reports, the victor over Carthage, looked down. And despite the honors to come, he frowned in displeasure at the mud on his floor.

End of the sample

### A note from J. Clifton Slater

Thank you for reading *The General's Tribune*. This is the 8th book in the *A Legion Archer* series. When combined with the *Clay Warrior Stories* series, it becomes the 27th book dealing with the Punic Wars. If you've read them all, I congratulate you. Your confidence in me to deliver a compelling story set in actual history warms my heart and challenges me to live up to your trust.

***

And now let's separate fiction from history. We'll start with the sea lanes to Rome from the east and from the west.

*The Cyclades*

The Cyclades islands in the Aegean Sea were a wealth of ores for ancient civilizations. Each island offered different mixtures of elements. Copper, iron, silver, gold, pumice stone, plus other minerals were harvested by miners throughout the ages.

*Serifos Island*

Serifos sits on the western edge of the Cyclades. One reason I started the book on this island is the White Tower. A Hellenistic marble watchtower built in the 3rd Century B.C., displays graphically the wealth of the Cyclades. Today the tower has been partially rebuilt and can be found on the road a mile and a half northeast from the town of Megalo Livadi on Serifos.

*Cyclops' Cave*

The cave is an eroded depression in the rock formation on the shoreline downhill from the White Tower. About a mile west from Paralia on Serifos Island, I used the cave as a searchable location for the introduction of the pirate, Diceärch from Aetolia. Cyclops means 'water fleas' which tells us the cave in antiquity had a tidal pool at the bottom for the tiny aquatic crustaceans.

*Diceärch from Aetolia*

A short note in the writings of Historian Polybius mentioned Dicaearchus of Aetolia. Diceärch is the Greek spelling and the easiest form for me to write and reader to read. Diceärch as a pirate worked under Philip V of Macedonia from 205 – 196 B.C. We know he left two altars when he landed. One to *Asebeia* meaning impiety or blasphemy and a second altar to *Paranomia*, meaning

319

lawlessness or self-delusion. In 196 B.C., Diceärch was captured by the Egyptians, put on a rack, and scoured to death. Although we don't have records, in order to earn such a cruel death, we can assume Diceärch committed some very evil acts.

*Goddess Cybele (cyb-e-lee)*

Prophecies are difficult for historical fiction writers to decipher. In one version the words are clear and give specific instructions. On the other hand, they typically are muddled, leaving much to be interpreted.

I need to assign motivations to characters' actions but when the actions are arrived at by a committee reading from an arcane book, it presents a problem.

The Sibylline Books, written by the Sibylline oracles around 520 B.C., were offered to the last King of Rome. Tarquinius Superbus purchased three of the nine original books of prophecies. The other six were burned to spite the King's refusal to buy them at a decent price. And the books were lost and replaced later during the Roman Empire, leaving us without a sample of the original as a guide.

When Romans experienced bad omens in 206 B.C., the ten caretakers of the three manuscripts consulted the Sibylline Books and somehow arrived at the idea to go East, find a Protective Mother Goddess, and bring her back to Rome. In *The General's Tribune*, I assumed the Senate and people of Rome didn't know Cybele when her black, spiky, meteorite stone, arrived in Rome.

Along with the Goddess Cybele, Proconsul Valerius Laevinus returned to Rome with a group of her priests, Galli. Loud fanatics, they went against the Latin practice of ritualistic prayers and regimented rituals. The Galli must have shocked the populace for a number of reasons. They wore bright saffron robes, played cymbals, pipes, and tambourines while they sang. And to prove their commitment to Cybele, each Gallus carried the same knife he used to perform self-castration. That was surely a tough job requirement. To counter the neutering of young Latin men, the Senate passed a law forbidding Romans from becoming priests of Cybele. Except for the Head Priest of her Temple, and he need not be castrated.

*Ten Days to Ostia*

Based on a description by Historian Livy about distances traveled by ancient ships: From Messina in Sicily to Alexandria in Egypt is 830 miles and takes a ship 7 days.

I judged that from the Island of Serifos to Ostia, Italy is a thousand miles. And from Cartagena Bay, Spain to Ostia, Italy coming from the west is also about a thousand miles. In the story, this placed both Valerius Laevinus and Cornelius Scipio 10 days from Ostia at the beginning of the tale.

*Lynx*

The cats are solitary creatures, and almost exclusively, night hunters. Except for females, when they're training their young to hunt. Birthing from one to six kittens, the mother lynx teaches during the day. It's how she was spotted in the story. Along with history, I enjoy facts about nature, hopefully you do as well.

*Marcus Livius*

The Senate tried Marcus Livius in 219 B.C. for malfeasance concerning war spoils during a mission to Carthage. Convicted, he was stripped of his Consulship and promptly retired. At forty-five, he was recalled to the Senate and next elected as a Consul in 207 B.C. Along with his Co-consul, Claudius Nero, they defeated Hasdrubal Barca at the battle of Battle Metaurus. I have no reason to believe Tiberius Longus was at Livius' headquarters. But the tale Longus told about the Consul's past was accurate.

*Battle of Metaurus*

I shortened the battle to a single attack. In history, the Battle of Metaurus took place over three days with Hasdrubal clashing with the Legions of Marcus Livius before Nero's Legions arrived.

After running battles against Hannibal near Grumentum, Claudius Nero marched his Legions 290 miles north and joined with his Co-consul Marcus Livius at the Metauro River near the city of Senigallia. The interception of the couriers carrying the message from Hasdrubal to Hannibal happened down south by forces commanded by Tribune Caius Claudius. And Nero forwarded the message to the Senate. It was the Senate that sent Marcus Livius' Legions to block Hasdrubal's army. In *The General's Tribune*, I compressed the history and made Veturius Philo, who did become the Co-consul the next year, the focus of the revised story.

Arriving at night, Nero's Legions combined with Livius caught Hasdrubal Barca by surprise. Seeing the large force against him, Hasdrubal didn't fight that day. In the night, he attempted to locate a fording place to cross the Metauro River. His guides either couldn't find the crossing spot or they intentionally turned on the Carthaginian General. Livy said the guides found the shallow during the night, jumped in, and swam across, leaving Hasdrubal's army lost on the south side of the river. The next morning, Nero and Livius trapped Hannibal's brother on a plain between the river and the foothills.

Hasdrubal Barca was killed, his army defeated, and Claudius Nero had his head cut off. The head was carried south to Hannibal's stronghold where it was flung over the wall.

The next year, 206 B.C., Veturius Philo and Caecilius Metellus were elected Consuls of Rome. And while Philo stayed in the city to deal with the bad omens and manage the fear of Hannibal Barca, Metellus returned to Bruttium, where he kept Hannibal caged in the south.

*Greeting Cybele*

We don't know how the committee selected the people to greet Cybele, but we do know who was chosen. Cornelius Scipio Nasica was selected as the best man in Rome. For clarity, I renamed him 'Nasica Scipio' in the book. The son of deceased General Gnaeus Scipio, twenty-one-year-old Nasica was a cousin of Cornelius Scipio. For the female, they named Quinta Claudia the most virtuous maiden in Rome.

Research on Quinta Claudia varies from her being a maiden to her as a married woman. With the age for marriage at fourteen for males and twelve for females, I figured they would have chosen a young teenage girl as the most virtuous female. To ease modern sensibilities, let me report that history shows most women married in their late teens and the men in their early twenties despite the law.

When people accused Quinta Claudia of not being virtuous or chaste a legend began. On the trip up the Tiber, the Goddess Cybele's boat ran aground. In a display of faith, Quinta jumped out of the boat, took a rope, and towed the boat off the mud bank. Claiming divine intervention, the citizens of Rome understood Cybele had accepted Quinta and the rumors of her impurities were ignored. I hope you enjoyed my rendition of Quinta Claudia's fable.

*Cornelius Scipio*

After the Carthaginian forces were driven from Iberia, the Senate denied Cornelius Scipio a triumphant parade. Considering the treatment of Cornelius over the years, I could not understand his miraculous promotion to Consul at twenty-nine. With thirty-two being the age requirement for a Senator how did Cornelius ascend to the position? We know Rome had lost Consuls, officers, and leaders in the war with Hannibal. The shortage of qualified candidates allowed for Consuls under the traditional age of forty-two.

At first, I assumed Cornelius was made Consul to take advantage of his talents as a field commander. Yet one of the first arguments about his Consulship dealt with serving his term in Rome. The debate fell apart when it was pointed out that Crassus Dives, Cornelius Scipio's Co-consul, held the position of Pontifex Maximus. As the elected head of all the temples in Rome, it was against the law for the Pontifex Maximus to leave the city. Fighting to keep an underaged Consul Scipio in Rome and limit his growing fame made no sense. With the election of Consul Scipio and Consul Dives, the anti-Hellenistic crowd had already lost the argument.

Did Cybele's arrival have anything to do with Cornelius Scipio's election as a Consul of Rome? Probably not, but the job of a historical fiction author is to find motivations and link historical events. In *The General's Tribune*, the Goddess Cybele and Consul Cornelius Scipio were linked to create a story.

*Goddess Bellona*

The Temple of Bellona occupied a plot on the Field of Mars outside the Servian Wall. Between the defensive wall and the Tiber River on the western side, the land was designated as not belonging to the Republic. This allowed Senators and Consuls to meet with enemy diplomats while not allowing the ambassadors into the city.

As the Goddess of War, Bellona had followers from the Roman Kingdom to the Republic, and into the Imperial period. Called Bellonarii the priests of Bellona boasted scars on their arms and legs from ritualist cuts to honor the Goddess. Two festivals celebrated Bellona. A public festival happened in June. But on March 24th, her followers celebrated with the Day of Blood. By cutting and bleeding in the name of the Goddess Bellona, they showed respect and adoration.

*205 B.C.*

On March 15, the ides of March, Consul Veturius Philo presided over the election of Crassus Dives, the Pontifex Maximus, and Cornelius Scipio, recent Governor of Iberia, to Co-consuls of Rome. Detractors of Cornelius wanted to hold him in Rome under a barrage of political issues. But the Pontifex Maximus, by law, was forbidden to travel outside the city of Rome. Meaning, of the two Consuls, Cornelius Scipio would be the field commander of the Legions.

During the argument against Cornelius Scipio, Rome's first invasion of Carthage was mentioned. I wrote about the commander of that campaign, Marcus Regulus, in the *Clay Warrior Stories* series book #17 *Tribune's Oath*. The ill-fated invasion, 255 B.C., didn't go well for Carthage until the Carthaginian's hired a Spartan General. He took command and claimed victory for Carthage.

*\*\*\**

At this point in *The General's Tribune*, we'll shift the notes to Egypt and Jace Kasia.

*The Lighthouse of Alexandria*

Mostly the lighthouse is pictured as a three tiered, 330-foot or 101-meter, structure with a wide covered porch surrounding the base. I made two assumptions about this wonder of the ancient world.

Considering the nightly operations, the colonnade must have been more than decorative. It likely held an enormous amount of drying wood. To feed the furnace, they had to bring in lumber, probably from the regions we know today as Lebanon and Syria.

My other concept delt with the nature of humans. I couldn't find any references to a nightly street party. But with a bright light miraculously beaming out to sea, the citizens and sailors in Alexanderia probably gathered to watch the amazing light in the evenings. Mix the light with an audience, add beverages and food, and you have an ongoing lighthouse festival.

*The Rebellion in Egypt*

A rebellion materialized in 205 B.C. The leader, who took the name Horwennefer, would face off against an army of the Pharaoh at Luxor, then called Thebes. After defeating Ptolemy IV, Horwennefer declared himself Pharaoh and made Luxor his capital. Defeated and humiliated, Ptolemy IV returned to Alexandria where he died under mysterious circumstances in 204 B.C.

*Problems Setting Scenes in Ancient Egypt*

The chronology of Egypt creates a quandary for historical fiction writers. While we know the names of places Jace Kasia went to in *The General's Tribune*, the question remains, would Jace or anybody living in the region around Luxor know the history of the ruins in 205 B.C.?

We don't know where Horwennefer had the camp of his rebel army. I placed the army's bivouac at the Colossi of Memnon. The two massive stone statues of the Pharaoh Amenhotep III (14th century B.C.) were mistaken by Romans and Greeks in 20 A.D. as being statues of a Greek General of lore named Memnon. The statues are old enough that the priesthood of Amenhotep III would have faded with time, leaving no one to explain the statues.

Not far away from the giant statues, Jace guides the chariot through Deir el-Medina. Active from 1,550 B.C. through 1,080 B.C., the city housed workers during the construction of tombs in the Valley of the Kings. With the story occurring in 205 B.C., the city would have been buried under sand and dirt as the excavation didn't begin until 1905 A.D.

Egypt presented a challenge for me as an historical fiction writer. I attempt to identify locations and features by names for the benefit of readers who use maps to follow the journey of the characters. Because of its age, Egypt foiled me from the start of Jace's journey up the Nile River. For example, Cairo, Egypt's largest city and home to ten million people, did not exist in 205 B.C. Near Cairo, the pyramids and the Great Sphinx were in Giza. But they date from the 26th century B.C.

We know from explorer reports, over centuries and across continents, that when ancient ruins are discovered, often times, the locals don't know the names or the history of the locations. Egypt presented a classic example. Horwennefer's army wrecked and looted temples, being unaware of the religious or historical importance of the tombs. I can only imagine people in 205 B.C. had no idea of the significance of the visible structures.

How then do I have Jace Kasia identify the Mortuary Temple of Hatshepsut? And how much of the grand staircase was visible at the time of the book? If it's not apparent, I had problems setting scenes in ancient Egypt.

*Dragonflies*

National Geographic reports that dragonflies are important to the ecosystem because they eat mosquitoes, need fresh water to lay their eggs, and their larvae require water to survive. Since they rely on clean water, dragonflies are considered an indicator of a healthy ecosystem. I don't know whether you could follow a dragonfly to clean water. But if lost in the desert, a Nile blue dragonfly would be better than nothing.

*Moloch*

An ancient Canaanite God, Moloch is mentioned in the Hebrew Bible. The reference is that Moloch and his followers are an offense to Yahweh. Research guesses that the worship of Moloch might have included the sacrifice of children. That's about as evil as possible, making a Soldier of Moloch, the perfect cover for Jace to lure the pirate Diceärch into a trap.

*Dice Water Snakes*

Eurasian nonvenomous snakes, Dice snakes are solitary water creatures. Durning mating season, however, they cluster in groups. Females are the largest of the species, growing between 1 – 1.3 m (39 - 51 inches). They have three defensive mechanisms. They bite, but it's not poisonous. They play dead when frightened. And they spread a foul-smelling aroma to fend off predators. Dice snakes were the perfect, creepy swimming companions for Jace as an archery student.

*Mitilini, Lesvos*

The city of Mitilini on the Island of Lesvos, since the fourth century B.C., had bridges over a channel. Thirty meters or ninety feet wide, and seven hundred meters or over two thousand feet long, the canal connected the north harbor with the south harbor. The channel has long since been filled with dirt and covered with streets and buildings.

Historians only noted marble bridges, leaving out the numbers and names of the structures. To help Jace Kasia navigate Mitilini the city, I named the southernmost bridge Ermou. "One could argue that the channel transversed what is now called Ermou Street," per the Kids Encyclopedia of Facts.

Adult research documents were not helpful on the location of the canal. The Kids Encyclopedia on the other hand gave the best guesses. For anchoring an adventure story, I'll take any reference I can find.

*Berenice II of Cyrene & Queen of Egypt*

The ancient kingdom of Cyrene is located near modern day Shahhat, Libya. In 252 B.C., King Magnas of Cyrene feared an invasion by Egypt. To protect Cyrene's sovereignty, he proposed a marriage to a Prince of Egypt. Before he could make it official, the King died, and his Queen Apama came into power. Going back on the proposal, Apama sent for a Prince of Macedonia, Demetrius the Fair, the half-brother of the Seleucid King.

Demetrius, a handsome man, arrived, married Berenice, became King of Cyrene, and started an affair with Queen Apama. History tells us that after arguments with both, Berenice led a revolt. Durning the fighting, Demetrius the Fair died in the arms of Apama.

We have little record of the palace revolt. I inserted the fictional character of Rodas of Haîma, translated to Rose Garden of Bloodshed, and invented his part in the murder of the King of Cyrene.

After the death of Demetrius the Fair, Berenice II moved to Egypt, married Prince Ptolemy III Euergetes. She became Berenice the Queen of Egypt and the mother of Pharaoh Ptolemy IV. History does not tell us what became of Apama, but it's believed she moved to Egypt with her daughter.

*Sosibius, Chief Minister of Egypt 221 - 204*

The vast army of Ptolemy IV defeated the army of the Seleucid Empire in 217 B.C. at Rafah. Modern Rafah is a Palestinian city in the southern end of the Gaza Strip in Israel. Durning the battle, Chief Minister Sosibius commanded 20,000 Egyptians trained to fight like Macedonian phalanxes. As an advisor to Ptolemy IV and a loyalist to the Pharoah, Sosibius helped with the smooth transition of power for Ptolemy V after the death of his father, Ptolemy IV, in 204 B.C. Without a doubt Sosibius would have been with the Army of the Pharoah when they marched south to face the rebels.

We have little details about the battle and the defeat of Ptolemy IV at Thebes / Luxor. I trust you followed my logic in building out the story around the victory of the rebels and the part played by Sosibius in the fictional account.

*Cult of Berenice*

Shortly after marrying Ptolemy III, Berenice of Cyrene / Egypt was inducted into the Ptolemy Religion. As such she became the Benefactor Goddess Berenice. Although she died by poison in 221 B.C. when Ptolemy IV ascended to the throne, her Priestess, the Gift-Bearer, continued to walk in the fourth position in religious processions. First came the priests of the great King Alexander, then priests of the Ptolemies, followed by young unmarried women, and then the Gift-Bearer, representing Berenice.

*Eratosthenes of Cyrene*

The scholar was a renowned philosopher of geography and created the first globe of the world. In 204 B.C., he was the head librarian for the Library of Alexandria. As such, Eratosthenes would have been the teacher for the Pharaoh's children. It's not impossible that the scholar would have been in the palace during the mysterious fire that took the life of Ptolemy IV.

*Ptolemy V Epiphanes*

When his father died in a mysterious fire, five-year-old Ptolemy V Epiphanes ascended to the throne of Egypt.

History tells us his mother, Arsinoe III, was murdered soon after the death of Ptolemy IV. The suspected assassins were Agathocles, Head Priest of the cult of Alexander the Great, and Chief Minister Sosibius. Initially, they kept the death of Ptolemy IV a secret.

Within the year, Agathocles killed Sosibius, leaving Agathocles as the Regent for the underaged Pharoah. His rule as Regent lasted until 203 B.C. when the military mutinied. They put Agathocles to death, as well as his family, and anyone associated with the demise of Arsinoe III. No one was punished for the death of Ptolemy IV.

*205 B.C.*

*The General's Tribune* mostly occurred in 205 B.C. with part set in early 204 B.C. Here's hoping you enjoyed the story and the notes. Euge! Bravo, to you for going on this journey with me.

*** 

I appreciate emails and reading your comments. If you enjoyed *The General's Tribune,* consider leaving a written review on Amazon or Goodreads. Every review helps other readers find the stories.

If you have comments e-mail me.

E-mail: GalacticCouncilRealm@gmail.com

To get the latest information about my books, visit my website. There you can sign up for my monthly author report. In every newsletter, I start with an article about ancient history before giving you updates on my books.

Website: www.JCliftonSlater.com

Facebook: Tales from Ancient Rome

I am author J. Clifton Slater and I write historical military adventures.

Other books by J. Clifton Slater:

Historical Adventure of the 2nd Punic War

*A Legion Archer* series

#1 Journey from Exile

#2 Pity the Rebellious

#3 Heritage of Threat

#4 A Legion Archer

#5 Authority of Rome

#6 Unlawful Kingdom

#7 From Dawn to Death

#8 The General's Tribune

#9 When War Gods Battle

Historical Adventure of the 1st Punic War

*Clay Warrior Stories* series

#1 Clay Legionary

#2 Spilled Blood

#3 Bloody Water

#4 Reluctant Siege

#5 Brutal Diplomacy

#6 Fortune Reigns

#7 Fatal Obligation

#8 Infinite Courage

#9 Deceptive Valor

#10 Neptune's Fury

#11 Unjust Sacrifice

#12 Muted Implications

#13 Death Caller

#14 Rome's Tribune

Printed in Great Britain
by Amazon